All
Are
Welcome

All Are Welcome

a NOVEL

LIZ PARKER

LAKE UNION
PUBLISHING

Published by Lake Union Publishing, Seattle

www.apub.com

Amazon, the Amazon logo, and Lake Union Publishing are trademarks of Amazon.com, Inc., or its affiliates.

ISBN-13: 9781542029889
ISBN-10: 1542029880

Cover design and illustration by Bethany Robertson

Printed in the United States of America

For Sarah

THE FLIGHT DOWN

TINY

Tiny was actually tiny. She liked this because she was also a story of contradictions and being tiny meant the same thing to everyone. Her father was large and her mother was small, and on most days, this was the only thing the two women had in common. And even then it was a stretch: Tiny was *tiny*. Her mother was small. It was different. Her mother was not diminutive, nor did she look positively juvenile, nor was she often asked if she was old enough to sit in the emergency exit row. Tiny was thirty-four, and it had happened that morning, on the way down to her own wedding.

She'd been sitting next to Caroline, her bride-to-be, and they were both deep into their respective onboarding rituals. Tiny liked to make sure she had a water, entertainment device, and book perfectly placed in the seat pocket. She knew this pocket was a cesspool and she didn't care. She liked knowing exactly where everything she wanted might be. Caroline boarded an airplane equipped with a stack of magazines; a large bottle of water with lemon, the bottle and lemon from home, the water from inside the terminal; Beats wireless headphones, and a playlist designed specifically for the flight at hand. Today's was a retrospect of moody albums from 2009. Tiny would be lying if she didn't wish her fiancée had opted to listen to more upbeat music on the way to their wedding. If not for a moment when Caroline leaned over to kiss Tiny's shoulder when they first sat down, they looked like nothing more than two women boarding a flight. They moved like a couple fluent in independence.

The flight attendant appeared from the back of the plane.

"Hey, y'all, I just wanted to make sure this one is fifteen?" She glanced suggestively at Caroline and nodded toward Tiny, as if she were in charge of the row.

"Sorry, yes, I am," Tiny responded, reaching down for her wallet. "Do you want to see my ID?"

"Oh, I believe you, I think. We just have to be sure, you know, in the case of an emergency."

When Tiny was honest with herself, she hated southern accents. She hated most accents.

"Luckily, we're equipped." Caroline reached over and touched Tiny's arm. The universal couple code for *please shut up; you are this close to embarrassing yourself.*

The flight attendant didn't pick up on the gesture.

"Y'all sisters?"

Tiny looked over.

"We aren't, actually," Caroline said.

"Girls' trip?"

"No. I mean, yes. Sort of? We're getting married?" Tiny said, holding up her ring finger (admirable diamond) and looking at Caroline a little desperately. Caroline raised her left hand to show her own admirable diamond. The flight attendant looked between them and opened her mouth to say something, then closed it when no words came out.

"Don't worry—it's legal," Caroline said.

"I know! Of course it's legal!"

Tiny debated whether she could physically fit underneath the seat in front of her. Crumple herself into a human hedgehog and disappear. The flight attendant walked away without even going through the safety demonstration.

"2019, ladies and gentlemen."

Caroline was bristling, and Tiny's cheeks were so flushed, she felt faint.

"You didn't have to do that, you know," Tiny said.

"I did, actually."

Caroline crossed her legs and opened the latest issue of *US Weekly*.

"I'm sorry I'm not as political as you are," Tiny said, trying to figure out where this all had gone wrong. It was the flight attendant who had been both ageist and homophobic and yet Tiny had somehow messed it all up.

"It's not political. It's a willingness to stand up for myself," Caroline said, looking down at the magazine while she turned the page.

Tiny looked out the window. She knew the tension would lift. Caroline was a woman of real integrity, for better or for worse. It's what made her such a fearless attorney for the ACLU. And Tiny loved this about her, she thought, stealing a glance as Caroline turned a page of the magazine. And an attorney for the ACLU was a lot more impressive than a first grade teacher, even if Tiny had been awarded Best Elementary Educator in the state of New York in 2017.

~

The flight attendant returned an hour into the flight, clearly dreading seeing these "sisters" again.

"What can I get y'all?" she asked, putting packets of almonds on their trays before either answered.

"Club soda," Caroline said, not glancing up from the latest issue of *Vogue*. Her love for fashion and gossip magazines was something Tiny found fascinating. Caroline limited her own wardrobe to cotton and shapeless-yet-hip-hugging pants but knew every move Victoria Beckham ever made. She picketed Washington over Proposition 8 and also never missed the latest Instagram Story from Chrissy Teigen.

"White wine," Tiny all but whispered. It was ten in the morning and her mother kept her petrified of becoming an alcoholic. Her brother did too, for that matter. Tiny didn't look at the flight attendant until she was passing the wine-filled cup, lest she catch the judgment no doubt on the flight attendant's face. Of course, she should have looked up sooner: the flight attendant's hand missed her own and the wine came pouring down, soaking Tiny's lap and damaging Caroline's *Vogue*.

"I'm so sorry!" Tiny yelped.

Caroline yelled, "What the *fuck!*" and jumped out of her seat, allowing the magazine to drip more wine onto Tiny's lap.

Tiny jumped up too and immediately tried to save the *Vogue*, haplessly rubbing napkins over the cover. The wine soaked through her white jeans and into her underwear. Caroline stood glaring. The flight attendant looked like she was wondering at what point she was allowed to ask them to get back in their row so she could continue the beverage service. A small amount of the wine had gotten onto Caroline's navy-blue V-neck, and she was furiously blotting it with a napkin. Still no attention had been paid to Tiny's lap. She was still muttering "sorry" over and over.

"Y'all, I'm so sorry, but I need to push this thing through," the flight attendant finally said, going so far as to lightly nudge Caroline with the cart.

Caroline turned around and locked her eyes on the flight attendant.

"You will *not* first accuse my fiancée of being a minor; then forget that you're in 2019 and gay marriage is legal; then spill wine on my fiancée, ruining her pants and my magazine and my T-shirt; then nudge me with your frankly outdated beverage cart and not expect us to file a serious complaint with the airline."

Tiny thought she saw the flight attendant's ankle wobble.

"I will not, ma'am," the flight attendant finally said.

"I expect a miles compensation to both our accounts, my fiancée's wine replaced, and a voucher to replace the clothes you've ruined. Trust me, that's a whole lot easier than the airline issuing a statement about why one of their flight attendants was directly homophobic to two passengers flying down to their own wedding."

This garnered claps and "uh-huh"s from the passengers in nearby rows. Tiny wasn't sure she'd ever felt so proud. This was her woman, standing up for what was right in the world. She took a step to the left so she could stand next to Caroline and help stare down the flight attendant.

Tiny mouthed, *I love you*, and Caroline took her hand and mouthed, *I love you*, back and smiled through the side of her mouth.

TRIP

By the time the plane was starting its descent, Trip was on his fifth whiskey soda. His wife was not here. Nor were his twins, and he realized with a start that he'd forgotten to tell Tiny that they couldn't be her flower girl and ring bearer. He wasn't supposed to be drinking; it had been his wife's last straw, even if he told her repeatedly he had everything under control. She was too rigid, too set on keeping him in a neat little box with her friends' husbands. Even if those husbands were unbearably boring and barely took home six figures. The six-figure part wasn't true—most of them were pretty successful—but they were boring as hell and he could barely take those dinner parties drunk. Forget sober. Lucky for Trip, he had always believed that nothing counted in the air, and as the booze coursed through his blood, making his arms droopy and his neck increasingly weaker, he looked around for anyone who might be interested in joining the mile high club. The other first-class seats were mostly occupied by graying men and a couple clearly on their first trip together or their honeymoon.

He looked at the woman sitting next to him by the window. He had noticed her as soon as she came onboard, and over the past hour, he had kept pretending to look out the window so he could catch another glimpse. She was leggy, daring to wear shorts on a plane, and he could see that her toenails were painted hot pink. His eyes traveled up past the shorts and he saw a white sweatshirt covering a solid set of bosoms. He'd always liked that word. *Bosoms.* Her neck was long and slender; her chin jutted out at an angle. He'd reached her eyes, closely met by a brown bang, when she finally looked over.

"Can I help you?" Her voice was deeper than he'd expected. He coughed and sat up, smoothing his white-and-green-striped Augusta National golf shirt and travel khakis. His legs were crossed at the ankle, his Tod's driving loafers just visible under the seat in front of him.

"Flying down to Bermuda for my sister's lesbian wedding," he said proudly, hoping "lesbian" would get her attention or at least afford him some social currency. He often used his sister's sexuality to appear more progressive than he actually was. She nodded and looked neither interested nor uninterested.

"That right."

He took another sip of whiskey.

"My wife taped a sign to our front door that said 'This House Is Not a Storage Facility' and then threw all my belongings onto the front stoop. Some stuff even hit the sidewalk. The neighborhood thought we were having a yard sale." He was proud of this joke and waited for the woman to laugh. She did not.

"That right," she said, turning back to her video.

He would not be deterred. "We've been having problems for a long time, you see. But the twins are three and her parents were divorced and frankly she never got over it so I stuck around because I think kids should be happy. But if she wants me to leave, then I guess I'll have to go." He puffed out his chest. He was a good father and a good husband and Daphne could screw herself.

"That sounds like a lot," she said, moving her body as close to the far edge of her seat as she could.

"I've done well for us, if I'm totally honest. I manage almost a billion in assets and own a house outright in Cobble Hill and another one on the Vineyard. My uncle owns a golf club up there, you see. It's a bit of a family island. The kids will be in private school and I can join any golf club I want to." Daphne had served him papers yesterday morning, packed up the car, and taken the twins to her parents' house near Boston. At least she'd gone quietly.

The woman was fully facing her video. Trip poked her shoulder.

"Yes?" she said, turning her head.

"Where are you staying in Bermuda?"

She grimaced and then responded, "I'd honestly rather not say."

Trip nodded and considered this. Took another sip of whiskey.

"I'll be at the Coral Beach and Tennis Club for the weekend," he said, making sure to accentuate the club's proper name. "We're not members, per se, but membership has been *offered*. We've got the whole place. Or most of it. If you're interested, my last name is McAllister. Like the Connecticut McAllisters."

The woman stared at him a moment before he continued.

"Well, I live in Brooklyn now, but my family is still in Connecticut. We've got a lot of wedding stuff all weekend, of course, but if you wanted to come by for a drink or something, I'll be around."

At this, the woman actually laughed, an openmouthed, head-back, full-throttle laugh, and Trip joined in because he didn't know what else to do. He expected her to say something when she finally caught her breath, but she put her earbuds back in—both ears—and turned to her video. He knew, even in this fog of airplane drunkenness, that he was one shoulder poke away from harassment. The last thing this divorce needed was a headline about him being escorted off the plane.

He looked over her and out the window. The waves shimmered before they broke into luscious white streams of foam and sand. He noticed bodies (maybe kids? Would kids make the moment more or less bearable?) playing chicken with the water and losing, and for a brief moment, he both wanted to be playing with those people and for the plane to crash. His was the type of maudlin that found rain too hopeful—it quenched the world's thirst—but it was *also* the type that couldn't resist chasing anything that might help.

It felt odd going to his sister's wedding when his marriage was officially over. Like the snake eating its own tail. But Tiny was more balanced than he was. Even-keeled and loyal and desperate for all the tidings that adults clung to. She'd always been fine waiting her turn for things, he thought, deciding he didn't want the plane to actually crash, but he wanted the news to say it had crashed so Daphne would hear and know she'd made a horrible mistake. Trip pressed the "Call" button for one more whiskey soda before they landed.

TINY

Customs had taken over two hours and they were late for the welcome lunch, and as they snaked their way from the airport through the skinny part of the island before it widened into more of a thumb, Tiny was unnerved because she hadn't thought about whether or not there might be traffic and she liked to think that she thought of everything. Caroline was nonplussed. She'd been texting her parents, who were happily settled in at Coral Beach and rolling through midday rum punches with Tiny's parents, all morning. That was the benefit of marrying the daughter of your parents' friends: life got set up around you.

So excited to see you and Tiny! her mother had texted. I've got Bitty taken care of. Caroline was looking out the window, her hand resting lightly in Tiny's lap. Tiny leaned over and kissed her shoulder. Caroline turned around and smiled like she'd been waiting all day for Tiny to kiss her shoulder.

"You look pretty adorable, you know," Caroline said, shifting her weight so her arm was around Tiny. They sat like this, watching the sea against the hill, and Tiny felt heard and seen and loved all at once.

When the car came to a total stop, the traffic jam like a multicolored rope hogging the street, Tiny looked at her watch. She didn't know why she was surprised: Bermuda was a hotbed of construction, especially midday on a Friday.

"My mother is going to be so annoyed," Tiny said. She could already see her mother, alight in pink slacks and perfectly white pearls, a lighter shade of pink sweater tied loosely around her shoulders. White Jack Rogers to perfect the island look. She would also have her hip slightly cocked to the side, to match her disappointment.

"It doesn't take much to annoy Bitty."

Tiny came from a family of women whose names ended in *y*.

"Don't," Tiny said firmly.

Caroline failed at hiding an eye roll. "This is our weekend. *Our weekend.* You and me. We only get to do this once. Who cares about the rest? Who cares about Bitty? You were always going to annoy her. We always annoy her. Bitty is *always annoyed.* Let Mabel take care of her." She stressed this point like the litigator she was.

"But I didn't want to annoy her *today*," Tiny emphasized, already seeing Bitty's thin smirk upon their arrival, a quippy line about how Tiny had never been one for time management. Tiny had been slow to walk as a child—nearly three years old—and Bitty had never forgiven her. The real issue was that Bitty had wanted them to arrive on Thursday, when she and Dick and Mabel and Peter had flown down, so she could organize a welcome barbecue.

"Wedding weekends need to be properly commenced!" Bitty had said, even bringing Caroline's mother, Mabel, into it. She'd flung the four of them onto a conference call three weeks prior.

"It would be a good idea to have enough time to settle in," Mabel had said, giggling at Bitty's intensity but also not saying she was wrong. They'd been friends for nearly thirty years, since Caroline was a preteen and Tiny was learning to ride a bike. Peter and Mabel had arrived at the Country Club of Connecticut Young Members dinner and the foursome had never looked back.

"We're flying down Friday," Caroline said, using her lawyer voice to impress their final decision.

"Stop lawyering us," Mabel said. "Bitty raises a very good point. It is important guests know what's to come for the weekend."

That Caroline happily assumed the role of Tiny's protective shield— *she* was lawyering their parents, not Tiny—all but made Tiny overflow with devotion.

"First of all, besides the four of us, sixteen other people are coming. They know it's a wedding; they know it's a wedding between Tiny and me. I'd say everyone, except clearly you two, knows exactly what's to come."

Bitty sniffed and Tiny could see her bristling into the tufted chair in their living room. Tiny clung to Caroline's ability to ask for what she wanted. The concept was utterly foreign. Caroline gave Tiny's hand a squeeze while she waited for their mothers to concede. Tiny felt safest when her hand was in Caroline's.

"Very well," Bitty said after too long. "We'll do a welcome luncheon on Friday and that is that. I suppose guests won't be too confused."

Bitty was *excited* for the wedding. It both made sense and did not make sense. Bitty was a woman from a certain world, and in that world, mothers planned weddings for their daughters. So even if this particular daughter happened to be marrying another daughter, Bitty had a wedding to plan. Naively, Tiny had thought Bitty was excited for *her*, but a few weeks into the engagement, when Tiny had raised the idea of wearing a brightly colored dress instead of white, it was like Bitty had seen right through her. Tiny was hollow, and at once she saw how Bitty saw her: a nice-enough girl, modeled on inconvenience, who would do. What little was left of Tiny's gumption shriveled up after that moment, and she began a long round of the Yes Game, hoping against hope time and again that the next yes would be the one to finally get her mother's attention. Mabel put no such notions on Caroline.

"We've already broken the mold with two girls," Mabel said so proudly, Tiny wished she were her actual mother.

Tiny was wearing white.

14

Her hair was long and freshly highlighted. She felt like a doll in her own clothing, a jumble of limbs beneath fabric.

"When does Trip arrive?" Caroline asked.

"I think right around now. We probably should have waited for them."

Caroline looked at her kindly while Tiny remembered that Caroline and Trip did not get along. How could they? Caroline had taken a girl Trip had been seeing right from under his nose during college. Tiny played *Groundhog Day* when it came to uncomfortable family dynamics.

"Will they make lunch?"

Tiny smirked despite herself. "They better."

"And Robbie?"

At Robbie's name, Tiny's shoulders fell.

"You know I haven't heard from him since we got engaged," Tiny said, biting the inside of her lower lip. It had been longer than that even. Caroline's hand went right back over Tiny's.

"We'll get through this, my love," she said. "Robbie will come around or he won't, but either way, it's you and me."

Tiny looked at Caroline and fell in love a little bit more.

WELCOME BAGS

BITTY

The Coral Beach & Tennis Club was right on the coast in Bermuda, sprawled over twenty-six acres and perched atop a cliff, lined with cutely named cottages like Bay Grape and High Tidings. It was as much a club as it was a hotel, and the grounds were teeming with things to do. Muted pink matched the buildings to the island's famous sand, and Bitty had always loved how the ocean's blue bled into green bled into light pink. Like nature's rugby shirt. She and Dick would stay in Surfsong, the largest of the cottages, with two floors and three bedrooms that sat on the cliffs above the beach. It was the kind of lodging that new money found shabby and old money found familiar. They could see water from nearly every window, so close that Bitty could stick out her hand and touch it.

Dick was writing on their porch, squinting through his tortoiseshell glasses. Bitty had no idea what he actually wrote when he "was writing," but his recent paunch poked boldly under his white polo. She knew he would look up at any moment, asking if it was time for a sandwich.

Caroline's parents, Mabel and Peter, were ambling down the path toward their cottage and Bitty was so taken by excitement to see them that she almost ran out to pick them up and carry them the rest of the way herself. They were staying in Stowaways, close enough that they could shout from their porches. Mabel was so comfortable with everything, Bitty wanted to ride her coattails until the weekend was over. She had initially been discouraged by a wedding in Bermuda, it being so familiar, she couldn't get over what to do if they ran into someone they knew. Bermuda was a place people *went*, though Dick did remind her they most often went earlier in the year, before the heat settled onto the island. Then she leaned into the fact that Bermuda wasn't terribly fond of gay marriage. Mabel reminded her that neither was Greenwich, Connecticut. To which Bitty said, "Why not get married in Greenwich, then?" She knew Tiny didn't care about Bermuda. They'd come as a family once and Tiny was so distraught by the high-socks-and-long-shorts rule, she all but ran away. It was Caroline who loved to travel and explore and put on new hats and most of all *prove a point*. Getting married in Bermuda proved a point. Then they'd scheduled it for the weekend after Labor Day during hurricane season, and renting the resort had been a steal.

"Mabel! Peter!" she called from the porch before she thought twice and decided she didn't want to seem desperate.

Mabel reached up a moderately worked-out arm and waved. "Ahoy!"

The four of them had arrived the night before and Mabel had already transitioned perfectly into flowy resort wear. Bitty envied Mabel's versatility: she was not afraid of change and she was not afraid of changing. And yet: she fit in wherever she went. Bitty had never met anyone like her. Despite Mabel's social aptitude, Bitty had always found her future daughter-in-law slightly unbearable. In a word, Caroline was lawyer-y, and Bitty hated, absolutely hated, contrarians. The world was hard enough; people didn't need to sniff out disagreements.

Peter walked just behind Mabel, rolling up his paper and swatting Dick with it when he stepped onto their porch. He was already wearing a CBC polo.

"Peter!" Dick said, getting up and taking off his reading glasses in one motion. The men shook hands and nodded and looked down and looked up in the sniffing ritual male WASPs do when greeting one of their own.

"How's the morning?" Peter asked, taking a seat in one of the rattan armchairs, his legs spread at a comfortable distance. Bitty had recently learned the term for this was *manspread.*

"Fine, fine," Dick said, sitting down in another chair and spreading his legs two inches farther. Between the two of them, they'd taken up the entire porch and Bitty and Mabel stood off to the side after air-kissing.

Bitty looked at her watch. Eleven. She could stave off her hunger for another three hours at least, maybe even five, the arrival luncheon at one be damned. Just because her daughter was marrying a letdown did not mean she needed to get fat. Bitty's dietary routine had been fixed since the mid-1980s: hard-boiled egg with salt and pepper in the morning, tuna salad made with mustard and not mayo over a bed of lettuce at lunch, a fish and two vegetables at dinner. In 2000, when hummus had exploded, she had taken to adding a dollop to her egg, but beyond that, the only part that changed was what kind of wine she had with dinner. Currently it was sauvignon blanc from South Africa, one glass consumed quickly with ice, three glasses sipped intermittently between 6:00 p.m. and bed. She'd worked the amount to a tee: just fuzzy enough to slip from day to evening, never so buzzed that she'd feel compelled to pick up the phone and call one of her children.

"Caroline let me know they landed," Mabel said. Bitty had not received the same text from her daughter. She checked her phone again to be sure, going so far as to unlock it and tap into her messages to make sure nothing had been missed.

Two figures took shape in her periphery, walking closer to their villa.

"Bitty! Mabel!" the figure on the far right said loudly, her hand up and waving.

Okay, so these figures were familiar. Bitty squinted. One woman, one man. Or two men? Or two women? Both tall. Both brunet. Both short hair. Both wearing the same unfortunate outfit of short-sleeve button-down shirts and dark shorts. It was a fine line between tomboy and homely, she thought, realizing it was definitely one man and one woman, and the man was slender and fitted and the woman was not, and Bitty wanted to know what the big deal was with presenting oneself in a feminine manner. It wasn't that hard.

"Well, hi!" she said loudly back, her own hand now waving. "Welcome!"

"This place is gorgeous! I can't believe you rented out the entire thing," said the man, his voice somewhere between a screech and a whistle.

Dick and Peter had taken the tack that two brides meant the two fathers would split everything down the middle, making the entire weekend that much more luxurious. She couldn't call Dick wrong, but it didn't feel right taking the Schells' money when they, the McAllisters, had so much more of it.

"When did you get in?" asked the woman. She was familiar, Bitty decided, but she couldn't tell if it was because they'd had dinner before or because she looked like Bitty assumed most lesbians looked.

"Oh, yesterday in the late morning. Dick? Peter?" She interrupted their man chat. "Come say hi to Tiny and Caroline's friends."

"We got in late last night," the woman responded and her counterpart nodded along. So the brides' friends knew to arrive on Thursday, just not the brides. And they hadn't had a single event to welcome them. Bitty felt a small pit in her stomach balloon to the size of a peach.

What were these people's names? Bitty screamed to herself, desperately cataloging her recent memory. Something with *C* kept coming to mind.

"Connie!" Dick said brightly, engulfing her in a hug. Dick was very good at seeming comfortable in uncomfortable situations. Peter hugged her next and Mabel after that. Bitty felt like her bones were about to fall off her skeleton.

"I didn't know you were coming," Mabel said to Connie, holding her a beat too long and patting her on her back.

"Tiny invited me, actually," Connie said, trying a little too hard to sound confident. "She thought it would be a fun surprise for Caroline."

Mabel held her gaze, her lips slightly squeezed together. "That's lovely," she said.

"Connie!" Bitty offered, deciding too late to hug instead of shake hands. The man stood off to the side, smiling like he was trying to catch up.

"Andrew," Dick said, sticking out his hand. "Thanks for making the trip."

How did everyone but her know these people? She swore her husband had an entirely separate life from hers.

The group was now cloistered around a table on the front porch.

"Please sit down." Bitty motioned to the overstuffed white linen couch and armchairs behind her. "What can I get people to drink?"

She willed someone to request a real drink.

"Is it too early for Dark 'N' Stormys?" the man named Andrew said. Andrew was someone who had not had a choice as a child.

"Not at all!" Bitty could have hugged this man. "Should I make six?"

Connie nodded.

"Skip me, please," Mabel said. "When I drink during the day, I fall right asleep."

Dick offered a smirk that said, *Count me in, but if you get drunk before tonight, I'll kill you.* Forty years of marriage meant they could go days without speaking and the conversation never stopped. He was excited about this weekend, and Bitty felt like she was under a microscope to prove to him that she was excited too.

She hurried back to the bar, a rattan rolling cart situated in a small closet off the living room. Normally, day drinking was not an option—too much risk of overdoing it and picking up the phone or, worse, venturing into town or the club and actually seeing someone. But this was a special occasion, of course it was, and what better way to get to know her child's friends? Plus, none of her friends besides Mabel were here. She was safe. Maybe this weekend wouldn't be horrible. Maybe Tiny and Caroline's friends were as nervous about this union as she was. Maybe Tiny would call it off, though even as she thought this, she knew it was impossible. Caroline had spiraled into Tiny's life with such attention and intensity, Bitty was smart enough to know lovestruck when it was right in front of her. They'd had a spirited courtship, Caroline impressing Tiny around every corner. Tiny had no choice but to tattoo herself onto Caroline. Anyone would. Bitty didn't hate Caroline, but she was too hard for Tiny, unyielding and more like a drill sergeant than a spouse. Plus, she always had to be right, and that was an utterly exhausting trait. She was pretty, though. And clearly intelligent. And came from the right stock. There were worse things than being pretty and right.

But Bitty knew enough about love to know that when someone finally comes around after so many years, it doesn't matter what they bring with them.

She poured generously, first a little rum and then a little more, then adding ice to even it out and then topping up the drink with floaters, which resulted in the glasses nearly overflowing, which in turn resulted in Bitty sucking small amounts from each glass through a metal straw intended for stirring. Before returning outside, she stole away to their bathroom and grabbed a few Adderall for her back pocket. This day was about staying even.

Andrew's phone buzzed on the table.

"The brides are here!"

CAROLINE

A team of attendants welcomed their taxi when they arrived at the Coral Beach Club. They'd wound around most of the central grounds, passing the tennis courts and bar and an almost unbelievable amount of grass cut in different formations. Caroline had been here as a young teen for a family vacation and she was struck by how little the club had changed. Even the hut outside the tennis courts that had seemed antiquated at thirteen years old remained equally and, she supposed, adorably antiquated.

"Welcome, welcome, to the McAllisters," a middle-aged man with a sharp gray crew cut said. "I am Simon, the manager for CBC." Clearly the club had been briefed for political correctness. He held out a hand to help Tiny out of the car. Caroline let herself out on her own side. She wasn't planning on taking Tiny's name, but Tiny didn't know that. Caroline Schell suited her just fine.

Tiny and Caroline followed Simon into the main reception area, their hands lightly clasped.

"It's our wedding!" Tiny said when they walked through the clubhouse and onto Longtail Terrace, which overlooked the cliffs and beach below. She beamed. Caroline squeezed her hand and kissed the side of her head and tried to catch up to Tiny's excitement. Correction. She was excited, of course she was, but she wanted to show excitement like Tiny showed excitement.

"We have you in Breakers, one of our best cottages," Simon said. He had a printed map of the resort on the counter between them and started circling various locales: their cottage, the kidney-shaped pool, the tennis courts and tennis house, the croquet field, the putting green, and the dining room, where afternoon tea was served on the main terrace. A young woman appeared behind Simon holding two welcome bags.

"For the brides!" she said gladly. Too gladly? Caroline looked at her polo tucked into the knee-length khaki shorts uniform and her dark hair in a low ponytail. It was impossible to tell—both female golf attire and preppy hotel uniforms overlapped significantly with a lot of lesbian wardrobes, so her intuition was always off. Caroline and Tiny each reached out to take one.

Caroline briefly looked inside and saw two plastic water bottles and various bagged snacks. This had Bitty and Mabel written all over it. Tiny caught her eye.

"Clearly our moms got drunk and made these?" she said.

Caroline nodded. "Clearly."

~

Their cottage was beautiful by any account, made more so by the fresh-cut flowers and strawberries and bottle of champagne waiting for them on their private porch facing the water. Everywhere Tiny looked, she saw green lined up with blue. She gave the entire space a once-over, opening every drawer and commenting on every feature while Caroline sat on the plush white linen couch and went through the welcome bag.

"How drunk do you think Bitty and Mabel were when they made these?" she shouted from the porch, not waiting for an answer.

First there were two small bottles of water. Fine, hydration was always important. Next came a small tube of nontoxic sunscreen and two pairs of cheaply manufactured sunglasses embossed with Tiny and Caroline 2019. Caroline tried on a pair but they wouldn't stretch across her head. There were two bags of trail mix and two bags of potato chips—Planters and Cape Cod, obviously purchased stateside—a map of the resort, countless brochures of nearby activities, a tube of ChapStick with the CBC logo on it, and finally, a welcome letter and itinerary.

> Welcome to our wedding weekend!
>
> We are so grateful you are here to celebrate with us, and we can't wait to celebrate with you all. If there is anything you need over the weekend, please don't hesitate to ask.
>
> And remember: stay hydrated while you dance the night away!
>
> Love,
> Tiny and Caroline

"Hey, Tiny," Caroline said. Tiny walked out onto the porch. "Did you write this welcome letter?"

Caroline held it up so Tiny could see.

"Definitely not," she said, a little laugh escaping.

"But it says it's from us?"

"They probably thought it would be better with a note, and your mom probably convinced my mom to stop asking us to do stuff." Tiny was already back to cataloging their room.

"Why would Bitty have written the letter from us?" Caroline looked at it again. "And couldn't she have been a little bit more articulate?"

"She probably just thought it would be weird if she wrote it, given that it's our weekend and everything. But she didn't want to make it too long."

It was meddling without meddling. Of course: WASPs loved to invite guests to their country house and offer directions only after they've arrived.

Caroline read on. The schedule was typed, with clip art graphics, and looked like it had been printed at home. She could see Bitty doing this, Mabel leaning on the chair next to her, their sauv blancs on ice leaking condensation by the keyboard.

Wedding Festivities

ALL ARE WELCOME

Friday, September 13, 2019

MORNING
Arrival

ONE O'CLOCK IN THE AFTERNOON
Welcome Luncheon *(Casual Attire)*

THREE O'CLOCK IN THE AFTERNOON
Snorkeling Excursion *(Swimsuit Attire)*

SIX O'CLOCK IN THE EVENING
Rehearsal *(Island Attire)*

All Are Welcome

Six Thirty in the Evening
Cocktail Hour & Hors d'oeuvres *(Island Attire)*

Seven Thirty in the Evening
Rehearsal Dinner *(Island Attire)*

Saturday, September 14, 2019

Nine O'clock in the Morning
Breakfast on the Terrace *(Casual Attire)*

Ten O'clock in the Morning
Tennis *(Whites)*

Eleven Thirty in the Morning
A Celebratory Boat Ride *(Festive Attire)*

One O'clock in the Afternoon
Ladies' Luncheon *(Smart Attire)*

One Thirty in the Afternoon
Men's Golf *(Golf Attire)*

Five O'clock in the Afternoon
Wedding Ceremony *(Formal Attire)*

Six O'clock in the Evening
Cocktails under the Palms

Seven O'clock in the Evening
Reception under the Stars

Sunday, September 15, 2019

TEN O'CLOCK IN THE MORNING
Farewell Brunch *(Casual Attire)*

TWELVE O'CLOCK IN THE AFTERNOON
Checkout of Coral Beach & Tennis Club

It was like reading the Wedding Frankenstein of their mothers. The exact times and attires were all Bitty, the attempt at playful titles for each event her mother. She knew she was the groom in all this, but the schedule was goddamn ridiculous.

"Tiny!" she called out. Tiny appeared immediately.

"Yes?" Her wife-to-be was nothing if not dutiful.

"What is this?" She held up the schedule.

Tiny read it thoroughly.

"Looks like a pretty normal wedding weekend schedule to me," she said, about to turn away again. "Remember Lucy's wedding in Northeast Harbor? I wasn't even in the wedding party and we had four days of events."

"Lucy had three hundred people at her parents' coastal estate." Caroline knew she was playing with fire and she couldn't help it.

"It's hardly an estate. There aren't more than six bedrooms in that house. Lucy always wanted a wedding at home."

"And didn't we want a casual and intimate wedding not at home? This is all a little much."

"What is a little much?"

"The letter, this itinerary—I feel like I'm on a business trip. I feel like I'm a guest at this thing."

Tiny looked at the schedule again. "I don't see what's wrong with it. And you shouldn't feel like a guest—everyone is welcome at every event. It's very inclusive."

Caroline looked at Tiny looking at the piece of paper.

"Do you want to say that again?"

"Say what?"

"Just that bit that everyone is welcome at every event. That it's very inclusive."

"It is. Bitty was adamant about that, you know. Everyone is invited to everything."

"Might you want to reframe that given that I am one of the brides?"

Tiny's eyes widened, and she let her arm fall with the schedule.

"Of course, you're right. I meant I don't think the activities are anything against you or us or anything. They're just meant to fill up the time for everyone else. We can do whatever we want."

Caroline softened with Tiny's discomfort. Maybe she was overreacting. What made her a great litigator made her a hard spouse; she knew this. And she knew Tiny was gentler than she was, more dependent on love languages and feeling wanted. She had known this from the moment they'd started dating. What Caroline wanted was a fighter like she was. What Caroline got was Tiny, smoother of surfaces.

Tiny looked at her.

"It's okay. I just wish you were a little more thoughtful about how I feel in all this. It's a big deal for me, and I want you to see that," Caroline said.

Tiny looked down, ashamed.

"Of course. I'm so sorry. We don't have to do anything you don't want to do."

Caroline picked up the schedule and looked at it again. She all but whispered, *Don't be cruel.* "What's the light at the end of the tunnel?"

"You get a wife," Tiny said, standing over her. "And we'll probably get a pretty nice gift."

Caroline perked up and tried to hide it. The McAllister fortune was not often talked about, though she knew it ran deep. Her parents kept reminding her.

"Oh?" she said as casually as she could muster.

"Trip and Daphne bought their old apartment in Tribeca with it."

"So the gift is . . . money?"

Tiny kept unpacking. "I'm pretty sure. We really don't talk about it, but I bet we learn more on Sunday."

Trip and Daphne had lived in a converted loft, complete with an industrial elevator and a doorman, an almost unheard-of combination. Caroline started calculating highs and lows of the gift in her head. The real question was whether the gift was just a down payment or a purchase in all cash. Mabel would be happy to hear this.

Tiny was looking at her expectantly. Caroline needed to confirm that everything was okay.

"There's no reason to miss the welcome lunch. We need lunch, and the group is probably ready to welcome us." She used her pointer finger to underline the event.

Tiny was back to beaming and went so far as to kiss Caroline on the cheek before disappearing inside.

~

"Should we go to the terrace?" Tiny asked a few minutes later, having switched from her travel outfit to a simple white eyelet dress and a pair of nude TKEES. What she really said was, *Can you please be more excited for our wedding?* Caroline heard this, and by getting up and putting on a pair of rolled-up white jeans and a gingham button-down, she said she would do her best.

BITTY

Andrew told them the brides had arrived. The brides. It was 2019 and she'd had fifteen years to prepare herself, but the plural word still stuck out. The table talked around her. Dick jumped up immediately, wondering if the girls would go to their room first or come here. Andrew did a little jump that reminded her of a small dog. She liked him. But she also liked that Trip and Robbie were more *boyish* boys.

"Shall we go meet them in the lobby?" Bitty finally said, the Adderall kicking in and making her entire body rigid. Her jaw clenched, and her bowels loosened. She debated whether she needed to figure out a way to make everyone else go ahead of her.

"Let's," Dick said, getting up. "We can just leave the glasses for housekeeping." The two friends followed suit. Mabel and Peter were already on the steps leading down to the path.

"We need to quickly change," Mabel said, leading Peter in the opposite direction of the clubhouse. Peter smiled and gave a small wave.

"I'll meet you all there too," Bitty said too brightly. Dick looked at her.

"Why don't you come with us?" he said.

"I'll just clean up quickly. What if the girls want to come back here and there's a mess on the porch? They'll think we've just been partying here without them!"

"Leave it for housekeeping—lord knows we paid enough," Dick said again. "Tiny and Caroline will *hardly* think we've been *partying* all morning."

Bitty squeezed her butt cheeks together.

"Okay, let's go, then."

She could hold it. She'd been here before.

They walked up the path like six ducklings, no one knowing who to lead and who to follow. Connie finally went ahead and walked in front.

"I'm excited to see them," Dick said quietly to Bitty, the two of them now taking up the rear.

"I am too!" Bitty said in the brightest voice she could muster.

"Get more excited," Dick said, quieter this time.

~

"Ladies!" Andrew burst into the lobby first. "Ladies, ladies, ladies!" By now he was waltzing with his arms outstretched, his hips swinging easily from side to side. "Are you ready to get married or what!"

Caroline visibly brightened at seeing him and moved in for a hug. Andrew pulled in Tiny as well.

Bitty didn't understand the need for all this movement. She watched the three start to do an awkward dance with their arms and hop from foot to foot. It was dramatic. Caroline looked tired. Tiny looked skittish. They were both underdressed.

"Mom." Tiny saw her and stepped out of the trio. "Hi."

"Darling," she greeted her daughter, kissing her quickly on the cheek. Tiny moved in for a proper hug, which Bitty welcomed without actually letting her body touch Tiny's. She'd spent sixty years mastering this hug.

"How was the flight?"

"Easy enough. How was yours? How's Daddy?"

"Oh, we're fine. Dick," she called behind her, "come say hi to Tiny."

Dick and Tiny embraced, Dick lifting Tiny a few inches off the ground.

"Daddy!"

Bitty could pretend she didn't hear how much lighter Tiny's voice was when she spoke to her father, but she heard it. Dick never told Tiny he wished she were stronger. He loved that she was light as a feather.

Caroline tapped her softly on the shoulder. "Hi, Bit!" she said brightly, kissing her on the cheek but knowing well enough not to try anything more. Bitty had known Caroline since she was a middle schooler trying to wear her father's jeans. She was a pretty girl, if a little plain, but raised well. Not a color on her body or a stitch of makeup, but her hair was a beautiful shade of chestnut brown and she'd somehow hung on to her lithe running figure twenty years after actually running cross-country.

"Caroline, hello! Thanks for coming!"

Caroline cocked her head slightly and Bitty realized what she'd just said. "I mean, it's so good to see you. Of course you'd come to your own wedding!"

"Where are my parents?" Caroline asked.

"Quickly changing for lunch, dear," Bitty said.

The girls now stood together, Caroline's height an inverse complement to Tiny's. Bitty's daughter leaned slightly into Caroline, like she was looking for protection. Caroline let it happen, but she did not cave her body around Tiny's, and Bitty noticed this and wished it were different.

Suddenly Caroline registered Connie being there and let out a small gasp. "Hi!" she said. "What are you . . . what are you doing . . . why are you here?" The words rushed out and Tiny started laughing.

"Surprise!" she said, gesturing toward Connie and linking them into a hug. "I know we wanted to keep this weekend intimate, but then I figured, Andrew needed a plus-one, right?" Andrew stood off to the side with his hands in his khaki shorts pockets and a closed-mouth smile.

Caroline took in Connie for a second before Connie stepped back and gestured toward the group. "I'm so happy to be here! Congratulations."

No one quite knew what to say next.

"You must be hungry?" Bitty finally ventured, uncomfortable with assigning anyone, especially a young woman, an appetite.

"Oh yes. Yes, I think I am. I think we are," Tiny said.

They started filing from the lobby onto the terrace, the recently arrived guests like a line of ants.

Bitty caught Caroline staring at Connie.

FRIDAY LUNCHEON

CAROLINE

The group fit around two large, round tables, and Caroline asked to keep the two seats next to her empty so she could sit between her parents. Bitty situated herself one seat over so she could be next to Mabel. Regardless of her upbringing, Caroline had always thought WASPs participated in far too much salutation. It was the small talk that killed her: the near-constant stream of easy questions intended to confirm that both parties had no interest in discomfort. She had no problem with discomfort, especially if it meant she got to prove her point.

They were clustered on a tumbled-marble-tile porch overlooking the beach and ocean, a narrow swath of perfectly hydrated grass rolling right to the edge of the cliffs. Pale-pink, white-trimmed cottages lined the property in a meandering horseshoe stemming out from where they sat. Below, there was a proper beach bar and chairs and umbrellas resting on the sand, and Caroline could make out a figure walking out of the water. She surmised it was Trip, clearly unconcerned by the start of lunch. Behind them was a preppy dream: a nineteen-hole putting green, a croquet court, and no fewer than eight tennis courts. The pool sat wedged between the tennis and squash courts.

Andrew planted himself next to Connie and made a big point of them being dates for the weekend. There was a glistening around his dark crew cut, which would have made a healthier-looking man positively glow. Especially with his dark-olive skin. Caroline looked down at her exposed ankles and they were basically translucent, and she desperately wished she'd at least gone for a single spray tan before her wedding day. She hated when Andrew was unbearably jumpy. He'd promised her he would keep it together this weekend.

She couldn't believe Connie was here. Connie, with her Upper West Side predilections and decidedly frumpy style, did not look like someone ready for this weekend. Connie seemed comfortable enough, sitting next to Andrew and starting conversation with whoever caught her eye, and Caroline caught herself looking once, twice, and then three times, unsure if Connie being here made everything all right or all wrong. They were like a conversation that kept getting interrupted, and by the end, neither participant quite remembered her original point.

"Remind me how you and Caroline know each other?" Dick asked Connie, snapping Caroline out of her reverie. Connie glanced at her before answering.

"You know we went to college together," Connie said. Dick nodded and took a sip of his beer, a signal he wouldn't need any follow-up. Caroline exhaled and then inhaled, not realizing she'd been holding her breath. He wanted only to source people. He didn't need particulars.

~

A few minutes later, Trip glided up onto the terrace and to the table, all hugs and cheek kisses, his hair wet and sandy from the ocean. Caroline had always found him to be an unbearable asshole—sharing a high school and lusting after the same girls (her in secret, of course) will do that—and also gamely attractive.

She looked over at Dick, smoothly going between Tiny and Trip, his uniform in full force: a white-and-navy-striped golf shirt, this one from National Golf Links of America; Nantucket Reds; a golf-themed belt Bitty had needlepointed for Christmas two years ago; and perfectly worn-in classic Gucci loafers. He matched this with perfectly parted sandy-blond hair and an easy tan. Dick was a man who appreciated country club leisure, not unlike her own father, whom by now she was ready to see. A familiar face and all that. Tiny came from old money, the type that didn't even like to get spent lest it disappear. They both did. Her parents were just one more generation removed from the real wealth and so were used to working for it. Still. Old money was not no money.

"Where are my grandkids?" Dick asked, giving Trip a firm handshake.

"On their way, Dad," Trip said, blending his answer with a laugh and immediately turning to give Tiny a hug that was more of a back pat.

"Have you seen my parents?" Caroline asked Dick, touching his shoulder to get his attention. He startled.

"What's that?"

"Sorry. Have you seen Peter and Mabel? Any idea when they'll come?" She didn't mean to sound so eager.

He nodded and said, "I'm sure any minute. *Bit.*" He waited until she turned her head. "Do you know where Mabel and Peter are?"

"Dressing," she said, going back to Trip, who was in the middle of some sort of story.

"So when do you fly back?" Dick asked no one in particular, his fingers drumming rhythmically on the table.

"Sunday afternoon or so." Connie responded first. "But this weekend should be beautiful. So long as the storm stays off the coast. Or at least that's what the weather is saying."

"Now, what app do you use for the weather? Is it Storm Tracker?"

Caroline sniffed a challenge. How much small talk could Dick and Bitty throw around before the following words would be said out loud: *wedding, women, lesbian*? Knowing Dick and Bitty, a lot.

"Personally, I love Weather Maven," Connie said, as if she'd heard Caroline's thought. Game on.

"Tell me about that one." Dick was all ears.

~

Caroline looked over at Tiny on the other side of Bitty. She looked like she was waiting for someone to talk to her. Caroline looked under the table, found Tiny's sandaled foot, and nudged it with her own.

Hi, she mouthed.

Tiny lit up. *Hi,* she mouthed back.

How's it going over there?

Tiny did a little shrug and pointed to her wineglass. Caroline nodded her approval.

Mabel and Peter arrived like a gust of wind, and Caroline jumped up immediately, thrilled and relieved and comfortable in the same moment, the feeling falling over her head like a wave.

"Hi!" she said, hugging them both. Peter and Mabel hugged back, each supporting half her body the way they'd done for nearly forty years. It had been the three of them from the start, a "trio of supporters," as Caroline had dubbed them after a middle school assembly on self-esteem.

"How's my bug?" Peter asked, ending the hug first. Caroline and Mabel followed suit, and Mabel backed up to welcome Tiny into an embrace.

"We're good; we're good," Caroline said, nodding too much.

"How was the flight?" Mabel asked, her arm loosely around Tiny's shoulder. The two women had always been close, and Caroline knew Mabel was more of a mother to Tiny than Bitty.

"It was easy enough," Tiny said.

"Well, except for when you were mistaken for a child and the flight attendant was a total homophobe," Caroline corrected. Tiny was so afraid of conflict, she'd sooner apologize to a driver for hitting her with his car.

"It wasn't that bad," Tiny said, but Caroline was shaking her head before Tiny finished speaking.

42

"No. It was that bad, and you didn't deserve it. We're going to make a fighter out of you one day." Caroline said this kindly, cocking her head to the side and grabbing Tiny's hand for full effect.

Mabel was undeterred. "With skin like that, you'll be mistaken for a child even after you've got babies of your own." Tiny and Peter laughed and Mabel joined them. Caroline caught on just before it became obvious she wasn't also laughing, but the air suddenly felt stifling, like the oxygen had been zapped completely from her breathing space. Her mother had said *babies*, plural, and she realized that she and Tiny were expected to have children and she had never thought about that before. Of course children were a factor in any marriage—whether or not to have them had to be decided—but she'd always avoided the thought altogether. What scared her was not the idea of children but the idea of children with Tiny.

Caroline stepped closer to Mabel. "I'm so excited you're here," she said. "Thank you for the weekend."

Mabel looked at her daughter closely before leaning into her ear. "What is that woman doing here?" Her eyes gestured to Connie. Caroline felt herself wincing and tried to reverse the process. Marrying Tiny was supposed to finally make her mother proud. She took a deep breath.

"Tiny invited her—you know that," Caroline said. "And she's one of my best friends," she added.

Mabel smirked. "Is that what you call it now?"

Caroline leaned forward to pick up her glass. Mabel pulled her back by her shoulder ever so slightly.

"You promised you wouldn't mess this up," Mabel whispered in a singsong voice. The words tickled Caroline's eardrum and she shivered.

"I won't mess this up, Mother," she singsonged back.

Mabel did a subtle nod and turned her attention back to Tiny. "You really do look absolutely marvelous, dear!"

~

A few minutes later, everyone was seated back at the table, Mabel and Peter talking easily with Connie and Andrew. Caroline sat back for just long enough to appreciate that she was engulfed in the sounds of her favorite people. It felt good, sitting here, Tiny across from her, this weekend expanding into so many possibilities.

"Where's Daphne?" Caroline asked Trip, wondering as she opened her mouth if she was poking the bear.

"She's on her way," he started to answer, then took a sip of his drink. "The kids have so much going on right now, the three of them are flying down tomorrow. First flight in, I think?" He failed at keeping his voice light.

"Isn't that risky? What if they don't make it?"

Trip didn't miss a beat. "You'll understand when you have kids of your own. It's a lot of responsibility. Sometimes we have to make sacrifices."

Caroline held up her hands in mock surrender.

"Now we don't have a flower girl or a ring bearer," Mabel said, almost to herself but just loud enough for Bitty to hear.

"What did anyone say about not having a flower girl or a ring bearer?" Bitty said. "They'll be here. Daphne wouldn't let them miss it."

Trip tapped his fingers on the table. "They'll be here!" he said, forcing the enthusiasm in his voice. "Now, who can I convince to play a little tennis this afternoon?"

~

Caroline watched Bitty watch the waiter hand out a tray of Dark 'N' Stormys. She was all but salivating, yet also watching to make sure everyone accepted the beverage. WASPs and their booze. There was no other culture on the planet so simultaneously dependent on drinking and having others drink with them. For these people, tragedy was drinking alone.

"Stormy over here!" Andrew yelped, likely taking advantage of Bitty's desire for a drinking buddy. His unencumbered gait was that of a poodle puppy. He lightly touched Bitty's shoulder and Caroline watched her flinch. WASPs and their physical touching. Not that she was any different, but Caroline had always prided herself on at least noticing her people's tried-and-true rituals.

Connie leaned across the table and whispered, "Check your phone."

If I decide to write a feature about WASPs and wedding culture, would you be willing to go on the record?

Caroline typed back. I can't believe you're here.

Me neither.

Caroline's phone buzzed in her hand.

So . . . can I count on you to provide some sound bites for the article?

~

If you use my alter ego, Halsey, then we're a go.

Halsey was the name Caroline and her college friends used to reference anytime Caroline got out of hand. She was the free-spirited, outspoken side of Caroline, and someone rarely seen since the mid-2000s.

What would Halsey think of this weekend?

Caroline read the text four times before putting her phone back in her pocket without responding.

The drinks were distributed and immediately consumed.

Caroline had grown up with Dark 'N' Stormys, but her parents didn't drink like their friends drank. They were both take-it-or-leave-it types, utterly rare birds for a town like Greenwich, and Caroline had inherited their preference for good sleep and fried food.

She tuned in to the table and heard the small-talk game still going strong.

"I did hear we might get some rain tomorrow," Caroline said, deciding to play the game.

"The hotel mentioned the rain," Trip said, clearly past the point of humiliation for being here alone. "But we can handle a little rain, can't we?"

"I can't," Andrew said, sucking the last sip of his drink through a straw. "I melt."

Dick laughed harder than anyone, himself especially, expected.

"You melt! Now that's something!"

"Oh yes, Dick, we *all* melt." Andrew looked conspiratorially at Connie and Caroline and Tiny. Bitty looked ready to fall off her chair. Dick was as amused as ever. He raised his glass.

"Well, then I think we should toast to it! To melting!"

"To melting!"

Everyone played along, joyously clinking their glasses together and laughing as Dick laughed the loudest and kept saying, "Cheers!"

"Hello, brides!" came a voice from behind her. Caroline spun around and saw Daisy with an obviously drunk Hank. Tiny leaped up to greet her best friend and the girls embraced as only friends from childhood do. Trip got up too and awkwardly shook Hank's hand and kissed Daisy on the cheek, his gait suddenly as jumpy as Andrew's.

Mabel leaned over to Caroline.

"How does Tiny seem?" she asked.

"Good. Excited. Definitely excited," Caroline said. "It's going to be a great weekend."

"Good girl. And you'll keep her excited?" Her mother was speaking so quietly out of the corner of her mouth, it didn't look like they were talking at all.

Caroline looked at her first. "You don't have anything to worry about."

DICK

He could do this. He, Richard Franklin McAllister III, could do this. He was a respected man in the community; he belonged to four golf clubs and had a pool that went from outdoor to indoor, as well as a driveway they kept heated in the winter. He had been married to a beautiful woman for forty years and raised three debatably functioning children. He ran a fund that was often written about in the trades, and he gave exactly 25 percent of his earnings back to charity. He maintained a nine handicap, had kept the same group of friends since grade school, and prided himself on being the only man over seventy he knew who was still allowed to eat red meat. When Trip had asked at the age of eight whether they'd ever move from Sandwich Road, Dick had replied, "Change is for the birds."

Dick sat back in his chair and looked around the table. This was not a table he ever thought he'd be hosting. Not that he was against alternative lifestyles. He wasn't, at least in theory. But it was a lot to wrap his head around, he thought, his eyes subtly moving from one person to the next. The thing that confused him was how the men looked a little like women—he could see Andrew was clearly wearing mascara—and the women looked a little like men—Connie was a beanpole in a button-down. It was confusing, putting Connie next to, say . . . he scanned the table until he saw Daisy, who sat quite normally and looked quite like a woman should.

His eyes caught Tiny's and she gave a little wave, knocking him out of his trance. He just wanted her to be happy. Like all parents want for their children. But this table made him feel completely old and out of touch and like the world had changed one night after he'd fallen asleep in front of the local news.

People had started to order, finally putting his suggestion of a casual chicken salad sandwich lunch to rest. Bitty had been horrified when he'd suggested sandwiches and insisted everyone be offered the full menu.

"Shrimp cocktail!" Andrew said, making a point to stroke his chin in contemplation. "That sounds perfect! I'll start with that and also do the cobb salad with lobster."

The shrimp cocktail got the table's attention and sent a wave of ordering all the way to Dick. Daisy's husband, Hank, asked loudly if maybe he should order two.

"Can I get a show of hands of who would like to start with shrimp cocktail?" the waiter, who sensed an opportunity, asked. Everyone except Dick raised their hand. He'd never seen the point in shrimp cocktail, not when there were oysters or caviar. Shrimp itself tasted like very little, and then you were stuck with the tail, like a secret you never wanted to know.

"And can I get a show of hands of who would like to double their order?" All the men except Dick raised their hands.

"Dick," Bitty said, and he realized this was not the first time she was saying his name. He raised his eyebrows in answer.

"I've ordered a bottle of the burgundy and two bottles of the pinot grigio. Do you want a beer as well?"

This started another onslaught of orders as people requested beers and vodka seltzers and rosé and Hank, drunker than a skunk, ordered a martini.

"He didn't mean that," Daisy said to the waiter, course correcting the martini into a light beer. "Could you pour it into a plastic tumbler for him?" she said next, patting Hank's back in the way wives did to tell their husbands something wasn't up for discussion.

"Oh, let him have some fun!" Andrew cut in, ignoring Daisy's panicked look. "Martinis for all!"

"Andrew, stop," Caroline said quickly and sharply. Andrew put his hands up in mock surrender.

Hank looked between Daisy and Andrew, angel and devil right there on his shoulders, and looked again at Daisy for long enough that she took advantage of the moment. The waiter was still standing behind him, smart enough to know that Daisy had the final word.

"Let's do a light beer in a tumbler and we can have a martini later, okay?" she said to her husband, like she was offering a candy bribe to a small child. He nodded along and Andrew returned his attention to Bitty.

~

Dick's only daughter was marrying a woman. His little girl, the one with the pigtails and the affinity for gymnastics and soccer. She wasn't supposed to marry a woman, Dick thought, looking at Tiny momentarily, then looking away before she looked at him and risked catching him thinking this. No, his feelings about Tiny had been long kept inside, away from view. It was his only choice.

The table talked around him, ignorant to his sweating palms and his upset stomach and his swollen feet.

Trip looked at him expectantly. Dick didn't realize they'd been talking. His ability to tune out reality for his own thoughts was one of Dick's favorite skills.

"So what do you think?"

Dick searched his mind for what his son might be talking about. "I think this weekend is going to be really nice."

Trip rolled his eyes. "What do you think about putting me up for Wing Foot. Jesus, Dad, we've been talking about this for months."

Dick repositioned himself in his chair and took a sip of beer before responding.

"It's not the right year, I don't think."

Trip's eyes flared, his eyebrows so furrowed, they were almost touching.

"Not the right year?" he said through gritted teeth.

Dick had no choice but to sit up straighter and puff out his chest.

"As I've said, this club is hugely competitive, and timing is everything. It's not something where I simply march into the clubhouse and sign you up. There's a process."

His son looked like he was about to lose it and Dick debated whether he needed to put a hand on Trip's forearm and remind him that this was not the place.

Daisy poked her head around Hank and interrupted them. Dick could have kissed her.

"Trip, Bitty just told me you closed the Cooper account. That's fantastic! Truly." She beamed kindly.

Trip loosened his shoulders. "Thanks, Daise. Yeah, it was a ride, but we made it."

"Well, I'm proud. I know you've been working on that for a long time."

"Thanks," Trip said again. "How's work for you? The museum?"

"You wouldn't believe the number of kids who aren't exposed to the arts," Daisy started, putting down her fork and shaking her head for effect. "I'm just trying to get through to some of them."

Trip nodded along. "So true."

"How are the twins? Are they in music classes and the like?" Daisy asked.

"That William has a real ear for music, I think," Dick said, and Trip smiled at the thought.

"Lucinda not as much," Trip said. Both Daisy and Dick laughed politely.

~

Hank spilled his beer glass on the table. The liquid spread out like a blanket, traveling far enough to hit the other side's edge and utterly soaking Daisy. Dick should have said something: Don't give a drunk man a glass. Give him a sippy cup.

"Hank!" was all Daisy said, jumping up, grabbing the tumbler, and pushing Hank back into his chair in the sort of fluid motion only the wife of a drunk can do. The rest of the table was stuck between getting up to help and hoping that if they pretended everything was fine, everything would be fine. Daisy continued to mop up the liquid, the wheat and the hops emanating into the tropical air. Hank still hadn't moved.

"What just happened?" she said much quieter, almost to herself, and Dick felt guilty for hearing it at all. Hank sat there with a bewildered look on his face. There were two shot glasses between his and Andrew's seats. Andrew was equally silent.

"We did a quick tequila shot while you went to the bathroom," Andrew said, feigning apology.

Daisy touched Hank's shoulder, leaned down, and whispered something in his ear. He partially used his arms to get up from the chair and mostly let Daisy guide his body into a standing position. The two hobbled off the terrace while two waiters made sure any remnants of the spilled beer were properly disappeared.

~

Daisy and Hank weren't totally gone before the table resumed its conversation, glasses clinking and utensils scraping plates like nothing had ever happened. The most Dick saw was a raised eyebrow and eye roll from Bitty, like this sort of thing happened all the time.

Trip turned his head back to his father. The brief lightness in Trip's face at the mention of his kids was long gone. "Will you make the call or not?"

Dick felt frozen in a way he'd never been before. He knew the answer: of course make the call, of course help your son continue his journey toward legacy. But his mouth felt physically closed, his lips sewn together so tightly, it was hard to believe they'd ever been apart. He chided himself. *Speak! Say something!*

Trip had waited long enough. When no response came, he sneered and shook his head. "You're unbelievable, you know that? I just asked for some help from my dad. Thanks for nothing."

Sometimes, he wanted to say to his son, smug with youth, *sometimes you can work for your entire life and things still go terribly wrong.*

"Trip, it's not that—" he started, but Trip cut him off.

"You're the one who always talks about legacy. I can't uphold my end of the bargain if you don't open any doors."

Dick let Trip get up and move to a seat at the other end of the table. He couldn't tell his son that he had made the call, that he'd made it several times, and Trip was not going to be offered membership. He'd been just rowdy enough as a young man to cast too long a shadow to walk alongside his father.

By now, the table was littered with remnants of items served: wineglasses, bread baskets, salad plates, the dreaded shrimp cocktail, entrée plates, silverware strewn about. Andrew was refilling Bitty's wineglass at the other end of the table and Dick hoped this would result in Napping Bitty versus Angry Bitty.

The wind had picked up enough that the waiters were pulling down the clear plastic flaps around the periphery of the terrace, and for the first time since arriving, Dick really looked up at the sky and out toward the water. Noticing things was typically at the bottom of his to-do list: he figured he'd see what he needed to see when it was in front of him. The place was lovely; there was no other word for it.

Dick looked back toward the table as the waiter opened another bottle of the burgundy. Trip was now talking to Bitty, and Tiny was looking concerned as she watched Daisy and Hank fade from view. At this moment, Robbie was his favorite child, regardless of whether he hadn't been home in three years. If Robbie didn't come home, it meant Dick couldn't disappoint him.

SNORKELING EXCURSION

TRIP

Daphne ignored his sixth call of the day. He threw the phone onto the bed and paced for the umpteenth time between the far walls of the cottage. He could see a playground from the living room and it felt especially cruel. It was nearly three. He knew he was supposed to be at the main clubhouse by now, that a hotel van taking them to the snorkeling spot was leaving at three sharp. But he couldn't break this cycle: dial, listen, throw phone, pace. Dial, listen, throw phone, debate hopping on a plane back to New York, pace. She did this to torture him: she hadn't blocked his number or turned off her phone; otherwise his calls would be going straight to voice mail. Instead, the phone would ring and ring and ring, each time Trip thinking maybe Daphne would answer, until he heard the now-familiar notification that the voice mailbox was full.

The irony that he was down here to officiate his sister's wedding was not lost on him. At some point, everyone was going to find out that his wife had left him. Divorce papers and all, served to him on his own front stoop. He was humiliated. He was furious. But mostly he had been so lonely for so long that he couldn't right himself, like a kayak stuck upside down.

"What's happening in there?" a voice from outside called. He looked over the railing. Daisy stood on the path leading down to the clubhouse, her blue-and-white vertical-striped cover-up revealing just enough to remind Trip of how they used to know each other.

"Just wiling the day away," he said, trying to lean on the railing in such a way as to accentuate his torso.

"Where's your family?" She asked this innocently and it took every ounce of self-control for Trip to keep his cool.

"The kids. They're so busy right now. Daphne's bringing them tomorrow."

Daisy stood in place and didn't say anything back. Trip smiled and wiggled his eyes up and down to break the tension. It worked.

"Well, are you coming snorkeling or what?"

"Are you?"

She held up her hand like a visor. "Of course. I'm the maid of honor or whatever. I go to all the events."

"Where's Hank?"

"Writing the next great American novel." She said this dryly, which gave Trip pause.

"Taking a nap?" he offered.

"Jet lag is a beast," she said.

He turned back to his room and looked at the iPhone on his bed. His number was so ignored by Daphne's, even social media notifications weren't popping up.

"Hang on—I'll come around. We can walk together."

"We're already late. I'll see you there."

She turned and started walking, not looking back and not like someone hoping to be followed. Daisy wore her hair differently from the last time they'd seen each other, and Trip caught himself replaying all the hairstyles he'd ever seen her with as she walked out of view. He realized he was posing and stood up abruptly, a little embarrassed.

He tried Daphne once more while he traded Nantucket Reds for a sky-blue Patagonia bathing suit with red lobsters all over it and threw whatever looked snorkeling-appropriate into a white canvas beach bag.

"You have to stop calling me."

"You picked up!" he said. "You picked up," he said again, calmer and more serious.

"I mean it, Trip. Stop calling me."

"I miss you."

"You don't, actually. How could you? This has been over for a very, very long time," she said, raising her voice when she sensed he was about to interrupt. "We need to let the lawyers figure it out." Her voice was like crushed ice falling into a glass.

"But what if I don't want this to be over?" Trip hadn't realized how desperate he felt. He didn't want to be alone.

"Trip, stop it. Please. For me. For the kids."

"Well then, fuck you, Daphne. See what your lawyer is actually able to get, given you *abandoned me.*"

"Abandoned you! Please. I'm raising our children. You stopped coming home—"

"Because you changed the locks!"

Spit had gathered at the corners of his mouth. It didn't matter how often they had this fight—it always felt like the first time, and Trip imagined sticking his hand through the phone and pulling her hair.

"This is good, Trip. Get angry. Yell. We all know it's what you do best."

"I don't have to put up with this, you know," Trip said, haughty.

"THEN STOP CALLING ME!" Daphne screamed so loudly, Trip half expected the bedside lamp to shake. He heard the line go dead, and then the only sound left was his panting.

He threw the phone on the bed (again) and paced one more time before finally making it to and out his door.

CAROLINE

The group agreed to meet at the main clubhouse at three, where a van would bring them to a choice snorkeling spot fifteen minutes east. The ride was uneventful, and when they arrived, they learned the boat could hold twelve comfortably and fourteen if people squished and CBC could provide snorkeling equipment to anyone who wanted it. Drinks and canapés too. Caroline wondered who among this crew had brought their own swim masks. At what point on the wealth scale does someone start to buy resort toys? She looked at Bitty and Dick, wrinkly and elegantly tanned under big sun hats. Dick held up a monogrammed L.L.Bean canvas bag and she realized with as much horror as chagrin that, in fact, her future in-laws were exactly the type of people who brought their own snorkel equipment. She rubbed sunscreen into her face and neck and shoulders.

Daisy and Trip also carried monogrammed L.L.Bean canvas bags and they also traveled with their own swim masks and snorkels. Of course they did.

Mabel and Peter ambled up the path to the dock, Peter also holding a monogrammed L.L.Bean canvas bag; when Caroline intercepted her parents to look inside, she saw that they also had their own swim masks.

"When did you become people who own your own swim masks?" she asked, horrified and jealous that she was the only one using resort-issued equipment. They even had water shoes on. The kind for scuba diving.

"Don't be ridiculous," her mother said. "We've always had masks. You used to have one too until you left it at that beach house we rented in Antigua."

"When I was a teenager?"

Mabel nodded.

"Why didn't you get me a new one?"

"You said you were over water sports," Peter said, looking around for Dick and Bitty. He spotted them and walked away.

Mabel pulled out her mask and handed it to Caroline. "Do you want to use mine?"

Caroline took the mask and started sizing it to her head. "Thanks, Mom," she said and walked to the boat.

~

Connie came up behind her. "Hey, you," she said into Caroline's ear. "Are we the only people here who didn't bring our own snorkels?"

"Speak for yourself. I stole my mother's." Caroline held up her mask. "I'm so embarrassed to not have brought a snorkel to my own wedding." The word *wedding* struck Connie and Caroline felt guilty for saying it. "But thank God Coral Beach will let us borrow theirs!" she said in a rush, trying to bring a smile back to Connie's face.

Connie was tall and radiant, her sandy-brown hair falling in waves around her face, tropical humidity be damned. Their friendship was like two trees wrapped around each other, fused and imprisoned at the same time.

"How was your flight down?"

At this, Caroline started to speak quietly. "It was fine, but the flight attendant thought Tiny was a child and Andrew never showed up, so I thought he had disappeared. Imagine my surprise when he beat us here. I think he's the only person I know who can run so late that he somehow makes an earlier flight than he'd meant to."

Connie rolled her eyes.

"He was also supposed to help me pack last night but never showed up."

"Because he caught an earlier flight and forgot to tell you?" Connie said, her wit immediately hitting Caroline in that spot she thought was gone.

"Exactly. He flies down and I'm left to pack alone."

"I would have helped you pack," Connie said.

"I didn't know you were coming! Remember? And plus, it wouldn't have been fun for you. Just a bunch of white outfits. Plus Tiny was there and all anxious because Bitty was rapid-fire texting after too much wine. I wish she wasn't so desperate for approval, you know?" Caroline emphasized "you know" too much, which made the words come out so loudly, others sitting on wooden benches on the dock near the boat turned around.

"It's okay with Tiny, you know." Connie nearly whispered this. "The three of us can hang out. I won't do anything crazy." She flared her eyes in an attempt to lighten the moment.

Caroline looked at her and scrunched her eyebrows. "Of course we can."

"Tiny was the one who invited me, after all," Connie said, still whispering.

Caroline clenched her jaw and tried to breathe. "I know she did. I know. And it's great. I just didn't expect it and my mind is spinning out a little bit."

"Because it would be easier if I wasn't here?" Connie asked.

～

Caroline was about to answer when she caught Mabel staring at them.

"Mom," she said, interrupting the gaze. Mabel sat up straighter. Connie was leaning back to trail her hand in the water.

"Mm?"

"Oh, nothing," Caroline said, shrugging. "I forgot what I was going to say."

Connie sat back up. "I need to find my date! Andrew!" she called, getting up and leaving Caroline with her mother.

~

The Coral Beach attendant started ushering the group onto the boat and giving snorkeling instructions. Her parents were the first on and situated themselves at the stern, where they could sit together and see everyone else boarding. Her father's hand rested lightly over Mabel's. They looked happy, Caroline thought, feeling at least partially responsible. Bitty meanwhile stayed on the bench on the dock, her legs wrapped like a pretzel and her foot tapping against the wood.

"You all have fun!" she said, waving with her whole hand flapping up and down. "The water is just not for me!" Dick barely registered her goodbye as he stepped on board and gestured approvingly toward the sea.

As Caroline stepped onto the boat, Mabel was suddenly there to offer a hand, the happy look in her eyes from a second ago all but disappeared.

"We need this marriage," she said. "We need it," she said again.

"Jesus," Caroline said under her breath. "Stop breathing down my neck." She walked to the bow before her mother could do anything.

~

Tiny came and sat next to her, squeezing her hand and leaning a little into her chest.

"Hey, babe," she said, kissing the top of Tiny's head. She still smelled like home.

TINY

The weekend *was* heavily planned, Tiny thought, leaning on the edge of the boat and taking in the seascape around her. It had been Bitty's doing: she hated downtime unless it was structured, and she found nothing ruder for guests than when they didn't know where to go next. The McAllisters had once thrown a party in Manchester, Vermont, that was so elaborately planned, it took place over three days, included a pig roast and a scavenger hunt, and everyone who attended—nearly 250 people—called it the McAllister Family Wedding. Tiny had come out shortly before, and one of Dick's favorite jokes was that this might be the only wedding he'd have to pay for.

"It's our job to tell them where to *go*," Bitty had told Tiny after she asked if maybe they could forgo either the snorkeling or the boat ride. It felt indulgent.

"Don't be ridiculous," Bitty said. Tiny could see her mother rolling her eyes.

"What about the men's golf, then? Who will even play?"

"Tiny," her mother said, now annoyed, "you don't invite a group of people down to an island for a wedding and not offer golf. It's not done. Plus, at the very least, Trip, your father, and Peter will play. Hank too if he's up to it."

"Couldn't that exact foursome play at CCC any weekend they'd like?" Tiny hated golf. She hated that it couldn't be casually played: either you golfed or you did not golf. And if you did not golf, you needed to ensure that anyone in your life who did golf had adequate time to play golf.

"The men will play golf on Saturday. I've already found the course."

The conversation was over. There would be snorkeling, boating, croquet, and golf. Tennis on Saturday. Spa for the women, and four scheduled meals between two restaurants. Now, as Tiny sat wedged between Trip and Caroline, she almost laughed out loud at the number of sightseeing brochures Bitty had put in the welcome bags. Who would have the time?

"Should we go?" she asked Caroline after the boat driver dropped the anchor. Caroline looked faraway.

"Let's do it!" she said, getting up from her perch too quickly and nearly falling over the side.

The Coral Beach snorkel coordinator offered a brief instruction and pep talk.

"When you're swimming," he said, mimicking something between a breaststroke and a doggy paddle, "best to keep your hands at your sides. The fish are not for petting." At this, he mimicked a petting motion, to which Trip and Andrew both started petting the air and laughing when they saw the other doing it too. Tiny considered how often common ground presents itself almost by accident.

The group outfitted themselves with flippers and masks and snorkels and one by one stepped out into the water. Tiny paddled and kicked over to Caroline.

"Hiya!" she said with the snorkel in her mouth. She held up her fingers in a peace sign.

Caroline nodded and winked and started swimming toward the shore, where the boat driver promised the best fish sightings. Tiny followed suit and was swept away by the underwater. Fish were everywhere, striking in their yellows and blacks and reds and blues. It was like a little pride aquarium and Tiny took it as a good omen for the rest of the weekend. A stream of her ex-girlfriends swam past, all different versions of what she understood *alternative* to mean, the short hair or the tattoos or the Peter Pan approach to life. She'd always been like Goldilocks, looking for someone who could fit into what she was already trying to build. She never liked the idea of running away from home to be her true self. Why couldn't she be who she was where she was from? Caroline had appeared like a mirage right there on the street. Someone who already knew where she'd been and where she was going. It would be fine, the wedding and everything that would come after, she thought, kicking her feet a little harder against the current.

She lost herself in the reef, coming as close as she could bear without touching it and trying to follow a particularly striking yellow-and-black-striped fish on its course. She paused, her thoughts and the water colliding for one utterly silent moment, and realized she was very much alone. Caroline was not to her right or her left or up ahead, and Tiny swung around jaggedly to see if she was behind her.

She didn't want to be alone. Not right now, not when she knew there could be an eel or a barracuda lurking just beneath the reef. She tried to remember what the instructor had said, whether she should try to remain perfectly still or splash her way to the surface should a creature intersect her path. She was a guest in this ecosystem, not a member.

You can do this, she told herself, her heart beating wildly. She was too far from the others, so she squinted to really look, and she could see figures too many yards away, pairs of swimmers ambling around. Tiny turned her body again and started kicking in that direction, doing multiplication in her head to calm her thoughts. It was her wedding weekend: she couldn't possibly be attacked now.

Tiny finally reached the other swimmers closest to where she'd started and was surprised to see Caroline's feet kicking alongside Connie's. Daisy wasn't anywhere to be seen, until Tiny realized they were nearly back to the boat, and the missing snorkelers were simply out of the water. She counted again in efforts to slow her breathing, not wanting to be panting when she got back on board. Caroline popped her head out of the water and saw Tiny.

"Why, hello there," she said, now smiling, her eyes bloodshot from the salt.

"You swam away from me," was all Tiny could say. The boat driver offered her his hand out of the water.

"I got distracted by the fish!" Caroline said to her back, her hand grazing Tiny's foot as it stepped up. "I didn't mean to leave you behind." Her voice sounded hollow and faraway.

DRESSING FOR THE REHEARSAL

TINY

The rehearsal was supposed to start in an hour, at six on the dot, and Caroline was still not back from the beach. After snorkeling, Tiny had come back up to shower, expecting Caroline to trail behind a few minutes later, but that had been over an hour ago. She stretched out her getting-ready ritual as long as possible, but even with shaving and looking in the mirror, it was all over thirty minutes later. She even shampooed and conditioned twice, then dried her hair with a brush, as opposed to turning her head upside down and frenetically moving the blow dryer around until her hair was dry. High-maintenance was not like a switch that could be turned on or off. She looked out from the balcony and saw Caroline sitting with Connie and Andrew and Mabel, the four in deep conversation. Trip ambled over too and sat down next to the group. She kept watching in case Caroline looked up and saw her.

~

A few minutes later, there was a knock on the door as Tiny was zipping up her dress (picked out by Bitty, disliked by Caroline). It was white, sleeveless, and very fitted. Tiny felt swaddled. Caroline was back, finally.

"Coming!" It was Daisy. Tiny's heart fell a few inches toward her stomach. Daisy was already dressed and she looked rich. Pretty too,

Tiny thought, but mostly rich and, like Tiny, not overly done up. They'd always shared a lack of fussiness, even when boys were lining up for Daisy and Daisy was determined to make them line up for Tiny. Of course, when Tiny had finally told Daisy the truth of who she really wanted to line up for her, Daisy had simply raised her hands over her head and said, "You're the first lesbian I've ever known! And you've been right under my nose this whole time!" Tiny hadn't known what to do with such blanket acceptance. Years later, when Daisy started getting increasingly protective of Hank and Caroline couldn't understand the girls' friendship, Tiny couldn't begin to explain what it felt like that her friend never missed a beat. You don't leave behind a friendship like that.

"I thought we could sneak in a little toast just the two of us," Daisy said, revealing a half bottle of Veuve Clicquot.

Tiny fumbled around the minibar until she found two flutes.

"Well, this is fun!" she said as Daisy poured the champagne. They clinked glasses and each took a sip. It was quiet, almost awkwardly so despite a twenty-year friendship. "Should I put on some music?"

Daisy nodded as she said, "Sure."

Soon a Paul Simon song started playing through a Bluetooth speaker in the corner. Both women sat on the edge of the bed and watched where the music was coming from.

"I'm so glad you're here," Tiny said after a few moments.

Daisy leaned in to Tiny's shoulder. "Of course, friend. It's your big weekend."

They were quiet again.

"How's it going really?" Daisy said this like she'd dared herself to speak. Abruptly and all at once.

"You know how Caroline is," Tiny said.

Daisy nodded. "But how are you?"

"I feel like if we can get through the wedding and this weekend, then everything will be okay. Once Caroline and I are actually married, I can take comfort in that when she is moody or stressed or something.

Because we'll be married, so that means whatever is making her moody or stressed or whatever isn't me."

Daisy nodded more and squeezed her lips together. Tiny drank her champagne. They both looked at the speaker again, now crooning a Van Morrison song.

"I get it," Daisy finally said.

"I'm not being fair," Tiny said, tapping the side of the champagne flute with her pointer finger. "She's not that moody. She's just focused."

"She's really focused," Daisy said, nodding and taking a sip. "Hank's the same way," she said after a moment.

"Really?" Tiny asked, nervous that Daisy was comparing Caroline to Hank, even if it was just in her own head. Hank was a drug addict and perpetually underemployed as a novelist.

"Really. He gets totally moody and it took me forever to learn that nine out of ten times, it wasn't me." Daisy looked right at Tiny as she spoke. Tiny took it in, nodding as the words registered. It was exactly like Caroline.

"People only get married when they're in love, right?" Tiny faced Daisy so she knew it was a real question.

Daisy didn't miss a beat and put her hand over Tiny's.

"Right."

~

Twenty minutes later, Daisy was gone and Caroline was now swimming. Tiny had drained the last of the champagne and was fussing with her shoes (even though it was a small heel, she preferred flats) when someone else knocked on the door.

"Coming!" It was Bitty this time.

"I thought you might want some jewelry?" Bitty said, letting herself into the cottage while Tiny tried to covertly toss unfolded clothes behind the bathroom door. Items, mostly Caroline's, lay strewn about haphazardly and Tiny was mortified. The women did not embrace.

Tiny considered her mother. She was beautiful. She did not simply look good for her age. Bitty was svelte, more so than Tiny, and far more physically disciplined. She had been exercising long before it was trendy. Tiny sometimes ran around a tennis court—a childhood spent at the club every summer ensured she was a deft tennis player—but the faster she moved, the more she felt like Bambi. Bitty was impeccably dressed in the sense that she did not throw on clothes—she wore outfits. Of the children, Trip was most like her: fit, groomed, and well presented no matter the occasion. Robbie was most like Dick: softer, nicer, and could fit in anywhere. Tiny fell in the middle. She was pretty but never stood out, fit but never first, blended in but also faded into the background.

Today Bitty wore a fuchsia Escada dress, despite Tiny's plea that the weekend be intimate and casual. Tiny recognized it from a recent blitz of texts late one night. Bitty had matched it with Van Cleef clover earrings, multicolored pearls, and Jimmy Choo glittery, sling-back gold kitten heels. Bitty was more dressed up than either bride. She was also holding a light-pink sun hat to protect her face until the sun went down. The hat looked ridiculous, but Tiny didn't say anything.

Bitty stood awkwardly, like she didn't know how to continue an interaction until she was offered something.

"I've got some wine?" Tiny said to her mother, taking a bottle of chardonnay out of the minibar fridge.

Bitty held the bottle and turned the label toward her, looking surprised and satisfied. Tiny was not a girl who knew her way around a wine cellar.

"This is a pretty good bottle," she said, looking up and then back down at the label. "Where'd you get it?"

"Oh, Daisy brought it in her luggage. She thought it would be fun to have while we got ready tomorrow. But we can open it now."

Bitty started uncorking the bottle before Tiny finished speaking.

"Great," she said, the cork making a slight popping sound as it slid up. Tiny held out two glasses and Bitty poured generously. They clinked glasses but didn't say anything.

Tiny turned back to the mirror. Her dress felt literally all-consuming and she wished Caroline were here so she could see what she was wearing. Caroline had insisted that their outfits stay a surprise until each event, a twist on the traditional bridal reveal, and Tiny swooned every time Caroline showed initiative with the wedding. Her high school self still couldn't believe she was marrying Caroline Schell, lacrosse star, untouchably cool, turner of countless curious girls.

Bitty started laying out pavé diamond earrings and strands of pearls on top of the dresser.

"Caroline is still on the beach," Tiny said, not sure why she felt compelled to explain her fiancée's absence.

"That's fine—it won't take her long to get ready," Bitty said, her focus completely on the pearls—one Mikimoto, one Tiffany, the rest family pieces—and two pairs of diamond earrings, one with sizable miner's-cut diamonds and one pavé in the shape of a butterfly. They were beautiful and Tiny felt silly wearing them, like she was still playing dress-up with her mother's clothing.

Bitty moved behind Tiny and clasped one strand around her neck after the other.

"These look nice, don't they?" she said, clasping a final strand she'd gotten from a dealer in Hong Kong.

They really did look beautiful, the pearls a brilliant white against Tiny's lightly tanned skin.

"Don't you care?" Tiny asked, her fingers lightly caressing the pearls over her collarbone.

"Don't I care about what?" Bitty asked.

"That Caroline isn't here yet getting ready?"

Bitty took a sip from her wineglass and looked at Tiny through the mirror.

"I think you should wear Mimi's pearls," she said.

"We can't decide if I should take her name or not. Or if she should take mine. Ours."

Bitty stood up a little straighter.

"I think you should do whatever you'd like." Bitty unclasped the Hong Kong pearls and lay her grandmother's strand around her neck. Tiny traded out one diamond earring for the other. Tiny thought she looked exactly the same.

"So I should be Tiny Schell?"

The name sounded ridiculous.

Bitty took another sip of wine.

"If you'd like."

Tiny searched her mother's face for something that looked like love or pride or ownership over her daughter. Her mother's eyes wouldn't meet hers.

"Mom."

She watched her mother clench her jaw and raise her eyebrows.

"Yes?"

"Were you nervous when you married Dad?"

Bitty nodded and Tiny immediately exhaled. Nerves were normal.

"But I also knew it was the right thing to do."

Tiny would wear the white pearls that had been her grandmother's and the vintage Tiffany diamond drop earrings.

"You look beautiful, Tiny," Bitty said, still standing behind her. Tiny felt like her mother was looking at her for the first time.

"Thank you," she whispered back, unsure of what to do with Bitty's gaze.

Bitty caught herself out of the moment and started collecting the unused jewelry. She set the cup of wine down on the vanity.

"So we'll see you on the patio in a few minutes?"

Tiny got up to walk her mother out.

At the doorway, Bitty turned around suddenly, nearly knocking into Tiny.

"We all deserve to be happy," she said, her head cast slightly down.

Bitty turned around and walked through the door.

CAROLINE

Nothing felt right. Not the light-blue seersucker blazer (too tight in the shoulders), not the white silk short-sleeve top (she carried her weight in the middle), not the matching seersucker pants she'd thought would be perfect for tonight (they pushed the weight up and out, making her feel like a doughnut). She couldn't decide if she was clammy or hot and she knew this was another instance in which the vision in her head and the one in front of her were horribly out of sync.

Tiny was humming a little in the bathroom, hair gels and makeup splayed by the sink.

"How much time do I have?" Caroline called into the bathroom, pulling at her top again.

"You have exactly fifteen *minutos*," Tiny called back, her voice almost still in a hum.

"You know when you use words in foreign languages at random times, that could be construed as appropriation," Caroline said. Why was she saying that? She flared her eyes at herself in the mirror and waited with bated breath for Tiny to say something back.

It felt like a year passed until, "You now have thirteen minutes and we shouldn't be late." The hum was gone but she didn't take the bait.

Tiny was a gigantic step in the right direction. At least that's what Caroline had been told at least once a day since they finally started dating three years previous. It was not unexpected: Caroline had known Tiny her entire life; the girl was practically family. Until she wasn't, and now she supposed it was lucky that they weren't. When Caroline had come out, it was a nonsecret secret: her parents loved her, Mabel especially was excited for the opportunity to flex her socially progressive muscles, but it was also agreed the Schells would be quiet about Caroline's *lifestyle*.

"We don't disapprove," her father had said, "but there is absolutely no harm in a little discretion." He said this like he was selling it. Caroline nodded along, and together they decided who they would tell: Caroline's friends from college, people she met in her post-college life, and who they wouldn't tell: the extended family, close family friends, anyone from Greenwich. Caroline had been good enough at keeping it quiet until she got drunk at The Ginger Man and was caught kissing a bi-curious high school friend right there on Greenwich Avenue.

When Tiny had come out five years later, Mabel picked up the phone and dialed her daughter.

"You and Tiny McAllister have something in common," she'd said, nearly breathless.

The news hadn't yet hit the lesbian mafia of Greenwich, Connecticut, so Caroline was legitimately confused.

"Tiny McAllister?" she asked, making sure she'd heard it correctly.

"Tiny McAllister!" her mother exclaimed.

"What on earth would Tiny McAllister and I have in common?" Caroline did a mental rewind of everything she knew about this girl: much younger; cute but, again, younger; not known as a partier or a nonpartier; not known as particularly cool or uncool. She was like any other younger version of Caroline's old classmates.

"Oh, just think about it," her mother said coyly. And then it clicked. Of course.

"Did Bitty and Dick just find out?" Caroline asked, wondering how that family meeting had gone. She imagined Trip as a smug teenager wielding his lacrosse stick like the status symbol it was only to realize he had a gay sister.

"They did. And Bitty called—of course she would. I think I'm the only person she knows who understands." Mabel said this conspiratorially, proud and emphatic with social justice.

"That's interesting." And it was. If she remembered correctly, Tiny was cute, in a word. And the idea of dating someone from her world felt suddenly right. Refreshing. She made a note to start looking for her in that way lesbians, especially those from the same small towns, orbited each other.

"I think it's *very* interesting," her mother said, and Caroline knew what would come next. "You and Tiny McAllister could be perfect. Just perfect."

~

Caroline was still standing in front of the mirror mid-daydream when Tiny came out of the bathroom.

"You look cute," she said as she crossed the room to kiss Caroline on the cheek. Polite to a fault. Caroline squatted down a little and jutted out her hips to pull up her pants.

"I look like a preppy whale."

"Don't be ridiculous," Tiny said, nymphlike in her own white dress. Caroline looked at her and remembered that Tiny really was beautiful. Her hair was almost sparkling, her eyes catching the late-afternoon sun streaming in from the terrace. She was the girl Caroline never thought she could marry because girls like Tiny don't often marry other girls. Caroline, on the other hand, looking again in the mirror and wondering why on earth she'd thought seersucker helped broad shoulders, looked exactly like the kind of girl who marries another girl.

"You look beautiful," Caroline said a little abruptly.

Tiny first looked down at her feet and then back up and smiled. "Quiet, it's just this dress."

"You look beautiful and I look like a preppy whale and we need to be on the terrace in five minutes," Caroline said again, now debating whether to disassociate and wear this outfit or try on every single article of clothing she had brought down here.

"Do you think everything with Daisy and Hank is okay?" Tiny asked out of the blue.

"I think so, why?"

Daisy drove Caroline crazy but she and Tiny were like sisters, so she came with the package. That meant Hank and his pathetically drunken antics did too. All Caroline could do was hope to steer Tiny in a better direction.

"They seem nervous. Daisy is always nervous, of course; that's part of her charm, skittering and darting around like a squirrel. But Hank is usually calm, even if he is plastered. Today, even he was clipped to get out of view. And shots at lunch? He's never that bold."

Caroline considered this. They had breezed through the patio, barely stopping to say hello while everyone sat down for lunch, Daisy's knuckles white from gripping Hank's hand. If Dick hadn't gotten up and made a big show of their arrival, they may have skipped the meal altogether.

"Maybe you are nervous and Daisy just took it on like she does." Caroline finally settled on this as her theory. Tiny gave her a look.

"Why would I be nervous? Should I be nervous?"

"Don't act so clueless." Caroline hadn't meant to sound so cutting. For a second, neither woman breathed. Caroline knew she couldn't get away with both the appropriation comment and this one.

"I'm *not* clueless," Tiny punted back. "I'm serious. Why would I be nervous?"

Caroline put her hands up as surrender.

"It's a complicated group. I think anyone would be nervous if she was responsible for bringing them all together. I'm nervous! It's a lot with our families and everyone!" It was as close to the truth as she could get.

This placated Tiny, or Tiny chose to be placated. Her shoulders relaxed.

"Do you think it has anything to do with Andrew, then?"

"What on earth about Andrew?" At this, Caroline perked up.

"You know Andrew loves company; he always finds someone to keep the party going with him."

"Andrew promised me he would rein it in this weekend. Plus, he's got Connie to help keep him in line."

Tiny shook her head. "The day Andrew reins it in, Bitty will eat a hamburger with a bun and not talk about it."

Caroline had seen Andrew light up at Hank's drunkenness. She'd seen it so acutely, she'd kicked Andrew under the table and told him to back off.

"I didn't see it," she said instead, also deciding in the spirit of time to disassociate and wear the stupid seersucker suit.

"Well, I did," Tiny said, her confidence back with this tidbit of gossip. "And I would guess that Daisy did too, and that's why she got out of there so quickly." This was their sweet spot: the Analytics Olympics.

The women gave themselves another once-over before leaving the cottage. Tiny was positively picture-perfect with blonde hair and blue eyes, a little pilgrim nose like the cherry on the sundae. The McAllisters all looked like this, the sort of family who had been blond for several generations. Comfort and belonging really did come from the inside, Caroline thought, readjusting her shirt for the umpteenth time. The Schells weren't far off; they just had heavier-bodied genes. Wealth without genetic perfection, as it were.

"I think you look beautiful," Tiny said, her voice small and earnest. Caroline stopped them outside their door and cupped Tiny's jaw. Kissed her softly on the lips and then again with more of a point. Then kissed her softly one more time.

"You look great, Tins," she said, really meaning it. "Let's go practice getting married."

THE REHEARSAL

TRIP

The wind picked up as Trip walked the remaining twenty feet or so to the Wedding Lawn. The grass was unending, especially with so few bodies taking up space. He was the last one to arrive and pretended to jog for his final few steps. He knew he looked good: a tailored white button-down shirt tucked easily into slim-fitted navy slacks that fell just above the ankle and paired with worn-in Gucci loafers. A look that he'd inherited and made his own.

"Sorry, everyone!" he said, offering a half smile and little wave, geared mostly at Daisy, who he realized was not actually there. He hadn't stopped thinking about her since he'd arrived. It'd been ten years since they were anything more than distant friends to each other and six since Daisy told him she would feel better if they simply kept Tiny in common. He'd met Daphne three months later. Daisy looked gorgeous, though, he thought, scanning the lawn for her one more time, the kind of classic beauty who looks the same at twenty-five and forty-five. Bitty stood off to the side, tapping her foot and pulling on Dick's blazer, which she did when others—never her—were running late.

"You're here!" Bitty said, waving Trip over. She never came out and chided anyone for tardiness, preferring to pretend she was above things like caring what others did and when they did them, but Trip knew that someday they would be fighting—about what, who cares—and she would say as her final zinger, "At least I was not late to your sister's rehearsal dinner." She kept score like a child hides pebbles in his pockets, waiting for the perfect opportunity to throw them at someone else.

The horizon was pulling the sun down on a string, casting pink and orange and red in every direction. Trip still hadn't taken off his sunglasses, even as the Wedding Lawn was covered in shade.

He was confused why they were doing a rehearsal, seeing as it was an intimate, straightforward affair, but Bitty had insisted. Implored, in fact. "It doesn't matter if it's twenty people or two hundred people—no one appreciates a disorganized ceremony. It's not how it's done." So here they were, Bitty and Dick and Mabel and Peter and Andrew and Connie clustered in an awkward semicircle around the brides and Trip, the de facto officiant despite not being close to either bride, his parents, or anyone else in attendance. Andrew was beet red from the sun and looked like his knees could buckle at any moment.

"*This* is why I asked for assigned seating," Bitty said too loudly to Dick, who shushed her. She looked around for validation and found it in Connie, who nodded, and Mabel, who flagged down an attendant and asked if he could drum up some last-minute place cards. Trip realized he was staring.

Another gust pushed through the group, taking Bitty's hat right off her head and sending it nearly back to their cottage. Bitty took off after it, gesturing wildly for a hotel worker to save it.

"For the best, Bit," Trip said. "This isn't a Derby party."

Dick shot him a look.

Tiny and Caroline both looked beautiful in the way they could: Tiny was, well, she was tiny and pristine in a white dress that hung on her like a slightly built scarecrow. She was delicate, her wedges almost taking over her ankles, Trip thought, her stance birdlike. Caroline towered over her, wearing a seersucker suit that didn't say bride or groom, and Trip wished she could just be one or the other.

"You gals ready?" Caroline brooded at *gals*. "I mean ladies. Women. Sis and Caroline." He was rambling now, suddenly petrified that Daisy was overhearing this, even though she was still nowhere to be found.

"Yes, let's do this." Tiny spoke first.

Trip took out a ratty piece of paper from his pocket—a Q3 marketing budget from work—and pretended to read notes.

"I'll start by welcoming everyone to this beautiful place." He gestured around obviously and looked back down. "And then I'll probably talk a little bit about Tiny and Caroline."

"As an officiant is wont to do," Caroline said dryly, looking bored.

Trip stood up straight and squared his shoulders.

"Yes, well, if you'd had a single idea of who else could have officiated this, then I wouldn't be standing here, would I?" He spoke softly enough that only Tiny and Caroline heard him. Tiny look struck and he immediately felt guilty. This had been Bitty's doing, compelling both Tiny and Trip—Trip officiating sent the right message about how everyone felt about the wedding.

"For the pictures," she'd said repeatedly until finally Tiny looked at her brother and said, "May as well get the glory of this proud union, right?"

Bitty was appropriately perched off to the side, looking pleased with herself.

"I'm sorry! I'm sorry!" Daisy prance-jogged down the path toward the Wedding Lawn with such velocity, Trip half expected a door to burst open too. "I'm sorry I'm late!" Daisy looked disheveled for Daisy, which meant her hair could have been neater.

"It's okay," Tiny said, stepping forward. "You didn't miss much!" Her voice was no match against the wind.

"Don't mind me!" Daisy said in a stage whisper, walking backward a few steps to get in line with Bitty and Dick.

Bitty raised her eyebrows and mouthed, *You look great!* as if they were seeing each other across a tennis court midmatch.

"Daisy," Trip said, offering a nervous smile when she looked up. "I think Hank is saying a few words tomorrow, yeah?"

Daisy nodded while Tiny said, "We can deal with that part later."

"Well, he will come up at this point in the ceremony, right before the vows, yeah? Can you tell him?"

"Sure can!" Daisy said, her voice shrill.

Tiny and Caroline were standing too far apart. Their body language was all off and Trip wished he didn't notice. He also couldn't decide who to tell first or who he could tell at all. He should talk to Daisy.

"I actually think we can head up to Longtail Terrace for dinner," Trip commanded over the group, smoothly guiding the semicircle into a line behind him.

"Hank will meet us up on the terrace; he needed a few extra minutes," Trip heard Daisy say to Tiny, who simply nodded in return and led the way inside.

He'd try to sit next to her at dinner.

DICK

Dick pulled Trip aside on their way up to Longtail.

"Have you heard from Robbie?" he asked.

Trip shook his head while he replied, "I haven't. Have you?"

"Not yet."

Whether the youngest McAllister would attend Tiny's wedding had been a frequent topic among the other McAllister men. Robbie had disappeared into life as a missionary, condemning everything from Tiny's *lifestyle* to Dick's golf game, and both Dick and Trip tried to protect the McAllister women from this dismissive, judgmental side of him. WASPs didn't have sons run off and become missionaries. It was an entirely new blueprint.

"He really should be here," Trip said, obviously hurt on Tiny's behalf. Regardless of how they felt about the lesbian-wedding thing— let's just say they were both grateful it was small and intimate and far away from the Country Club of Connecticut—neither Dick nor Trip had ever dreamed of actually missing the occasion. Tiny was Tiny. Theirs to love and protect, and the men had made a pact years earlier to direct any quips or questions or off-colored jokes to each other.

Dick leaned closer to his son.

"Would Caroline be considered the husband?" They looked at her, clad in a suit and hovering awkwardly by the door. Trip smirked and inhaled a laugh.

"Would Andrew be considered the wife?" Trip asked, raising Dick on his own question. Dick looked at Andrew, dressed in a gingham button-down, bright blue shorts, and an orange-and-navy ribbon belt.

They both laughed at this, then quickly regained their composure. This was horrible, they agreed, joking at Tiny's wedding.

"But, Dad," Trip said, hushed again, "are all their friends gay? Do gay people really only hang out with gay people?"

Dick considered this. He didn't have any gay friends, but his gay contemporaries also didn't frequent the golf courses in Greenwich, Connecticut. Not that they weren't allowed to. Bitty didn't have any gay friends either, save for a gay hairdresser, which felt cliché even to Dick. He wasn't against gay people. He just didn't know any.

"I don't know. But that Andrew is funny."

Trip agreed.

"Robbie should be here," Trip said again, disappointment creeping onto his face. Dick felt this too.

"It's not fair to Tiny," Dick said, hating that he was siding with one child over the other. "If he doesn't show up, we'll have a family meeting the next time he's home."

"He hasn't been home in three years," Trip said.

"Well, then we'll have a family meeting about how to get him home."

"When was the last time you talked to him?" Trip asked.

Dick took a moment to remember, scanning out over the terrace and down the rolling green to the beach.

"We caught up a few weeks ago. He's in Georgia doing service work. He's still dating Ella."

"Jesus, he's in Georgia?" Trip sighed too loudly. "I was hoping he was at least far away, in Africa or something. But Georgia makes it all too ironic. This is awful."

Dick put his hands in his pockets and looked down over his feet.

"It's not good," was all he could say. Was Robbie simply acting out what they felt? That this whole situation was a little weird?

"I can't believe you didn't force him to get his act together," Trip said, turning abruptly and going inside.

Dick was the last one on the terrace, and he took a look inside before stepping over the threshold. Peter was standing easily in the corner sipping a longneck beer, talking with whomever walked by. Mabel stood next to him, a flute of champagne in her hand and her posture relaxed. They *looked* like a couple who had been married for forty years, as comfortable in silence as in words, a fixed unit. And yet, as he considered them closer, they stood more like marionettes, invisible hands above them calculating their next move. When Peter's head turned, Mabel's followed in the same direction, and Dick couldn't tell if they were in sync or simply mirroring each other. He looked around for Bitty, her fluttering from Daisy to Tiny to Mabel to Trip so intense, Dick swore she was levitating. What did he look like next to her, a woman utterly desperate for the world to look just so?

THE REHEARSAL DINNER

BITTY

The Coral Beach Club staff had decorated the dining room beautifully. It was an orchestra of white and green and pink surrounding two
round tables in the room's center. There would be six at each table, and
Bitty stifled a gasp when she saw her last-minute request for place cards
had gone unattended. She bit her lip and looked to Dick. He either
didn't notice or didn't care as he led her in a circle around the room,
personally greeting each person. He looked handsome, with a white-
and-blue (always white-and-blue) vertical-striped button-down tucked
into a flattering tan khaki. Dick had recently discovered the fun of a
fitted pant. The last sliver of the day's sun hit the gold of his cuff links,
and he wore a needlepoint belt with fly-fishing ties Tiny had made for
him for Christmas the year previous. He wore a gold ring with the
McAllister family crest on his pinkie instead of a wedding band. After
much deliberation, he'd left the navy blazer in the villa.

She hated this part of hostess, much preferring to hold court in one
corner. This was how she did it at their annual Christmas party: she
stood right by the Christmas tree with a never-ending glass of sauvignon
blanc and a brief anecdote per child she repeated on an even loop. She
had been doing this for years and it *worked*. But right now, even with
only a handful of people, she'd gone right through those anecdotes and
she had nothing more to say.

"This is fun, isn't it?" Mabel walked into her vision. Bitty stood up straight and sipped from a wineglass that had appeared by magic.

"It is!" she said, holding up her wineglass.

"What does this make us? Co-mothers-in-law?" Mabel beamed too much.

"I suppose so," Bitty said, taking two sips in a row.

"We wouldn't be co-mothers—"

"We would not be."

"We could just pretend it's like sisters-in-law and be sisters?"

Bitty looked away; Mabel's eyes were as wide as saucers as she waited for a response. Despite being five years younger, Bitty had always felt like the older friend in the relationship. Some days, Mabel's willingness felt like an abuse of power.

"Let's call it co-mothers-in-law, and then we get to be wise." Mabel nodded and held up her glass to cheers again before floating away.

～

Bitty watched Andrew and Connie sit down at the table closer to the door, no matter that everyone else was still mingling. They had matched earlier in the day and they matched tonight: instead of short-sleeve button-downs, they wore long-sleeve with white pants, Andrew's fitting near perfectly and Connie's both too loose through the waist and too tight around her thighs. She wanted to remind them that the beauty of a seated dinner was that everyone got fed at the same time.

～

"Shall we?" Dick gently touched her elbow. She loved this touch: it was the only time in public he claimed her as his own.

"Where should we sit?" This was an earnest question.

"Probably next to Tiny and Trip?" he answered simply, already guiding them. The answer was obvious now that he'd said it.

Her daughter looked beautiful, but she did not look radiant. Caroline next to her looked neither beautiful nor radiant in a suit that could be described only as ill-fitting, like the designer at J.Crew had been stuck in a horrible nightmare where the material was right but everything else was wrong. Bitty refused to look at her feet because she was afraid she would see those Chaco things Tiny used to wear as a camp counselor. While Bitty couldn't prove it, Tiny had gone to work at an all-girls summer camp one summer and had never been the same. What would her life be like if she'd gotten a job as a tennis instructor or a lifeguard at the beach club like her other childhood friends?

Caroline had a hand placed around Tiny's shoulder, but the women did not fall into each other like a couple in love. They looked like they were on display for an exhibit they knew nothing about. Likely they were nervous, Bitty thought, remembering her own wedding night. Caroline took quick sips of a drink, fresh enough that condensation had not yet formed on the glass, then waved the waiter down for another one. Bitty looked a few beats longer. Caroline was drinking *quickly*.

Bitty was seated between Dick and Daisy with Tiny and Caroline on the other side of Daisy. Bitty adored Daisy. Bitty, and this was not something she was ashamed of, wished that Tiny were more like Daisy.

"Tiny looks beautiful, don't you think?" Daisy said, wordlessly filling up Bitty's wineglass. Her hand shook ever so slightly as she held the wine bottle.

"She does! She does." Both women looked at Tiny, who was fussing with her hands in her lap.

"Hey, Tins!" Daisy called, nudging Tiny's shoulder for full effect.

Tiny looked up, her eyes flared, and a smile plastered on her face. "You excited?"

"So excited!" Tiny leaned back to put her arm around Caroline's shoulder. Caroline turned her head toward Daisy and Bitty. Tiny kissed Caroline's cheek. "It's our weekend!"

Caroline smiled a tight smile and sipped again from her wineglass. Bitty couldn't tell if it was nerves or something else, but then Caroline leaned over and whispered something in Tiny's ear before kissing her cheek. What did she know, the goings-on between two girls?

"You look so beautiful, Tins; I'm so happy for you." Daisy said this with real emotion in her voice, and Tiny thanked her in a near-whisper.

"Robbie should come tomorrow," Bitty said over Daisy to Tiny. Besides Daphne and the kids, he was the only missing person of the group. Tiny nodded. In fact, Bitty had no idea if Robbie really would come, but she had a tendency to will things into being. It had worked with Tiny taking out her belly button ring.

"I can't wait to see him. It's been so long."

Bitty turned back toward Daisy.

"Where's Hank?"

"Oh, he'll be here any minute! He was just utterly exhausted from the flight. He couldn't keep his eyes open!" Daisy began, taking a large sip from her glass. "He has been writing nonstop, you see, and I think the warm air and the sand just did him in. It's like his body absorbed the tropics and knew it was time to relax. A switch just went off, so I tucked him in and told him not to worry, that the real festivities are tomorrow anyway."

"It's good when we can take care of our husbands," Bitty said, now nudging Dick. "I have to take care of this one every day!" Dick looked up just in time to nod and politely laugh.

"How is his book coming?" Bitty asked, even though she knew from Tiny that the book was not coming at all. It hadn't been coming for years. Hank spent most days either huddled in his library or hiding in Central Park.

"You know, the draft is almost done. Hank thinks he'll send it to his editor at the beginning of next month."

"That's wonderful!" Bitty went along with the charade. She had to. Daisy was doing the same thing for Tiny.

~

When Dick sensed a lull in the room, he jumped up and started tapping his glass.

"I wanted to welcome everyone here," he began, taking a step back from the table and properly addressing the room. "And from so far! We've got New York, of course, and Trip in from Brooklyn. Connecticut is showing strong, as we knew it would. And Robbie—if he shows up!—from Nepal. At least I think that's where he is." The room laughed gently.

"This is a special weekend, and I'm so pleased to be celebrating Tiny and Caroline, surrounded by their favorite people in one of their favorite places. When Tiny first came to us and said she might want to live an alternative lifestyle, Bitty and I just wanted for her to have a happy, good life. The world is hard enough, you know, without adding to it. But Caroline presented herself as an ideal partner, with thanks to Peter and Mabel for raising a great girl, and we welcome them with open arms. So let's raise a glass to Tiny and Caroline."

Glasses raised, though Caroline's for some reason was raised the highest. Bitty watched her clink glasses with Tiny and Connie, Caroline's glass going in just a little too hard to the others, causing wine to fall out of them all.

"Thank you, *Dick*!" Caroline exclaimed brightly as she tried to stretch the toast on and reach Andrew's glass.

"Oh, you're welcome." Dick laughed nervously, sitting back down and pulling on his collar. Tiny looked mortified. But she typically was mortified in public situations.

Bitty wasn't sure she had ever seen Caroline drunk before.

Peter stood up next, clinking his glass and standing slightly hunched over.

"Mabel and I couldn't believe our luck when Caroline reported she and Tiny were seeing each other," he started, his face serious but his voice warm. "The McAllisters are a wonderful family, and we're happy to be uniting the families here." He looked around the group, holding up his glass.

Andrew offered a toast next, but Bitty heard only bits and pieces. She was too distracted by Caroline, a woman caught somewhere between fear and euphoria. A happy drunk and on the verge of sobbing. She was almost manic, looking between Tiny and everyone else. The room fell away, and she looked like a rag doll jostling in the wind.

~

Bitty started the walk back to their cottage on her own. Dick was king of the table and showed no sign of dethroning. He sat between Peter and Mabel, cigar and single malt in hand. Trip was on the outskirts, talking animatedly with Daisy, who was now lopsided from hours of drinking wine. Tiny was there too, looking happy enough to be sitting with them. The bottles of wine and discarded desserts strewn about the room suggested it had been a successful party.

It was fully night, had been for hours, and Bitty was ready to breathe the sigh of relief that she'd survived day one of the weekend. One day to go and then a flight out midday Sunday after the Farewell Brunch. She could do this. She could help her daughter get ready and attend the ceremony and feel glad when the girls kissed to make it official. She could do this. She could do this for exactly one more day. Then she needed a long rest.

As she walked, she saw four figures emerge from the shadows on the paths leading to the croquet field. They walked alone and with purpose, each of them, hands dug in their pockets and shoulders facing forward toward the ocean. She stopped in her tracks as their paths started to merge. Two men and two women, a sliding scale of comfort in their gaits. The women met by one tree and the men met on the veranda, the two couples thinking they were the only ones out here. Heads came close as she imagined whispers drowned out by the wind and the waves and the lush grass. She watched the two women come together in an embrace, desperation visible even from so far away.

She wanted so badly to reach out and touch Tiny.

TINY

Later in the evening, Daisy came to find Tiny at a table off to the side of the dance floor. Most everyone was winding down, except for Dick and Trip and Peter, who held court for just themselves in the corner.

"Can you help me with Hank?" Daisy asked quietly. Tiny looked around for Daisy's husband. She found him inexplicably kneeling by a couch.

"Let's go," Tiny said, getting up and walking with Daisy across the terrace. "Hanker?" she said, kneeling to his level.

"Hmm?" Hank looked at her, his pupils swimming around his eyes.

"How about we head back?" she said, her voice gentle. Daisy stood nearby, her eyes darting around the room, making sure no one had noticed.

Tiny helped Hank stand up and get his bearings. He was absolutely blackout, and she prayed he could get all the way to their cottage.

"Daisy," Tiny whispered, "here, grab his other elbow and let's lead him." She couldn't count all the bars and parties she'd helped Hank leave, and yet she knew even in a few minutes when she said something, Daisy would blame it on Hank being tired. Or jet lagged. Or stressed. Or anything that wasn't the truth.

The three of them plodded down a path like they were in a six-legged race, one girl taking one step with one of Hank's legs and the other then catching up.

When they reached the cottage, Hank was determined to be the one to unlock the door. He first fumbled for the key card in his pocket and then held it in front of the wall, not the actual lock, and after what felt like an eternity, Tiny finally took the card and opened the door. Hank literally fell into the room, skipping over the ledge, hitting the ground chest first.

"Ugh, Hank," Daisy said, the disgust dripping from her voice. She gave him a little tap with her foot. He moaned enough to signal that he was fine, just ready to rest somewhere.

"I hope he doesn't pee," Daisy said. She and Tiny were now trying to hoist Hank up to the bed, where they could undress him and put him down.

Tiny thought maybe this would be the moment Daisy admitted something was wrong. The air felt tense, like it does right before something important is said, and Tiny debated how she would handle it. With surprise? With denial? Whatever it was, she would help her friend.

"He's just so stressed about the book," Daisy said, taking Hank's pajamas out of the drawer.

"The book?" Tiny asked.

Daisy shook her head for effect. "He's working so hard, you know. He's so tired. I keep telling him he needs to relax and unwind. I hoped he would this weekend. But just look at him."

Tiny looked at Hank. He was lying on his back, dead to the world, a thin dribble of drool trailing down his face. Tiny looked back at Daisy.

"Look how tired he is," Daisy said, so seriously it was like she believed it. Tiny looked at her friend and she looked at her friend's husband, and she knew she couldn't keep pretending he was tired anymore.

He wasn't tired. He hadn't been tired in years. But Tiny looked at her friend again and saw someone resolved to cover up the problem.

"So tired," Tiny said, giving him a pat on the stomach. She stood and stepped to where Daisy was perched on the bed. She leaned down and took her friend into a hug much tighter than either girl was used to.

"I love you," she said. "I'd better go find my bride."

Daisy hugged back but didn't say anything.

BREAKFAST ON THE TERRACE

BITTY

Robbie wasn't coming to the wedding.

It's unwise for me to attend an event I do not morally support.

He communicated like a seventy-five-year-old man, Bitty thought, adding three years so he sounded older than Dick. Robbie had sent the text message to both his parents, asking them also to convey the news to Tiny. She kept opening the curtains and closing them again. Dick had already asked her to choose light or dark—"I don't care which!"—three times. She closed them. She opened them again.

Please know Tiny remains in my prayers.

Dick had seen the texts and immediately gone for a walk, not saying when he'd be back. This was how he handled stress: walking. Some men hit the bottle or found other women or ate all the meat off a cow. Dick got quiet and he got mobile, refusing to say a word until five, six, even seven miles later, with a thin layer of sweat covering his whole body. He'd done this when Tiny had come out, an unbearable conversation in which her words were so scattered at first, they thought she was very sick. And then the situation was clarified and it wasn't liver disease;

it was actually a young woman named Theresa. Tiny was beautiful. The entire scenario made no sense. Bitty had waited for three hours while he walked and she paced the kitchen.

"Well, I've decided what I think," he'd said, finding her inside.

"And that is?"

"I'd like our children to be happy."

And that was that. They'd never discussed it again, beyond Dick's one-liners that Bitty get with the times, or jump her beliefs ahead a few years, or even just a curt "be quiet" if she started ruminating on what it all meant. No matter that Dick's refusal to refer to Tiny as anything other than "alternative" was hardly progressive. He was so afraid of offending Tiny that he wouldn't discuss her sexuality at all or acknowledge anyone she was dating beyond referencing a "friend," forget the fact that Bitty only wanted someone to talk to. She wanted a party line. Were they for this or against this?

She had called Mabel Schell in a moment of weakness.

"Well, that's fun news," Mabel said before Bitty had even fully gotten the words out. "We should set up our daughters!"

Bitty was nowhere near ready for the idea of Tiny dating anyone. Just her *living* as a lesbian, out and proud and all that, was enough.

She'd eked out, "Maybe in time."

Mabel had promptly hung up and called Caroline, and, well, everyone knew what had happened next. Tiny dated a string of girls in a stilted and never-permanent way, each potential match further from Bitty's idea of a good spouse than the last. And then finally, minutes before Bitty gave up and years after her first call to Mabel, Tiny came home beaming, overwhelmed with pride that she'd found someone from Greenwich, Connecticut, to marry. Bitty still had questions, though, specifically the rules of dating between two women and when one of the women was a bit of an asshole. Caroline had always been surly; Bitty remembered her wielding her golf clubs like weapons at the Country Club of Connecticut summer camp, and it left her with the feeling that the girl would always live a little unsettled. Tiny and Dick both called her homophobic.

~

Dick opened the villa's door and grunted. So he was back. Bitty was still at the window counting clouds.

"I wish Robbie were coming," she said.

"Well, he's not," Dick said and shuffled into the bedroom.

"Can't you talk about anything?" Bitty stifled a sob and tried to cough down her tears.

Dick furrowed his eyebrows and held up his watch. "We need to get ready for golf." And with that, he walked all the way into the bedroom and started to change.

~

What Dick didn't understand was that Bitty needed Robbie at the wedding. He was the only one who liked her, or used to like her, or really, when she was honest with herself, he was the only one who ever liked her at all. From the moment he came out of her womb, he'd nestled into her chest in a way the other two never had. Tiny took so long to latch, she nearly missed out on breast milk, and Trip was so greedy that Bitty's nipples still hurt at the thought. But Robbie was a natural, latching on his first try and taking the milk so smoothly sometimes that Bitty thought he wasn't drinking at all.

There were other things too. Tiny and Trip both learned to crawl *away* from her, usually toward Dick or the nanny. They'd play hide-and-seek and find such obscure hiding spots, Bitty would come close to calling the police. They'd set Bitty up in public, pretending to run away only to find a store clerk and tell them their mother had left them behind, forcing Bitty to choose between disciplining her children and thanking the clerk profusely for saving the day. In either instance, she looked like a horrible mother, and her cheeks would still be burning several hours later.

Robbie crawled toward her. He tried food when she offered it. He smiled when she looked at him. And when he was walking (early, at a year), he took to following her around the house, his eyes fixed on her movements. When he started talking (also early, eighteen months), he'd talk to *her*, asking her questions, making sure he knew exactly what she was doing. Once, when Dick had been late and Bitty hadn't taken her pill and thought for sure something horrible had happened, Robbie sat right next to her, like a lap dog, waiting to make sure she was okay. This was not how two-year-olds behaved. Bitty shook her head at the memory, even now.

She willed herself to walk away from the window and at least go through the motions of getting ready for breakfast on the terrace.

Come on, Bit, get moving, she whispered to herself. But she was frozen at the window, counting one cloud after another. It felt like the weekend was falling apart.

~

Robbie had come to her first when he joined the Bible group. His eyes were positively alight. "Mom, for the first time in my life, I have a cause," he'd said, *proud*.

"I think that's great—I really do," she'd said, wondering where a casual Presbyterian upbringing fit into the equation, at Williams no less. His sister had fallen in love with a woman there!

Bitty always wondered how it started. He'd been a normal high school kid. He partied, he had girlfriends, he had good-enough grades and all-American lacrosse to get to Williams. He might have been the only child to truly like Bitty, but he was just like his brother and sister. She tried asking once, early on, what drew him to the group.

"They've got a cause bigger than themselves," he'd said simply.

"But, Robbie, there are so many causes out there; why this one?" Bitty had always been allowed to ask Robbie questions.

"I wanted something where the values would never change."

~

A door slammed.

Bitty watched a couple start to argue in the doorway and realized she was looking at Daisy and Hank. Daisy was pulled together with a sheer white cotton caftan and blush bikini and leather Grecian sandals, but Hank looked like a mess: all wrinkles and stains. She ducked slightly out of view.

~

"For once, I want you to look in the mirror and like what you see," Daisy hissed.

Hank stood there and looked down at his feet. "When was the last time you looked at me and liked what you saw?"

Bitty held her breath, waiting for Daisy to answer. This was quite a fight.

"Any day you don't mortally embarrass me is a good day."

"So today?"

"Today is already ruined."

Bitty listened to their feet crunch into the pebbles filling the path down to the beach. They hadn't known this was her cottage.

TINY

Tiny woke up early and tried to feel Caroline's body next to her before she opened her eyes. If she could brush her skin against Caroline's skin before her eyes opened, then everything that could possibly go right today would. A lot of Tiny's life was made up of these decisions: skip two steps up the stairs and pass the calculus exam; hide the phone in her underwear drawer and the girl from the bar would text back; make a series of perfect slalom turns down Avanti on Vail Mountain and, at dinner, Bitty would comment on how nice she looked. This morning was no different. She turned her body, eyes still closed, and reached out her hand across the sheets, rumpled and warm to the touch. She could hear Caroline breathing the breath of someone asleep, but she still needed their skin to touch. Her hand was now outstretched, and she inhaled completely before touching her fiancée. There was her shoulder, turned in against the bed.

Tiny opened her eyes and watched as she lightly stroked Caroline's skin, careful not to wake her. It was in these moments Tiny felt safest, with Caroline inches from her and wholly relaxed, her mind still shut off from the day to come. Tiny's finger trailed off her shoulder and onto her arm and Caroline stirred, her face scrunching up before she became awake.

Caroline's eyes found Tiny's.

"Hi," she said, burrowing into the pillow.

"Hi," Tiny said back.

"What time is it?"

Tiny had to look at the clock by their bed before answering.

"Six thirty."

Caroline let out a soft groan. "Too early. Come back later."

Tiny tried to position herself as the little spoon, hoping Caroline would instinctually put her arms around her. It worked; Caroline cocooned around and fell back asleep.

~

An hour later, Tiny got up from bed and walked to her suitcase. She pulled out a small red photo album and went back to the bed.

"I made you something," she said.

Caroline turned onto her back.

"What?"

"I made you something," she said again.

Caroline's eyes were open now, darting around the room and looking at everything except Tiny.

"What'd you make?"

Tiny held out the album.

"What's this?"

Caroline opened the first page and a handwritten coupon fell out.

Skinny-dipping at sunrise

She turned the page and another coupon fell out.

Piña coladas by the beach

"I thought it would be fun to have some activities this weekend that were just us. Some are just you, like a massage at the spa, and some are just funny, like skinny-dipping. I know this weekend is a lot for you; I wanted you to know that I really love you." Tiny's voice broke ever so slightly at the end, and she could tell Caroline tried not to notice.

Caroline shifted her body into more of a sitting position and kept leafing through.

Ten minutes in which we make fun of Bitty's overly done outfits

Croquet by the water with Daisy and Andrew

Scuba diving up the coast

"These are great, Tins, thank you."

Tiny felt her face go warm.

"Of course. I love you."

"You're so sweet."

Caroline got out of bed and walked toward the terrace.

"You love me, right?" Tiny couldn't help herself. She hated herself for asking.

Caroline cocked her head to the side.

"Of course," she said.

"Should we have done this differently?" Tiny meant the wedding. Maybe it would have been easier to stay in Greenwich. Caroline didn't turn around but instead leaned over the railing like she was reaching for the water.

"Should we go for a swim?" she said instead.

Tiny traced the water with her eyes and saw a lone figure swimming the perimeter of the buoys, her lanky arms in easy rhythm with her legs. Connie. The other guests, from here simply bodies on towels, surrounded them. Mabel and Peter were also close by, though they looked to be packing up versus settling in.

"You go," Tiny finally said, realizing quite suddenly that she was exhausted and the area behind her eyes throbbed, making everything feel insurmountable.

"You sure?" Caroline said, already putting on a swimsuit and throwing a book into her beach bag.

"I am. You go. Have fun. I need a second."

Caroline was already to the door when Tiny stood up from the bed.

"Wait," she said. Caroline stopped in her tracks. "Is it the album? Do you hate it?"

Caroline's face was perfectly guarded. Tiny couldn't tell one way or the other.

"I love it," she finally said, smile and eyes bright enough to back up her words. "It's just a big day. I'm sorry. I'm freaking out, that's all." She left the room before Tiny could ask what exactly Caroline was freaking out about.

~

The anxiety came like a wave, and Tiny had to physically sit while she braced for impact. She practiced the exercise Dr. Joan had taught her: identify the anxious thought, recognize it as an anxious thought, trust it's no more than an anxious thought. It didn't matter if she didn't know what the thought *was*, just that it took root in the bottom of her stomach and rose up like smoke through the rest of her body while her mind rushed to figure out how to put out the fire. She never should have given Caroline that album. It was a stupid thing to make, the sentiment drowned out by the hokeyness. Of course Caroline needed to get away from her as fast as possible. Anyone would; she'd cut and pasted pieces of paper like a scrapbook, complete with infantile drawings of girls holding hands. She was such a child.

She practiced the breathing: in through her nose, out through her mouth, over and over, her eyes closed so tightly, light had no chance of getting in. In through her nose. Out through her mouth. The album sitting on the bed.

~

"Tiny?"

She swung around, nearly startled out of her skin at the sound of her name. "Jesus!" she yelled, realizing it was Daisy and immediately feeling guilty because now Daisy looked startled and guilty for startling her.

"Sorry, sorry, the door was cracked and I didn't see you on the beach."

The women had walked toward each other and reached the middle of the hotel room. Daisy looked flustered, Tiny thought, her cheeks flushed and her legs unable to remain still. She was dressed for the boat ride, but Tiny had a feeling she had no intention of going near the water.

"Are you all right?" Daisy asked this gently. Tiny pinched her thigh until it hurt.

"I am totally fine!" She said this so brightly, it was almost too loud.

Daisy surveyed the room.

"We were both so tired after last night, we came back and sort of exploded out of our clothes," Tiny explained, her own eyes dancing over the clothes strewn about, the two wineglasses on their sides, the messed-up bed.

"I'm not judging," Daisy said. "I remember when Hank and I got married. We didn't spend the night before together, but God, we couldn't keep our hands off each other. We planned a get-together the morning of."

Tiny smiled because she didn't know what else to do. Daisy had this entirely wrong. She also knew that Daisy and Hank had always been able to keep their hands to themselves just fine, not that Daisy had ever said anything before.

"Where's Hank?"

Daisy's eyes fell ever so slightly, but she blinked and bounced back to her chipper self.

"He's napping. The sound of the waves just lulls him right off like a baby."

"Is everything okay? With Hank?"

The question hit Daisy square in the forehead and she almost doubled over.

"What do you mean?" Her eyes narrowed.

"I just mean . . . I just wondered. I just wanted to make sure that he's happy is all." It was like someone was pulling a string of words out of Tiny's mouth. She had no idea what she was saying, and from Daisy's expression, she just needed to stop. Both women stood facing each other.

"It's fine," Daisy said plainly.

"And with my brother, is that weird? Seeing him here?"

"Ancient history!" Daisy said, attempting levity.

"But it's still a lot." College for Tiny was dominated by two things: her realizing she was far more attracted to Jills than Jacks and Daisy and Trip falling in and out of love too many times to count. Each brought its own special strain of drama.

"Should we go up to breakfast?" Daisy asked abruptly. Tiny felt desperate for honesty but also knew she couldn't force her friend to say anything.

"We should. I'm sure Bitty is wondering where everyone is."

~

The girls spotted Bitty as soon as they reached the terrace. She was sitting at an empty table closest to the water and scrolling through her iPad. The sun hit the gentle waves against the rocks so perfectly, Tiny decided it had to be a good omen. Based on the place settings around her, either Bitty had been hopeful for company or the staff was exceptionally quick at turnover.

"Hi, Bitty," Tiny said.

Bitty looked up. "Morning, ladies!" Her voice went up slightly when she saw Daisy just behind Tiny. It was too bad Tiny couldn't go ahead and gift Daisy to Bitty for her next birthday.

"May we join you?" Daisy asked, already pulling back a chair.

"Of course, of course, sit, sit. I know there is a waiter somewhere, and they've got a bread basket to die for. Do you need coffee?"

Tiny looked at Bitty's place setting. A barely touched yogurt and tea. Bitty had not consumed a carb or cup of coffee in fifteen years.

"Your father should be up any minute; he was just walking," Bitty continued, her arm up to flag the waiter. "How'd you sleep?"

"Fine," Tiny answered, perhaps too quickly.

Bitty didn't seem to notice and continued on. "Can you believe this day, ladies? It's really something. I thought I might go for a kayak ride later."

Even Daisy was catching on to the charade. The coffee and bread basket were one thing, but Bitty was nearly allergic to bodies of water. Yesterday she'd waved like a madwoman from the dock while the snorkeling boat set off. No matter that she still owned a snorkel and mask and flippers. The last time her mother had been on a boat, Tiny had been in diapers, and Bitty was so seasick that she vowed never to step foot near water again. She'd barely wade into a pool. She also hated herself in a swimsuit. Daisy and Tiny knew this because Bitty loved to talk about it.

But Daisy was a pro, Tiny knew—her commitment to keeping conversations moving surpassed any curiosity about what might lie beneath.

It was her biggest complaint: that Daisy would never ask the questions Tiny was dying for her to ask. Are you happy? Do you feel loved? Do you wish you weren't so small? Do you wish you could disappear?

Tiny knew she wasn't asking those questions of Daisy either. They both hid in each other.

Mabel ambled in and sat down in one fluid motion, her hand already lifting a mug of coffee before anyone had properly greeted her.

"Morning!" she chirped, sipping the coffee, then putting the mug down. "What are we having?" She gestured at the bread baskets strewn around the table.

"Eggs, maybe?" Tiny said. Mabel both scared her and made her wish she were her mother.

"Might I say," Mabel said to Tiny, out of the blue, "you look great, and I'm so excited you're joining our family?" Her eyes actually shone while she spoke. Tiny looked down and tried not to smile too widely in front of Bitty.

"And we're so thrilled to be getting Caroline!" her mother said, squeaky and abrupt.

"The day is spectacular," Daisy said, her own arm motioning toward the water. Tiny saw Caroline was swimming now, with Connie laid up on the beach next to Andrew, both of them clearly recovering from the night before. There was a squat Red Stripe beer bottle by Andrew's head. Trip was nowhere to be found. She guessed Hank was not allowed to leave the hotel room.

The day *was* spectacular. The sky was a striking shade of blue, and the sun was bossing the world around. There wasn't a cloud in sight. Workers from the hotel were already setting up for the wedding. Bitty had done so much of the actual planning, not that she'd had another choice, but Tiny still felt like she was looking in on someone else's day.

Daisy and Bitty were deeply invested in small talk, Daisy about her recent bathroom renovation, Bitty about whether she would pick up tennis again in earnest. Mabel came in and out, deflecting whenever Bitty asked about her own home renovation or their upcoming travels.

"Is Robbie coming?" Tiny blurted out.

Bitty paused nearly imperceptibly before responding. "Of course, dear—he's arriving this afternoon."

Tiny was flooded with excitement. Her entire body warmed to the news, and her heart lifted almost to her throat.

"I didn't think he'd come," she said a little quietly.

Daisy touched her hand with hers. "Of course he'd come; he's your brother."

"But we haven't seen each other in so long. Not really since I came out," Tiny said. Her mother looked like she was swallowing a hot pepper, all pinched face and watery eyes.

"Well, he's coming!" she said.

If Robbie was coming to the wedding, that meant he approved of it, of her, which meant getting married was the right thing to do. He'd come around, finally. Tiny leaned back in her chair and, for the first time since she'd woken up, felt like today would be an okay day.

A BOAT RIDE

TRIP

Bitty had texted Trip early that morning—he wondered when was the last time she had actually slept past four—asking him to head up the boat ride. *Of course,* he thought. *I'm already officiating the entire wedding, so why not add Captain to my title?* Did anyone even want to go on a boat ride? He looked off the porch and could see whitecaps in the water. The wind had only gained momentum from the night before. The morning's starkly blue sky was already sharing its canvas with a few scattered bushels of clouds.

He called his parents' room. Dick answered.

"Is Mom there?"

"Your mother is bathing," Dick said.

"Will she be bathing much longer?"

Trip listened to his father shuffle away from the phone and ask Bitty as much.

"She's just gotten settled in. Another twenty minutes or so."

"Okay, well, can you ask her if she really thinks we should do a boat ride today? It's really windy and—"

"Hang on."

Dick shuffled away again.

"She said yes."

"What about the wind?"

Trip listened while Dick shouted to Bitty in the bathroom.

"He asked what about the wind?"

A beat.

"The wind! It's windy."

A beat.

"She said that we offered a boat ride to our guests."

"Yes, but does she think anyone will actually want to go?"

"Hey, Trip?"

"What!" He felt stuck in a game of telephone with mental patients.

"This really isn't my job. Can you either wait until your mother gets out of the bath or just do what she's asked? It's not exactly a tall order." Dick said this last part like he was giving directions to a tour guide.

Trip hung up the phone without saying anything. His parents were insufferable. Correction: Bitty was insufferable, and Dick inexplicably followed her around like a puppy dog, thus making him also insufferable.

He called Tiny and Caroline's room. His sister answered.

"Do you want to go on the boat ride?"

"The boat ride?"

"Whatever we were supposed to do this morning." Trip looked at the welcome letter. "A boat ride."

"I guess so?"

"You guess so?"

"Yes."

"Well, does Caroline want to go?"

"I don't know."

"Can you ask her?"

Trip was near combusting.

"She's not here."

"Well, where is she?"

"I DON'T KNOW, TRIP. I GUESS I AM THE IDIOT HERE."

Trip heard the line click off and imagined Tiny throwing the phone down. He shook his head to try to bring his nerves back from totally fried. His family drove him crazy. Between Bitty's ineptitude and Dick's inability to make a decision for himself and Tiny's inability to actually make sense, Trip felt like the lone wolf in a family of beavers. They were so busy building their dam or whatever that they forgot to find any food. Now he was pacing. And debating if he was allowed to pour himself a drink.

He called Daisy's room. Hank answered and sounded as confused as ever.

Daisy came to the phone a few seconds later.

"Do *you* want to go on a boat ride?" The question came out aggressively. "Sorry," he added. "Bitty is driving me crazy."

Daisy didn't say anything.

"Well, do you want to go, I mean? On a boat ride?"

"Thank you so much for asking," Daisy started.

Trip groaned. He did not need niceties or rejection at this particular moment.

"Don't worry about it," he cut in. "It's fine. It's nothing."

He hung up before she could say another word.

He called his parents back.

"Put Bitty on," he said.

"Now she's on a walk," Dick said.

"Then please tell her that it's windy as hell, no one wants to go on a boat ride, and that this weekend is overplanned and everyone just wants to chill out."

"Hang on."

Dick put the phone down and shuffled outside. Trip heard the screen door open and close. He heard Dick talking, which meant Bitty was not on a walk at all but sitting on the porch, probably laughing at her son, who was running around his hotel room like a lunatic.

Trip heard shuffling back toward the phone.

"She says to please go to the dock and wait in case someone comes."

"Well, is she going to come?"

Shuffling. Talking.

"She is not. She is going to prepare for the day. It's a big day for Tiny, you know."

Trip swallowed. He swallowed again. He practiced his breathing and tried to think about what his anger management coach had said: people will always be idiots, but we can choose how we react to them. (His coach hadn't said the idiots part, but it was true.)

"Okay. I will wait by the dock just in case someone arrives looking for a boat ride."

"Great, Trip, thanks." His father was clearly pleased with his work as diplomat.

"Oh, and, Dad?"

"What's that?"

Trip couldn't resist. "Grow a pair."

Trip put on the same blue swimsuit from the day before, the material crinkly from the salt. He'd be off this island in twenty-four hours.

CAROLINE

The water was as much a cushion as it was an engine, her arms and legs propelling her from one side of the cove to the other. Caroline swam with purpose: arms reaching high into the sky and slicing the water on the way down. Her legs kicked with a steady, ferocious rhythm, and the *one-two one-two one-two* of each kick gradually organized her mind into a long line of thoughts.

Last night had been a mistake. Caroline was not a cheater. And she hadn't cheated, she thought, reaching the north end of the cove and turning around, but Connie had asked for something she had no business asking for, and in that moment, Caroline hadn't known how to say no.

~

Connie had passed her a scrunched-up napkin during dinner, reached right over the table and dropped it near her plate. Caroline unfolded it, not expecting to see Connie's handwriting.

Meet me at the gazebo after the toasts. I need to talk to you.

Caroline didn't know if it was all the booze or the nerves or the sudden desire to break everything around her, but she went. As soon as Andrew finished his toast, she kissed Tiny on the cheek and said she was taking a very quick walk, so quick that Tiny didn't need to join her. Connie was already at the gazebo.

"What's going on?" Caroline had said, still innocent.

"Don't do this. Don't marry Tiny."

Connie came out of the shadows and Caroline could see she was shaking.

"What?"

"Don't marry Tiny." It came out as a whisper. Connie's face was pointed toward the ground, her brown hair falling around her, her hands dug deep in her front pockets. Caroline took a step closer and put her hands on Connie's shoulders.

"What are you talking about?"

There was a part of Caroline that couldn't believe this was happening: she'd been hoping for Connie to save her for the past ten years. It felt as thrilling as she'd thought it would.

"Do you love her?" Connie lifted her neck to ask this, meeting Caroline's eyes.

Caroline answered quickly, lying and also not lying. "I do."

Connie winced and then nodded. "Are you doing this because you want to? I know Mabel and Peter. I know them all too well. You're stronger than this."

Caroline took a step back, the distance between them her restored power.

"Where do you get off?" she asked.

"What?" Connie looked shocked.

"You come down here and then tell me not to do something? I didn't even invite you! Tiny did. Out of her love for me. And what do you do? You pass me what, a napkin? You don't do this to your friend the night before her wedding."

What Caroline wanted to say was, why hadn't she said something earlier? What Caroline couldn't say was that she had to marry

Tiny. That it was out of her hands, and it had always been out of her hands.

Connie put her hands up in surrender.

"Fair enough. I'm sorry."

"You can't just say things whenever you want," Caroline said, her voice back to its normally strong tenor. "What you say affects people. Remember that."

Connie was gone before Caroline realized she'd left. She and Connie had been tugging this rope for so long, it was impossible to know whose hands were more burned.

The entire exchange was so quick, Caroline couldn't be positive it had really happened. It wasn't until she was walking back up the path and saw two men dart away from her and toward the water that she realized Connie hadn't ever said why she shouldn't marry Tiny.

∼

Caroline didn't stop swimming until her entire body was trembling, her legs finally revolting against her mind and kicking toward the shore. She sat just up from the waves breaking for several minutes, her chest rising and falling to the beat of her internal metronome. She looked at her watch: 9:45. Seven hours to matrimony. She touched down at her stomach again, a nervous tic from when she was a kid that had never gone away. She used to touch it when she ate, and over the years, she'd touched it when she was laughing, when she was crying, when she was about to laugh or about to cry.

∼

Connie and Andrew and now a few others were deep in conversation a few feet away. Andrew was nearly skeletal, his green swim trunks hanging on his hips. Caroline wasn't sure she'd ever really felt her own hip bones. She caught the tail end of a sentence and knew they were talking about why she'd gotten so drunk. It was obvious, wasn't it? Caroline was on the fence about this entire fiasco and had no idea what to do about it. She'd caused it, after all: she was the one who had proposed to Tiny. She loved Tiny, she was in love with her, and marriage was what people did when they loved each other. It was what was done. Was she even on the fence? Had Connie built the fence, or had the fence been there all along? What about when you didn't have a choice? Her mandate had been clear, and she could hear her mother's voice echoing, "There are things we do for family."

~

Caroline stood up and walked to her friends.

"Hey, guys," she said, sitting down on the edge of Andrew's towel. He bristled slightly. "What's up?"

"Hey, hey," Connie said. She sounded forced.

"What are you guys talking about?"

Andrew inhaled sharply but didn't say anything.

"Oh, nothing," Connie said, forced again. "Just how great this weekend is and how beautiful the beach looks."

Caroline touched her stomach. They were so clearly lying.

"It is a great weekend, isn't it?" She played along. What else could she do?

"Where's Tiny?" Andrew asked, his eyes still closed and shielded from the sun.

"Having breakfast with Bitty and Daisy on the terrace."

"That Bit is a piece of work," Andrew said, like someone who had his shit together. Connie let out a laugh and agreed.

"She just likes things a certain way," Caroline said.

Neither Andrew nor Connie said anything, confirming Caroline's suspicion that she'd interrupted something. She stood up.

"I'm heading back. See you this afternoon, I guess."

"Can't wait!" Andrew said too brightly.

~

Caroline walked up the beach as quickly as her legs would allow her without breaking into a run. When she looked behind her, she saw Andrew and Connie were back on their sides facing each other, deep in conversation. Connie was probably telling him about last night and how this whole weekend was a mistake. But if Connie was telling Andrew, then it meant she couldn't be in love with Caroline—Connie would never admit that to Andrew. It meant something was wrong with Tiny that no one was telling her. If Connie were in love with her, and she wasn't sure whether that would be a good or bad thing, then the intervention would have been as secret to Connie as it was to Caroline. All she did know was that no one was about to tell her either way.

BITTY

"Why on earth would you tell Tiny that Robbie was coming to the wedding?" Dick asked incredulously, he and Trip both gaping openmouthed at her. They were standing in Bitty and Dick's villa debating what to do. Trip had unearthed the lie first: Robbie had texted him also, and when he went to console Tiny, she'd wrapped him in a big hug and said how happy she was that all the siblings would be together. He'd taken this information to his father, who knew immediately what had happened, and they came to find Bitty in the villa, conveniently a few minutes after she'd sneaked a little vodka into her seltzer and chewed an Adderall. She hadn't meant to lie, per se; she just didn't want to be the one to tell Tiny.

"I didn't want to hurt her feelings," Bitty said.

"Neither do I!" Dick exclaimed back. "But he is not coming! And Tiny needs to know! That her brother isn't coming! To her wedding!" Dick had not yelled like this for years, and it exhilarated Bitty a little bit. She wished he weren't yelling at her, of course, but she'd always liked it when he got amped up.

"Trip could have told her," she retorted, defensive and suddenly sick of her husband and son ganging up on her.

"Why would I have to tell her?" Trip glared at Bitty, his eyes squinty and sharp.

"I didn't say you *had* to do anything. But you *could* have. Just like I *could* have. We both chose *not* to tell Tiny."

Trip gesticulated toward his father. "She is un-fucking-believable!"

Dick didn't disagree with him.

"I'll ask you again." He turned to Bitty. "Why on earth did you tell our daughter that her brother—the one none of us can seem to get through to—is coming to the wedding?"

"I thought you should be the one to tell her."

"And why is that?" Dick was spitting a little as he spoke.

"Yeah, why is that?" Trip echoed, his stance like that of a football coach.

Can they really not see? Bitty thought, her turn to be incredulous. Did they really think that she, Bitty, had as much clout with her daughter as Dick? She tried to cling to a single memory in which she had been the listened-to parent. Once. When Robbie had taken off after the neighbor's dog and Bitty had cried out for him to stop, he'd stopped. He'd stopped, and he'd turned around, and he'd looked at Bitty and said a simple, "Mama?" And in that time it took her to reach her son in the street, she had never felt so loved.

"If I tell her," Bitty started, "she'll think I had something to do with Robbie's decision." Robbie had left home right after Tiny came out, and Tiny had always felt like Bitty had let him leave, that she hadn't forced him to come around and should have done more to stop him.

Trip was still confused and rushed to put some words out, but Dick let his shoulders leave his ears. He nodded very slightly and relaxed his brows. Even if he never said it out loud, Bitty knew that Dick knew just how out of balance they were in their children's eyes.

"Okay. I'll take her for a walk."

"What the actual *fuck*?" Trip yelled, his eyes darting between Bitty and Dick. "Are you really letting her get away with this?" he spat, his shoulders now squared against Dick. "Every fucking time! Every fucking time! Why are you so afraid of her?"

"Don't worry about it, Trip," Dick said, his allegiance returned to Bitty. "We'll work this out. Don't say anything to Tiny for now."

"You can't always protect her, Dad." Trip was seething. "This is why I never come home, by the way. Because she's never held accountable for her actions. Maybe Robbie really is the smartest one *not* here."

"Enough!" Dick put up his hand. "I will not allow you to speak to your mother that way."

"What else are you protecting her from, eh, *Pop*? What might you be keeping to yourself these days?"

Bitty furrowed her eyebrows. To her knowledge, Dick wasn't protecting her from anything. That was part of the problem. He never left her side, but he also never held her up.

"Dick, what's he—"

"Forget it," Dick interrupted. "Trip, I need you to take a walk. I need you to take a walk right now."

Trip murmured, "Fuck this," and walked out of the villa, letting the screen door slam behind him. Bitty hoped no one had walked by and heard them.

"You shouldn't have lied, Bit," Dick said, looking at the door. "You shouldn't leave all the hard conversations to me."

His anger had been replaced by disappointment and submission, and any excitement that had pent up during their fight dissipated from the room. Bitty wanted to shout for him to understand what it was like to be scared of hurting your children.

TENNIS (WHITES)

CAROLINE

Daisy and Hank were already at the tennis courts when Tiny and Caroline arrived. While the wind had picked up on the beach, the courts were set far enough back on the club grounds to shelter them from the weather. There were five courts, four in a row and the fifth tucked around the corner, and attendants dressed in CBC tennis uniforms stood ready to collect errant balls. The bleachers and surrounding lawns suggested this was a place where tennis players competed, and Caroline felt the same sliver of competition that hit her gut every time she reached a court.

The foursome was a study in white, each perfectly clad in an outfit featuring no less than 90 percent of the required tennis color. Their shoes had court-appropriate soles (no black markings here), Hank was sporting a CBC-logoed polo and shorts, suggesting he'd simply purchased the necessary apparel at the pro shop. Caroline was slightly askew, with a skirt that threatened wrinkles and a top that didn't do much for her shoulders, but Tiny and Daisy looked like a page out of Wilson's latest catalog.

"Ahoy!" Daisy said, greeting them with what Caroline assumed was her "excited salutation." She waved dramatically, like there was anyone else at the courts Tiny and Caroline could possibly confuse her with.

"Hi!" Tiny waved back, equally dramatically.

"Must we with the ahoys?" Caroline said out of the side of her mouth. Tiny nudged her in the hip. "Fine, ahoy!" she said, pulling Tiny in for a quick peck.

Hank and Daisy were debating which side of the court they should take when Connie walked up behind them.

"Room for one more?" she asked.

"Connie, hi," Caroline said, turning around to face her. Caroline thought Tiny had said it would just be the four of them playing. Tiny shrugged subtly to Caroline and gave a closed-lip smile. "Hey," she said again, trying to get her bearings.

Caroline took in Connie. She was not in tennis whites. She didn't even have on tennis shoes, and Caroline looked around to see if the attendant had noticed her arrival.

"Hi," Connie said. "Do you know where I can borrow a racquet?"

Tiny pointed up to the pro shop.

"They have some to demo," she said. Now Daisy and Tiny were trading looks, clearly about Connie's outfit and not knowing whether to say something now or wait for her to get caught. Caroline didn't want to say anything either, but she knew this would fall on her, and she could kill Connie for being so awkward and showing up like this.

As Connie turned around and started walking back toward the pro shop, the attendant intercepted her path.

"Excuse me, miss," he said, "but I see you are not wearing whites."

Connie looked down, then back at him.

"I am not," she said.

"Yes, see, it's club policy. We must be in whites for tennis. At least ninety percent—that's regulation."

Caroline and the others awkwardly cloistered around Connie through this exchange.

"Do you have whites for hotel guests to borrow?" she asked.

The attendant shook his head. "We do not; guests need to have their own whites."

"And what if they don't have their own whites?" she asked. Caroline shuddered, knowing Connie would shoot questions back at this man all day.

"I'm sorry for the trouble, miss, but every guest must wear whites to play tennis. It's regulation and it's club policy."

"Even though we've rented the resort?"

The attendant started to speak but Connie turned to Caroline.

"You rented the club. This is ridiculous, isn't it?"

Caroline looked down. She was horrified. Yes, she thought a 90-percent-tennis-whites policy was ridiculous, but she couldn't believe Connie had shown up in black. She could have at least worn a color, tried to make a go of it. Tiny and Daisy looked on, confused, clearly amazed at the idea that someone would try to play tennis not dressed in tennis whites. That was the thing about this culture: most of the time, it was only people from the outside who questioned it.

The attendant stood still in his position.

"You don't have anything that's white?" Caroline asked Connie, her eyes pleading that Connie take the hint.

"You've got to be kidding me," Connie said, now looking from Caroline to Tiny to Daisy to Hank. She turned back to Caroline. "Are you seriously going to let him not let me play?"

Caroline looked at the attendant. He shrugged. She had no idea what he actually thought, but he was definitely not giving in to this woman dressed in exclusively dark clothes.

"Sorry, Con," Caroline finally said. "I really am. But it's club policy and they are already doing so much for us this weekend. We'll catch up later, yeah?"

Connie's brow furrowed and her mouth hung open enough for Caroline to see her tongue hitting the back of her teeth. She hadn't expected this outcome. *Well,* Caroline thought, *I'm getting married tonight. I'm playing tennis with my wife-to-be and her best friend. That's what we're doing here.* She gave Connie a little wave and turned back to the other three. She swore Daisy looked a little impressed.

"Should we play?"

TINY

Hank started bouncing a ball between his racquet and the ground in a way that suggested he'd spent every childhood summer at tennis camp.

"Shall we start with doubles?" he asked, bouncing the ball quickly and then slowly and then quickly again.

"That sounds great," Caroline said, leaning over to stretch her hamstrings.

The four took their positions and Hank hit in the first ball. He wasn't a strong player, but he was a knowledgeable one, and his footwork made up for the clear deficit of too many hangovers in a row.

Time passed this way, pleasantly, for long enough that Tiny had visions of this happening for the next thirty or forty years. As a quartet, they worked: Caroline's acerbic wit relaxed Hank's neurotic tics, and Tiny and Daisy shared so much history that the words never ran out. They had similar-enough palates and similar-enough ideas that even disagreements never truly got out of hand. One of the four would end up walking away, most of the time Caroline and most of the time out of respect for Tiny.

"Hey, Tiny," Daisy said as she hit a ball perfectly crosscourt, "remember when you were dating that field hockey player who tried to convince all of us she'd been All-State in tennis in high school?"

Caroline snorted. She did not like any mention of Tiny's earlier girlfriends.

"Blair," Tiny said, hitting a volley. "Little did she know you actually were All-State."

"And little did she know that I'd seen her making out with that soccer player a few nights before."

"Are they always athletes?" Hank asked innocently, causing both Caroline and Tiny to start laughing too hard to keep playing.

Even Daisy started laughing. "They are mostly athletes," Daisy said, looking at Tiny for approval. Tiny nodded and shrugged.

"Maybe our demographic just has really good balance?"

~

It was during the second set, where Tiny and Caroline were beating Daisy and Hank by the thinnest of margins, when Trip meandered down to the courts. He too was dressed in tennis whites.

"Hey, guys," he said, jogging the last few steps to their court. He had a tennis bag slung over his shoulder.

"Hey," Tiny said, followed by the other three. "You want to play?"

Trip nodded and started to take out his racquet.

"Well, I need a bit of a break," Daisy said, a thin line of what could only be described as "delicate sweat" arched across her neck. Tiny doubted she ever sweat under her arms. Not really.

"Me too," said Caroline, already moving toward the seats on the left side of the court.

Tiny also wanted a break, now that she thought about it.

"Me too," she said.

Hank was still on the court, holding his hand like a visor. His panting was obvious.

"I'll play you," he said.

"Are you sure?" Daisy asked, her eyes signaling to him that maybe he should take a break. Unlike Daisy, he was pouring sweat, his shirt nearly soaked through. Tiny hoped some of that sweat might be the alcohol from last night.

Trip perked up and walked to the other side of the court. He started bouncing a ball with his hand.

"You want to serve or should I?" he asked Hank.

"Let's call it," Hank said, spinning his racquet.

"W!" Trip called.

Hank held up the racquet for the group to see. "M."

The game started in earnest, and Hank and Trip shuffled around the court like two dancers already fluent in the choreography. Even their mistakes felt familiar, Tiny thought, watching Hank hit a forehand crosscourt that sailed past Trip by an inch. Trip held up his racquet as if to throw it down, then stopped himself at the last minute.

"Game time," Trip said to no one in particular. Tiny and Daisy were both well versed in Trip's erratic competitiveness.

Hank, on the other hand, was very clearly losing steam. It was a miracle he'd played this much to begin with, his pale, spindly legs almost breaking under the weight of the rest of his body. He looked horrible, Tiny thought, taking in how pale his face was, how ashen his normally blond hair was, matted on his forehead. She looked over at Daisy, her cheeks flushed from the exercise. That was how they were supposed to look after exertion: flushed, sweaty, alive.

"Don't go too crazy," Daisy said, looking at Hank and clearly seeing what Tiny saw.

Trip flashed Daisy an undeniably charming smile.

"Nah, just having a little fun out here!" he said, going so far as to flip his racquet in the air.

Trip served a ball into the service box, bouncing and sailing past Hank so quickly, he barely looked up.

"Let's do this!" Trip shouted. Tiny caught him looking at Daisy.

Hank returned his next serve, a feeble backhand that Trip took in a forehand volley and wailed back, letting out an audible grunt while he did. The ball hit Hank in the leg, sending him down to the ground.

Daisy rushed over.

"Why would you do that!" she yelled at Trip. "What is wrong with you?"

Trip ambled up to the court's net.

"You okay, man?" he asked. Hank was still on the ground, spent.

Tiny and Caroline had joined Hank and Daisy, all three of them moving Hank into a sitting position, his back leaning against Daisy's knees.

"You okay, man?" Trip asked again, his confidence now like a deflated balloon.

Tiny stood up and walked toward her brother.

"I didn't mean to hit him," Trip said.

She shook her head and used her hands to shoo him. "I feel like you should probably head out," she said as nicely as she could.

He looked at her like he was waiting for her to change her mind, and when she didn't, he muttered, "This is fucking lame anyway," and walked back up toward his cottage.

LADIES' LUNCHEON

TINY

Tiny was the first person to show up to the ladies' luncheon. It was at the Frozen Hut, a tiki-bar theme, steps from the water lapping onto the beach. *Rejection comes in many forms,* she thought, sitting down at a beautifully if not offensively empty table. She clung to Robbie's impending arrival: his presence canceled out every other bad omen.

The last time she'd seen him had been like standing next to a house of cards and being the one to pull out the card that made the whole thing crash down. They'd been at dinner, and Robbie had just moved from Houston to Charlotte, North Carolina.

"How's the church hunt going?" Tiny had asked.

"It's going," Robbie had said, methodically cutting his chicken parmigiana into pieces before taking a bite.

"I imagine there are a lot to choose from, right?" Tiny asked. Her brother's religion made her nervous, the nonnegotiability of it, even if it technically grew from a place of love.

"Yes and no. I'm looking for one that's application-based," Robbie said, still cutting the chicken.

"What is that exactly?" Trip asked, looking up from his fish. Dick refilled his sparkling water. None of them were drinking that night out of support of Trip's newfound sobriety.

"It's a church that provides ministries across all areas of life. Where we can apply the Bible's teaching into everything we do."

Bitty slurped her soup and startled herself at the sound.

"Sorry!" she said, putting the spoon down.

"So then is it that the Bible is literal?" Tiny asked as gently as she could. She kept her face open, her eyes warm. Inside, she was all knots.

"We feel the Bible is a timeless document, applicable to all areas of life at all times and across time," Robbie said, finally eating his first bite of chicken.

"But, Robbie," Tiny said, already wishing she could stop from saying what came next, "what if you disagree with something?"

Tiny didn't know this to be factually true, but she was pretty sure the restaurant went black at that moment, the sound and light and air sucked right out through the windows, sending everyone inside to space. Robbie didn't seem to notice and kept breathing, and eating, and answered.

"I pray, and I talk to the pastor, and I realign myself with God's word."

The air hadn't come back yet for Tiny.

"What if the Bible is wrong?"

"That's the thing, Tiny. The Bible isn't wrong."

Tiny saw her mother close her eyes and inhale. She saw her father squish his bread between his fingers and squeeze little balls of dough onto the bread plate.

"What about me?" she whispered, her eyes wet and her voice shaky.

"I can't force you on a journey." His words were kind and his voice was loving, but Tiny could still hear it: *I reject you. God rejects you. You are wrong.*

Tiny had fallen into the background, waiting for dinner to end. Bitty and Dick and Trip carried the rest of the meal, and Tiny felt like there were crickets in her ears. She decided she'd let Robbie be the one to reach out next, and he hadn't. Not yet. Not for the past three years. And today, he would come.

She ordered an Arnold Palmer and asked for soft butter for her bread. Trip ambled down the stairs as if by accident, looking for a chicken salad sandwich before golf but instead finding Tiny. They saw each other and gave a little nod and a wave.

A few minutes later, Tiny and Trip sat opposite each other at the table. This wasn't how Tiny had envisioned her wedding day, especially her ladies' lunch, sitting across from her older brother, a man she found unbearably proud of himself.

"So are you excited?" Trip asked, cutting up his own shrimp salad into what could be described only as child-friendly bites.

"I am excited," Tiny said back, confused why Trip was asking in such a stilted way and even more confused that her voice sounded so stilted in return. Caroline had taught her the difference between small talk and conversation and how the most committed small talkers could make idle conversation of the deepest, most personal topics.

"It's all in how it's asked," Caroline had coached. "Take your aunt Margot. Remember that time she wanted to know if Amy was coming for Christmas, and you answered honestly and she bristled, and you didn't know what you'd said? She didn't ask how you felt after the summer, when she knew very well you had just come out. She asked how your friend from Wyoming was doing and whether you'd be seeing her over the holidays." Tiny had stared at her, transfixed. "Aunt Margot was confirming that she knew you were a lesbian. She was also confirming that Dick had told her about Amy. She didn't want to actually know how you felt about Amy, or about your parents knowing you were gay, or even how you felt about being gay. But she did want to know whether she'd need to prepare herself to meet your *friend*, something that was relevant *only* if you confirmed that you would see your friend from Wyoming over the holidays."

Tiny's mind was blown, her memories of conversations flooding back at such a fast clip that she had to sit down. And Caroline was absolutely right. When Tiny had answered first with her name, Amy, and then that she didn't know whether they'd see each other and that things had gotten so serious so fast that she felt she needed a step back, Aunt Margot had abruptly changed the subject.

For a while, Tiny had thought she could change people. As soon as her mind expanded into real conversation, she determined Bitty and Aunt Margot and even Dick and definitely Trip simply didn't understand the difference. So she started to ask real questions, probing like a journalist into their lives.

"You have to stop doing that," Trip had finally said, a year into her journey toward honesty.

He said it with such finality, such a sharp look, daring her to say anything beyond *okay, you're right*, that she'd said exactly that. "Got it."

And that was the end of real conversations. Dick had hung on, in the way that fathers indulge their daughters. Tiny never stopped wanting to talk about real things with her family, but she got quite good at putting that desire in the box next to being five three and having special talents. The box lived under her bed, sometimes chiding her at night but for the most part leaving her alone.

"How's Daphne?" Tiny asked, instead of the question she really wanted to ask, which was, *Is your family really coming this weekend? Because all signs point to no.*

"She's great. She's great," he said between bites. "The twins are just super busy with school."

"Aren't they three?" This doubt slipped out, and Tiny wished she could grab the words back. What she really wanted to do was remind him that she'd asked if they would be the flower girl and the ring bearer and he'd initially agreed and then refused to talk about it ever again. When she called Daphne to go over the details and what the twins would wear and her sister-in-law asked Tiny to repeat herself not twice but three times, Tiny knew Trip had never even passed along the request. When Daphne had then asked out loud how that would work, a flower girl and a ring bearer at a lesbian wedding, Tiny knew whatever face Trip put on in front of her was not actually for *her*. It was so he would look more supportive than Robbie.

"Even at three, they need to be intellectually stimulated. You should know that as a teacher." He may as well have said, *There are things you have never been bright enough to understand.* They each took a few more bites in silence.

"How's work?"

Trip visibly relaxed. Work was a safe topic.

"It's really good, actually. Clifford thinks I'll be up for SVP soon."

Trip worked at a VC in New York, and Tiny had no idea what he really did all day, other than throw darts at a target and use a booming voice on calls—at least that's what he did when he worked from home—but whatever he did do resulted in living in a brownstone in Cobble Hill, even complete with a minuscule yard in the front, an unheard-of luxury and a step beyond the gigantic head start they had from being McAllisters. She and Caroline lived in a one-bedroom apartment in Long Island City. Caroline thought it made them more authentic. Tiny thought if they were really authentic, they'd live in Greenwich, because that's where they were from. Queens was notably *in*authentic.

"That's awesome, Trip," Tiny offered.

"How are the kiddos?"

Tiny taught at an egregiously expensive private day school called Seedlings, and despite promising herself every year that this would be the year she quit and went to grad school, she'd been at Seedlings since 2010. The problem with leaving Seedlings was that she'd need to do something else.

"They love blocks and they love snack time."

"It must be nice that the children are obligated to listen to you."

"What do you mean by that?"

Trip didn't miss a beat. "I know how Bitty is."

Actually, Tiny thought to herself, Bitty wasn't all that bad; Tiny just didn't have much to say she felt other people needed to hear.

"Do you know when Robbie is getting here?"

Trip looked up from his food and almost imperceptibly raised his eyebrows.

"What did Bitty tell you?"

"She said he'd be here before the ceremony."

"That's what I heard too."

"Did he text you?"

"Yeah, earlier today, when he was connecting flights."

Tiny leaned back. Why hadn't Robbie texted her? He hated Trip; she knew this. Trip had always been such a prick to Robbie—pre-DUI, he'd wailed on how lame Robbie was to not party more, and post-DUI he'd wailed on Robbie for not being more driven. Trip had done the same thing to Tiny, but she was exempt from things like frat parties and professional drive: latent homophobia and old-school sexism protected her from being held to everyone else's standards. If they didn't know how something worked, most people glossed over it and kept moving. This was why no one in her family ever asked Tiny if she wanted children. Ever. She did, for the record. So did Caroline. Two.

"How does Dick seem to you?" Trip shifted his weight so he was facing her.

"Fine, I think. Why?"

"He doesn't seem tired? Like he's letting Bitty get away with more than normal?"

Tiny considered this. "It's probably just weird for him that he's hosting a lesbian wedding."

This made Trip laugh out loud. He even threw his head back to let the laugh out of his throat, which made Tiny laugh, mostly out of surprise because she did not make people laugh very often.

"I guess you're right, Tins," Trip said, still laughing. "I think you might be the only gay person he actually knows."

"And Caroline. So he knows two gay people. Well, and Andrew and Connie, and I'm pretty sure he met Connie's girlfriend at the engagement party. That makes five. Nearly a quorum."

Tiny took advantage of the moment to ask the question she'd been dying to ask all day.

"Are Daphne and the kids really on their way?"

Trip didn't even take a breath before responding.

"I told you, yes, they're flying down." He was blustery and too emphatic. Tiny held his gaze and didn't say anything. "I don't think they're coming." Tiny cocked her head to the side. "They aren't coming."

Tiny exhaled and leaned back into the chair. "Did she leave?"

Trip drew his lips in a thin line and slowly nodded.

"I'm sorry, Trip." She meant it too.

Trip had started to say something else when Dick came up to the table. He was also dressed for golf but fancier. Pine Valley compared to Trip's Canoe Brook.

"Hi, Daddy." Tiny got up from the table to kiss him on the cheek. Dick and Trip regarded each other.

"Mind if I sit for a minute?" Dick asked as he pulled a chair over.

"Of course, of course," Trip said, shaking his head at Tiny to say that the conversation about Daphne was over.

All at once, the other women arrived: Daisy and Bitty, Caroline and Mabel and Connie, each stumbling over the others in apologies for being so late.

"I'm sorry," Bitty said the loudest, "but housekeeping took so long, it was impossible to get ready." Tiny only nodded. Caroline looked the most apologetic and sat on the edge of Tiny's seat.

"I am so, so sorry," she said. "I completely lost track of time, and I'm pretty sure my nerves are sabotaging my ability to get through this day as planned, but I am so excited to marry you in a few hours."

Tiny stayed quiet, enjoyed Caroline being so close. She smelled like salt and sunscreen.

"Tins?" Caroline said after Tiny had stayed quiet for too long.

"Yeah, it's okay; it's fine," Tiny said.

Caroline hopped up from the seat and sat down in the one next to her. She reached out her hand to Tiny's knee and squeezed. It sent a warm rush through Tiny's entire body.

Bitty had shooed Trip and Dick to another table: "Here, take your plates with you, and everyone else, let's sit and enjoy." The men did what they were told, Dick mumbling that they needed to leave for golf anyway.

"Will you two pick up Robbie on your way back from golf?" Tiny asked before they left.

Tiny thought she noticed a look trade between the men but couldn't be sure.

"Of course, Tins. We'll get him. See you on the veranda," Trip said, not totally meeting her eye.

She turned back to the now-filled table and took in her bride, who looked happy and sun-kissed.

She'd be a married woman in three hours.

CAROLINE

Female WASPs liked to gather for meals, but they didn't like to eat. Caroline considered the table. Her mother, Daisy, Bitty, and Tiny played with their food like synchronized swimmers, their forks and knives almost symphonic in their coordination. Caroline was tempted to start tapping her various glasses for full effect. Connie was the only one actually eating; she bit into a sandwich, and mayo and lettuce squeezed out of the other side and dribbled down her hand. Connie caught Caroline staring and mouthed, *Whoops!* and Caroline reached across to her plate and took a fry. Caroline mouthed, *I'm sorry about the tennis*, and Connie gestured *no big deal* with her hand. Connie didn't care about fitting in to this world, and it always stopped Caroline in her tracks. Imagine not caring about where you belong.

Her mother kept manually chopping her salad, placing a minuscule bite in her mouth, quickly chewing, and then craning her neck to either side of the table and saying, "Now, isn't this *lovely*!" The first few times, the other women put their own utensils down and agreed, Daisy even going so far as to side hug Tiny and say she'd been waiting a long time for this moment, but for the past ten minutes, no one had offered any sort of response whatsoever. It was official: Mabel Schell was the most excited for tonight.

The small talk at the table was going strong, and Caroline didn't know whether to sacrifice Bitty or herself to the Small Talk Gods. At this moment, Bitty and Daisy were deep in conversation about whether the Country Club of Connecticut would ever consider adding a third seating for their Easter brunch. No matter that it was September and no matter that Caroline was pretty sure Daisy and Hank didn't even belong to the Country Club of Connecticut.

"I just think," Bitty said, now getting conspiratorial with her fork pointed toward the ceiling, "that if the club is encouraging members to spend the holidays there, and they have to with how much they're paying the new chef, then they need to make sure everyone is accommodated. It's what you do." She emphasized this last part. Daisy nodded vigorously.

"I keep telling Hank how we need to spend more time over there. It's worth it for the community, you know?" Daisy was a fifty-five-year-old mother of four grown children stuck in a thirty-three-year-old body utterly devoted to SoulCycle.

Tiny kept crossing and recrossing her legs. Neither Daisy nor Bitty seemed to notice that no one else had said a word since their Cobb salads had been served. Even Mabel was barely exclaiming anymore, though Caroline knew for a fact that her mother found the club unbearably uptight, not to mention unaffordable.

"Has the club opened membership to gays or Jewish people yet, Mother?" Tiny asked. She asked the question so earnestly, Bitty didn't immediately register what she'd said. Caroline smiled; her body shot with adrenaline as she realized Tiny wanted to poke the bear. Tiny never wanted to poke the bear.

"You know how long the wait list is, dear. All are welcome; it's just terribly difficult to get in," Bitty said, her eyes betraying the calmness of her voice. Caroline wanted to lean over and kiss Tiny. This was the woman she fell in love with. The one who didn't let people hide from what they didn't want to see.

"It's just funny to talk about a club that doesn't allow gay people at a gay wedding. Don't you think?" She spoke with the perfect inflection of politeness. It was a true skill, Caroline thought, how Tiny could twist and bend herself into moments.

"Tiny!" Bitty said. "You know you could have had a reception at the club if you'd wanted it."

Caroline physically bristled at that memory: their parents pretending that a reception at the club would be their choice and Tiny tortured by the idea of hosting any kind of event at a country club that openly rejected so many different groups of people. "I'm sick of being the exception," Tiny had said, her words soggy and tearful. Caroline had held her on their rug, making Tiny into the smallest spoon that ever was. Bitty and Dick and Peter tried not to act relieved when the girls told them they wanted to do something small and far away, and Mabel openly acted relieved. "Have a party that's actually you two!" she'd said, hushing Peter when he said the club knew how to put on a good wedding. Plus, a destination wedding meant their engagement could be cut in half. Mabel wanted Caroline to marry Tiny yesterday. Dick had played it off by asking a string of *are you sures*. But Bitty had jumped up too quickly, settled on a number too quickly, and decided on throwing a larger party someday in the future too quickly. All six of them wanted the same thing for entirely different reasons.

"Luckily, it's not what we wanted," Caroline said.

Tiny reached over and took her hand. "Very luckily," she said.

"We didn't mean anything by it," Daisy said.

Tiny opened her mouth, but nothing came out.

"Of course you didn't," Caroline said on Tiny's behalf. "You just meant that you wished there was another seating at your all-white, all-Christian, all-straight club. And I get it: their raw bar is to die for, and it's a tragedy when it runs out before it's your turn."

Daisy and Bitty exchanged horrified looks. Mabel and Connie smirked, and Connie coughed to try to disguise a laugh.

Caroline was bolstered by coming to Tiny's rescue.

"Let's not forget whose weekend it is, shall we?" she asked, looking between Bitty and Daisy and reveling in the tension.

Caroline pushed her chair back and invited Tiny to join her.

"You and I have a date to get married," she said, kissing her square on the mouth in front of everyone.

MEN'S GOLF

TINY

Tiny and Caroline walked back toward Breakers arm in arm, and Tiny hadn't felt this light in days. Caroline seemed lighter too, even happy, throwing her head back and laughing as they reenacted the country club moment. It was almost like Caroline was back to normal, worlds away from this morning. Tiny didn't think anything of it when Caroline said she needed to grab something from Andrew's cottage, called Robbers Den and right next to theirs, and they stopped off the stone path.

"I've got a key," Caroline said when no one answered her knock, placing it in front of the fob reader. The door clicked and leaned open.

"How come you've got a key?" Tiny asked as they peered inside. It was dark with the blinds keeping out the day.

"In case Andrew overslept when he was supposed to help me get ready," she answered.

The room was dim with the blinds drawn, and a white light escaped through the cracks of the bathroom door. Tiny heard rustling and then laughter and then steps around the sink. She and Caroline exchanged confused looks.

"Hello!" Caroline called out, taking a few steps toward the bathroom. Tiny followed suit. The rustling continued, and it was clear whoever was inside was unconcerned about who was outside. When Caroline reached the door, she gave it a quick knock and opened it, only to find Hank midsnort of a line that could only be cocaine on the counter. Andrew stood just behind him, jumping from one foot to the other.

Tiny opened her mouth to say something but instead remained standing, transfixed. Caroline stood next to her, equally dumbfounded. Hank looked up only after he'd finished the line, and both he and Andrew stood looking between the women and the cocaine, also confused as to whether they should offer some or not. Tiny made the mistake of making eye contact with Hank.

"I don't think Trip and our dads have left for golf yet if you want to catch up." She didn't know what else to say.

The men fell out of their trance and started trying to explain themselves, Andrew going so far as to say they had found a more effective way to take Tylenol. "To prevent the hangover!"

Caroline and Tiny hurried outside, nearly falling over each other getting through the door.

"I'll be over soon!" Andrew called behind the closed door.

Caroline yelled, *"Fine!"* as the women broke into a jog, laughing and tripping over themselves as they got back to their cottage.

"Jesus," Caroline said when they returned, "Andrew literally has no limits."

"What do we do?" Tiny asked, letting herself fall into an armchair on the porch, the gravity of what she'd seen starting to sink in.

"What do you mean, what do we do?" Caroline asked back. She traded her luncheon polo shirt and long shorts for a T-shirt and board shorts. She'd have one more swim before the big event.

"We can't just let that happen, can we? What about Daisy? I have to tell her. Hank's gone too far. Hasn't he? Shouldn't we at least get him away from Andrew?"

"I assure you, you do not want to get in the middle of this," Caroline said, looking at Tiny like she was a child. "What's Daisy going to do? Thank you for being so concerned and calling out her husband's drug issues?"

Tiny winced. She hated it when Caroline looked at her like this.

"But he's the one doing drugs here, right before the wedding. Didn't he ruin it?"

"The ruiner is the messenger. She'll find out on her own, and then you'll support her like a good best friend."

"I don't think I can *not* tell her," Tiny said.

Caroline's face softened. "Trust me, Tins. There is no way you will come out of telling Daisy unscathed. Especially because she has never told you Hank is doing anything other than writing another award-winning novel. And it would break my heart to see you go through that. In my experience, we don't want to be told what we are already trying not to see."

DICK

Bitty had organized the golf game, delighting herself when she found out there was a course only two miles away from the hotel. Dick looked at the address and name again before walking over to the girls' table.

"Do you know anything about the course we're playing?"

"Just that it's the closest one. I'm sure it's fine," Bitty said. She was smart to get defensive.

"Do we have a tee time?"

"Two p.m., but they mentioned that resort guests get precedence for playing, so there might be a wait."

"What's the resort?"

"We'll have to ask. I called the golf course separately."

This was why nongolfers should not arrange golf for actual golfers. Bitty looked at him blankly, and he knew she knew exactly what she'd done, but off the technicality that she had found a course and organized a tee time, Dick had nothing to say. It didn't help that it was only he and Trip playing. Peter had dropped out at the last minute, saying he'd promised Mabel a walk.

"Since when does Mabel not let you play?" Dick had asked, some chiding in his voice.

Peter shook his head. "Sorry to miss this one." And he was—Dick could tell.

"Hey, Peter?" Dick asked as his friend started walking past him. Peter stopped in place. "I know this might sound strange, but is everything okay? With you?"

Peter looked at him strangely and then nodded, his mouth turned down in a frown. "Yup." He kept nodding. "Yup," he said again.

Dick let it go, and Peter headed down the path toward his villa.

~

"Okay, Trip, let's see what we find," Dick said. The men walked out of the dining room toward reception.

~

The shuttle ride was quick, and Trip and Dick exchanged raised eyebrows when they turned onto the grounds. They were playing at a Sandals, a resort both men were familiar with only through billboards and ads on TV. This would be far worse than even the public course they used to play near Bitty's grandmother's house in upstate New York. The course was clearly well taken care of, the grass green and the water blue, but people were everywhere, trolling the course without rhyme or reason. The golfers wore mostly versions of pajamas and jeans and loose-fitting T-shirts. Dick thought he saw a man sitting in a cart off the ninth hole actually watching television. It felt like a course where anything could happen. Not in a good way.

~

"Sir! Welcome to Sandals Golf and Country Club!" a resort attendant shouted far louder than necessary as he opened the door to their van. Dick did his best to keep up with the enthusiasm, but he'd never been one to leap into a new interaction. The attendant ushered them into the clubhouse, nearly falling over himself when Dick and Trip tried to pause just outside and trade sneakers for golf shoes.

"No!" the attendant exclaimed. "Here at Sandals Golf and Country Club, we invite the guests to use our state-of-the-art locker room to change their shoes!"

Dick shrugged. It seemed normal enough. They followed him inside.

"Welcome to Sandals Golf and Country Club!" another attendant behind the check-in desk said. Dick started a tally at that moment of how many times they'd be formally welcomed to the Sandals Golf & Country Club.

"Thanks," Dick said, pulling out his wallet. "So we've got two of us—"

The attendant began furiously typing.

"How many in your group today, sir?"

"Two."

"And are you staying at the Sandals Beach Resort?"

"We are not."

"I see."

The attendant's typing never stopped.

"Is that a problem?"

"No, no, no. No, not at all, sir. Not at all." He emphasized the last three words.

Dick didn't say anything.

"Will you be needing caddies today?"

Dick looked at Trip. "What do you think? We can just walk it, right?"

Trip nodded.

"Okay, we'll walk and carry our own bags."

"Caddies are mandatory, sir."

"Okay. So we'll take the caddies."

"Fifty dollars, sir."

"For both?"

"Each."

Dick nodded.

"Will you be needing a cart, sir?"

"We're good to walk."

True golfers played with four main codes of conduct: walk the course, play under four hours, best when alcohol comes after play, and long, serious, or uncomfortable conversations are never, ever to take place during the game.

"Carts are mandatory, sir."

"Why would carts be mandatory?"

"The distance between the holes, sir. It's too far to walk and to keep pace of play."

Dick let out a slow whistle to calm himself. "Okay. So we'll take a cart."

"That's forty dollars, sir."

"I imagine it is," Dick said under his breath.

"Will you be needing clubs, sir?"

The attendant had not stopped typing this entire time. Dick was tempted to peer over to see what kind of file this guy was starting on him.

"Yes, two pairs."

"Women's or men's, sir?"

Dick and Trip looked at each other, then back at the attendant.

"Men's."

"Will you need to change your shoes, sir?"

Dick held up his golf shoes.

"Yes."

"You'll need to change in our newly renovated men's locker room."

Dick nodded. Fair enough.

"We require guests to rent a locker to store their personal belongings."

Dick nodded again.

"It's twenty dollars to rent a locker."

"Can my son and I share one?"

The attendant looked struck. "I'm afraid not, sir. One locker per guest. It's policy."

"Is there anything else?"

"You'll need balls and tees, sir?"

"We will. Let's do a sleeve for each of us."

"What about the water, sir?"

"The water?"

The attendant started nodding vigorously and gestured outside.

"Our course boasts more water than any other neighboring courses. It's a delight!" Here he grew serious. "But also hazardous. For the balls. We recommend no less than three sleeves per player."

"We each need nine golf balls for the round?"

Dick asked it as an honest question.

"At least, sir."

"Okay, so we've got two sets of men's clubs, two lockers, two caddies, one cart, eighteen balls, a couple of tees, and the green's fees. Is that it?"

The attendant stopped typing and looked up.

"We also encourage guests to bring a cooler and beverages on the golf cart in an effort to avoid overheating."

Dick shook his head at this.

"We'll get water on the course. Perfectly fine."

"The cooler is mandatory, sir."

"Of course it is," Dick said, not politely, and pulled out his black American Express card to prove a point. The attendant didn't seem to notice, and this made Dick absolutely irate.

"I'm pleased to let you know that cold water is offered on a complimentary basis throughout the course."

"But we'll probably need to buy cups? Is that right?" Dick cracked.

The attendant furrowed his eyebrows. "Mr. McAllister, it would make no sense to expect guests to buy water cups."

The card went through and Dick heard the machine printing a receipt for him to sign. He'd never been so happy to hear such an ugly sound before, because it meant he could get out of this clubhouse. The attendant offered copious pleasantries as he showed the men into the locker room and explained how to operate the lockers (they were standard-issue school lockers, with a simple three-number code lock). By the time Dick and Trip were standing by the first tee, it was nearly two, and a string of resort guests was passing right by them.

Dick felt like he was stuck in the Spirit Airlines of golf.

TRIP

A foursome that could be described only as Tony Soprano and his cronies played directly in front of them. Based on where he was in life, Trip felt like he deserved this. His marriage had lasted six years and then dissolved, like lemonade powder in water: he couldn't recognize his life as his, only that it was entirely different. He was scared Daphne and he would never be civil again. He was scared Daphne would poison the kids against him. He was scared he would poison the kids against Daphne. He knew this divorce was his fault: he'd chosen work over Daphne too many times; he'd stayed out drinking too many times. He loved her, or he used to love her—he couldn't tell anymore. But what had killed them as a couple was his utter inability to do what she asked. If she asked him to come home early from work so they could eat dinner as a family, he would stay late to spite her. If she gave him a look to stop drinking at a party, he'd take the bottle and go find his guy friends. For the past year, he'd done the opposite of everything she asked for. How could she not leave? He'd all but shooed her out. He needed to tell his family and he didn't want to. He didn't want to tell them that he'd ruined his marriage.

Daisy was placed directly next to him all weekend yet entirely out of reach, due to his general failure of the past fifteen years and the existence of her husband. Of course he would be playing golf at a Sandals with his increasingly disgruntled father behind an increasingly drunk foursome. Peter had been brilliant when he opted out of golf to read a book on the terrace. Trip wanted to be reading a book on the terrace. Or maybe he just wanted to be on the terrace. Staring at Daisy.

Neither he nor Dick was on his game, but they had enough etiquette to keep their heads down and eyes forward.

They were at the sixth hole, a par four overlooking the ocean, with rolling hills and ideally placed trees. It was a nice course, if overrun by players who didn't know the difference between an iron and a wood. Their caddies lagged behind, either confused by the game or truly disinterested or both, and Trip was trying not to ask his caddy too many questions. He'd botched his drive and found his ball at the 150-yard mark.

"What club do you think I should use here?" he asked his caddy, regretting the question as it slipped out of his mouth.

The caddy shrugged.

"Are the markers accurate?"

The caddy nodded. "The markers are very, very accurate."

"Okay," Trip said, squeezing his lips together. "Is that marker to the front or the middle of the green?"

"Exactly," the caddy said, a little proud.

"Is it exactly at the front or exactly at the middle?"

"Exactly," he said again.

Trip pulled out his 150-yard club—a six-iron—and positioned himself over the ball.

Maybe things would turn out okay. Maybe his marriage with Daphne was always meant to crash because his marriage with Daphne wasn't lasting. The children would be okay; he'd do everything in his power to see to that, but he and Daphne deserved to be happy. Maybe they weren't meant to be happy together. Maybe it was all a ruse to get him back to Daisy.

He swung and made smooth, easy contact with the ball, sending it flying into the air. The ball flew up and out, coasting far past the green into the water on the other side.

He looked at the caddy.

"Didn't you say the markers were accurate?"

"You just hit the ball so beautifully, sir."

Trip shook his head and drove the cart in front of his father, who was setting up his own swing. The men didn't register each other, and Dick swung and hit, the ball sailing through the cart and hitting Trip square on his left biceps. He fell out of the cart to the left, rolling down the fairway, his right hand clutching his left arm. The cart swerved at the lack of a driver and sped into an exceptionally deep sand trap, nearly tipping over.

"God *dammit!*" Dick shouted, old-man-jogging to the sand trap to make sure Trip was okay.

"Do you have any idea how much they'll charge us for that cart?" So he was really old-man-jogging to make sure the cart was okay.

"Relax, Dad—everything is fine. Including me, thanks for asking, after you literally hit a golf ball *at me*."

The caddies ambled toward them, and Trip honestly wondered if they even knew what had just happened.

"You have to be careful!" Dick exclaimed again, his rage and nerves and frustration bubbling over.

Trip walked to his father and lowered his voice.

"Take a breath, Dad. Everything is okay. The cart is completely fine." His father was so panicked, Trip couldn't hang on to his anger. "What is going on?" he asked, looking closely at his father.

Dick was walking in small circles with his hands clasped behind his head. Trip went so far as to pat his back, but he didn't say anything. The anxiety passed a few minutes later. Dick stopped circling.

By now, the caddies were smoking a cigarette just off the fairway.

"You sure everything is okay?" Trip asked again.

Dick shook his head and moved from foot to foot. "I don't want to tell Tiny that Robbie isn't coming."

Trip knew how he felt.

The sun was holding steady in the sky, doing its best to warm the afternoon in spite of the wind. Trip could see that the ocean was rougher than earlier in the day.

"Hey, should we call this thing? It's nearly four."

Dick hated calling a golf game early, no matter how poorly it was going. It wasn't done: golfers kept score, didn't give themselves mulligans, and played for a buck. But his daughter was getting married in an hour. He nodded and Trip signaled to the caddies that they were heading back to the clubhouse.

"How should we tell her?" Trip asked as he drove them up the cart path.

"I don't know yet. But, Trip?" Dick asked, his eyes pointed straight ahead.

"Hmm?"

"You are the twins' father. It's your job to make sure they never grow too far apart."

Trip looked out at the course and swallowed.

"I know, Dad."

"You're their father. Remember that."

Trip looked at Dick, the thought crossing his mind that his dad knew more than he was letting on. They drove back to the clubhouse in silence.

"I wish Robbie's plane *had* gotten delayed," Dick said as they left the cart behind and got into a shuttle that would take them back to Coral Beach.

GETTING READY

BITTY

It wasn't fair that her children were always mad at her. And regardless of what Dick said about her needing to settle down and open up and catch up with the times, it still wasn't fair. He wasn't ahead of her. He refused to talk about anything! She was supposed to blindly accept everyone around her, but this felt like a double standard. In any case, it was an hour until showtime, and she would be damned if her daughter didn't look the part.

She gave herself a final once-over. She'd tried to dress down, *casual*, because she knew this was what the girls wanted, with a light-blue Max Mara shift dress and her most unassuming nude Louboutin kitten heels. There wasn't any use hiding the jewelry: a diamond the size of a skating rink thanks to Dick's first big year in 1986 (old money only ever produced old rings; new money bought new rings) would do that. But she'd understated everything with simple diamond studs. She'd been dropping vodka in her seltzer all afternoon, so Bitty chewed an Adderall to stay even, letting the metallic taste linger on her tongue. She could do this.

Bitty knocked on her daughter's door, and Tiny opened it quickly. She was nearly swallowed whole by the Coral Beach Club monogrammed robe. Positively tiny.

"Hi, Mom."

"Are you ready for hair and makeup?"

A woman Bitty had arranged through the hotel stood behind her.

"Yep, come on in." Tiny motioned the women inside.

"This is Barbara," Bitty said.

Barbara offered Tiny a wordless nod and began unpacking her rolling suitcase at the small table by the window. Tiny returned the gesture with raised eyebrows and a thin-lipped smile. The sliding doors to the porch and water view were open. Tiny had thought to put on some music and had some white wine on ice. She wanted to get married; Bitty could feel it pulsating off her body.

"Shall I sit?" Tiny asked.

Barbara nodded.

Tiny looked at Bitty for reinforcement.

"Sit." She swore that sometimes her daughter needed someone to remind her to go to the bathroom.

Tiny sat, looking diminutive in the chair. Her shoulders were hunched over, her face cast down.

"What are we doing here?" Barbara spoke, her voice at once deep and melodic. Bitty hadn't expected it to be so lovely.

"Tiny, what would you like?"

Tiny looked up but remained silent. After several seconds, she spoke. "I think something natural?"

"What about your hair being up in a bun, with a whimsical braid going around it?" Bitty had a picture prepared and Tiny said that looked fine. Barbara nodded and started taking out Tiny's ponytail. The three women sat in silence.

This was a game Tiny played whenever she was uncomfortable. She'd played it ever since she was a little girl. Rather than fighting, Tiny went silent, forcing Bitty to ask her what was wrong. Bitty used to indulge her, but after a while, she'd realized that she already knew, and every time she did ask, Tiny did not have to speak up for herself. So she stopped asking.

"Where is Caroline getting ready?"

"Andrew's room with him and Connie, I think," Tiny said, looking at herself in the mirror. "Daisy is stopping by here in a little while."

Bitty pulled out her iPad and started thumbing around. It was mindless, and she didn't completely register she was doing it.

"Can you not right now?" Tiny's voice sliced the air.

Bitty looked up.

"Can you not talk to your Twitter followers right now?"

"I'm not *talking* to my Twitter followers. I'm just checking in."

"Well, can you not check in with your fifty thousand Trump-loving Twitter followers while your gay daughter is getting her hair done for her gay wedding?"

Bitty's platform on Twitter had been as much a surprise to Bitty as it was to the rest of the world, and her presence was almost exclusively for her fellow conservatives. It horrified her daughter and absolutely exhilarated Bitty. Plus, it made her feel a part of something.

"Fine, I'll put it away," she said, closing out of Twitter and getting up to start taking pictures. Of Tiny, of Barbara, of the room, the view.

"So, Barbara, where are you from?" Bitty asked in her kindest voice.

Barbara looked at her and then around the room and then out the window. "I'm from Bermuda."

"Well, yes, I assumed that—"

"You *assumed* what? That someone like me would only ever be from here?"

Bitty was caught off guard and sputtered out, "I j-just meant, are you from near the hotel? Did you have to travel a ways to get here? Did you drive or maybe take the bus?"

"Jesus, Mom!" Tiny all but shouted. She looked horrified through the mirror.

Why would everything about today be difficult?

Barbara harrumphed and kept working on Tiny, who clearly saw her mother struggling to keep her composure.

"I'm sorry about my mother," Tiny said to Barbara. "She asks asinine questions when she's nervous, and I assure you, she is amped up because of me and not because of you."

"I'd hardly say I was nervous," Bitty said, now nearly shaking with nerves.

"Do you want to go for a walk?" Tiny asked, looking at her through a handheld mirror. It wasn't so much a question as a directive. Barbara did not try to stop her. This was Dick's doing: he'd trained every child to stab tension with a request that the other person *go for a walk*.

"Here is the jewelry we talked about," Bitty said, taking out the strand of Tiffany pearls and the other diamond drop earrings she'd worn when she married Dick. They were similar to but entirely different from the ones Tiny had worn the night before. She'd wanted Tiny to wear her grandmother's strand, but the Tiffany pearls almost jumped off her clavicle, they were so bright.

Tiny let out the smallest breath of submission.

"Thanks, Mom. I'll wear them."

"I just want you to be happy," Bitty said, not knowing what else to say. What she wanted to say was, *Don't do it! I'll take you home! We can save you from this hard life!* But Tiny looked at her, waiting for her to leave.

Fine. She'd go for a walk. *Good luck getting a tip,* Bitty thought bitterly. *Good luck looking as beautiful as I know you could look.* She showed herself out and could already hear Tiny and Barbara talking easily in her backswing.

She started walking with purpose. She would go find Trip and see if he was ready for his officiant duties. The pathways were quiet, though Bitty assumed it was because everyone was getting ready. The wedding was now just forty-five minutes away. She neared the croquet field and saw Daisy and Hank debating whether to play. Daisy was already dressed, and Hank was still in his swimsuit. As Bitty walked closer, fully intending to say hello, she realized they were not debating whether to play but were fighting again.

"You *ruined* our room and you are *ruining* this weekend," Bitty heard Daisy growl at her husband.

"It was an accident, and it was barely on the rug," Hank retorted, doing his best to stand up for himself.

"Barely on the rug is *still on the fucking rug.*"

Bitty walked with her head down and prayed they wouldn't notice her. No such luck: she missed a small crack in the pathway, stubbed her toe, and was propelled forward. She stumbled hard onto her left foot. Both Daisy and Hank looked up, alarmed.

"Hi, hello, hey!" Bitty said, regaining her balance.

"Hi, Bitty," Daisy greeted, her face in a forced smile. "How's the bride?"

Daisy was nothing if not composed.

"You should go now! She's in with hair and makeup and said she was expecting you. You look gorgeous," Bitty said, picking up her pace and realizing Daisy was wearing the same dress as the day before. "And, Hank, I have no doubt you'll look dapper out of those swim trunks!"

Hank gave her a quizzical look.

"In your suit! You'll look great in your suit!" She shouted it and was nearly into a jog to get away from them. Her ankle throbbed with each step. Was there nowhere safe for her on this island?

TINY

"You have to go!" Tiny said into Caroline's mouth, kissing her in between each word.

"I'm going; I'm going," Caroline said, breaking free of Tiny's grip. She'd sneaked in between Tiny assuring Barbara it was okay to leave and Dick arriving, engulfing Tiny in an embrace so tight, she thought she would disappear and burst at once. Of all the things Caroline did, it was make Tiny feel needed that got her.

"You look beautiful," Tiny said, her eyes casting down over Caroline's simple white dress.

"Technically, we aren't supposed to see each other yet."

"Does that mean you'd like me to look away and pretend we didn't just consummate our marriage before the fact or just say you look great again at the altar?"

Caroline smiled a wide smile and took a step closer so she could kiss Tiny again.

"At the altar would be great."

"I'm excited to marry you, Caroline Schell," Tiny said.

"And I'm excited to marry you, Tiny McAllister."

Caroline opened the door and slipped back outside, leaving Tiny to count the butterflies flying inside her stomach. It was 4:27. She had three minutes.

~

Their first date had surprised them both. First Tiny had seen Caroline on the street, Chambers and West Broadway to be exact, and had almost turned around so Caroline wouldn't see her. Tiny did this with most people, especially those from her hometown who were a few years older. Caroline didn't let her sneak away.

"Tiny McAllister, is that you?" Caroline said, looking trendy and bronzed in the late-September sun. It was midafternoon, that stretch of time between the end of business lunches and start of afternoon meetings, and Tiny was rushing back to her classroom after a midday errand. Caroline was headed back to the courthouse.

"It's great to see you," Tiny said after they'd stood on the sidewalk for long enough to disrupt the pedestrian flow.

"We should get together," Caroline said, pulling out her phone. "What's your number?"

Tiny gave it to her.

"What are you doing Tuesday? Should we do dinner?" Caroline asked.

Tiny looked around. Was she being punked? This was Caroline Schell, *the* Caroline Schell, her brother's age and always, always out of reach. Caroline had run the Greenwich lesbian mafia—a cool and cruel group of girls who took over The Ginger Man on Greenwich Avenue once a year—and Tiny had never even gotten a like from one of them on Instagram.

"I'd love that," Tiny eked out. She couldn't remember if she was wearing makeup or not or if the neckline of her T-shirt was stretched out.

~

They met the following Tuesday at Pure Food & Wine near Union Square. As Tiny walked down the few steps into the restaurant, she knew there was not a gayer spot for a first date. Tiny wasn't even sure she was gay enough for it, but she went inside, jeans tucked into little brown booties and a sweater that brought out her eyes (blue). Caroline was already waiting at the bar, a bottle of sake and small glass beside her. She looked hot in a black leather jacket and skinny black jeans and a designer high-top with a white sole. Tiny was smitten.

"You're here!" Caroline said, getting up and awkwardly kissing somewhere between Tiny's cheek and her ear.

"I'm here," Tiny said back.

They sat at a table on the terrace, an overly friendly waitress never going more than a few minutes without checking in. The conversation felt like a stream, meandering around bends from serious topics—growing up gay in Greenwich, careers, family—to banter—was *The L Word* realistic; was it watchable—back to serious—at what point does one stop apologizing for being oneself.

"And look at you," Caroline said during dessert. "You found yourself and blossomed into someone incredible." Tiny looked down at her cardamom spice cake. Caroline was trying to impress her. Caroline Schell was trying to impress *her*. Tiny looked up. Caroline was brave enough to hold her gaze, and Tiny felt like she could see her thoughts.

"I wouldn't go that far," Tiny said, shy and unused to flattery.

"Don't be ridiculous," Caroline said quickly. "And don't let your name fool you."

~

Her father arrived at her room exactly one minute later, at once dapper and like a man still figuring out how fitted pants worked, ready to walk her to the terrace. She had finished her own makeup after she sent the poor woman away, folding bills into her hand and assuring her that mascara was impossible to put on someone else anyway. Bitty had a way of ruining everything, most certainly getting ready for her wedding.

Tiny didn't look bad, she thought, turning around in the mirror and looking at her backside. But she was tiny; clothes fell off her, and she knew she got away with a lot. A taller woman with hips would never get away from the bug bites that constituted her breasts. A curvier woman would have to figure out what to do about her hair. But being this small meant she could hide in mousy.

"Hello?" her father said, letting himself through the slightly open door. Caroline wanted them to walk down the aisle together, without their fathers, so Tiny and Dick had decided they'd walk arm in arm to the ceremony.

"You look beautiful," her father said, kissing her on the cheek.

"Thanks, Daddy." His look helped her feel beautiful.

"Where is everyone?"

"Everyone?"

"I just figured your mother would be here, or Daisy at least. Caroline . . . ?" Dick started to trail off, clearly realizing that asking a bride where everyone was shared DNA with asking a woman if she'd gained weight. Obviously he hadn't intercepted Caroline on his way to the room.

"Mom did it again." Tiny couldn't help herself.

"With what?" Dick said.

"She made the woman doing my hair and makeup horribly uncomfortable when she basically implied surprise and wonder that *she held herself so well.*"

Dick grimaced.

"'You're so well spoken!' I cannot believe she said that, Dad. It was mortifying." He could hear Bitty say just that and Tiny knew it.

"Your mother means well, Tins."

"Does she? You say that; you always say that, but then nothing changes."

"Your mother has been through a lot."

"I'd hardly call her best friend moving away a serious trauma."

Dick shifted on his feet. Tiny was pushing him too hard.

"I just wish I was enough for her," Tiny said.

"You are, sweetie; I promise you are," her father said, assuming Tiny meant her mother and Tiny realizing she didn't know if she meant Bitty or Caroline.

She prayed Caroline was already waiting for her. She knew this was irrational: Caroline had literally just left their room dressed in white. But that was what happened when it felt like the other person might leave: you weren't safe unless they were touching you. And even then, it was all about how they were touching you and whether you touched them first. Tiny couldn't escape the images of Caroline and Andrew accidentally getting drunk on his porch, or Caroline deciding suddenly she needed another swim, or deciding she was starving and needed to take a car to that seafood restaurant in Pembroke Parish. Then she started in on Daisy, or rather Hank and Daisy or really Hank and Andrew, in a position that, after thinking about it, wasn't all that surprising to see. Tiny had no idea what to do about Daisy or how to tell her that her husband's drug addiction was hardly a secret, and very suddenly Caroline was back in her ear urging her to say nothing at all. Had Caroline known more than she was letting on? Tiny pushed away the thought. Not today. Not right now. She needed to get married.

"Did your mind race right before you married Mom?" Tiny asked.

Her father shook his head a little as he answered.

"Like a runaway train."

They'd nearly made it to a small veranda next to the Wedding Lawn, and Tiny could see everyone starting to sit down. For the first time all weekend, she felt excited and nervous and beautiful. She breathed in and the air entered her body with a gust. She stood up straight and pulled back her shoulders, the dress, lace and delicate, falling perfectly down her frame. She was a bride, finally, after all these years. Caroline stood off to the side, waiting. She was dressed far simpler than Tiny—a nondescript, below-the-knee white dress, sandals—but she was beautiful. Tiny counted her heartbeats.

"I promise you are good enough," her father said. "Your mother and I are so proud of you." His eyes were watering and Tiny watched him try to swallow back tears.

"Thank you, Dad," she said, meaning it.

He squeezed her hand. His eyes were still wet. He looked tired and sad.

She was about to ask if everything was all right, but Trip and Bitty were suddenly next to her, the family in a sort of huddle. She found Caroline's eyes and Caroline nodded for Tiny to stay where she was.

"What's going on?" Tiny asked.

Her father let out a breath. "We hate to tell you this." Tiny looked at her brother and mother, who were both looking at the ground. "But Robbie isn't coming to the wedding. I'm sorry."

All the good omens from earlier in the day evaporated.

"Did he say why?"

"It was the travel, sweetie. Too far and too many canceled flights." Dick looked crestfallen.

Tiny looked back at Caroline, who was smiling and standing between her parents, her eyes shining and her hair a perfect chestnut in the sun. Tiny didn't need Robbie to get married. She didn't need him at all.

"Thanks for telling me," she said, giving her dad's shoulder a squeeze.

"Let's get my little girl married." His voice broke as he said the words.

"Hey, Tiny," Trip said, reaching out and touching her elbow. Tiny turned around. "This is his loss. Not being here. This is his thing and not you." Trip's mouth was a thin line, his eyes serious.

"Thank you," Tiny said, more like a whisper.

Trip pulled her into a hug and whispered in her ear, "You're tiny, but you're ours. And we love you."

Dick walked Tiny to Caroline and kissed each woman on the cheek. Once everyone was seated, with Trip standing at the front of the porch, his back to the sea, Tiny and Caroline walked down the aisle together.

THE WEDDING

TRIP

Tiny and Caroline walked down the aisle holding hands, a quartet playing the song played at the start of every wedding. Tiny looked like a bride and Caroline looked like a bride-adjacent, and Trip wondered what two Carolines walking down the aisle would look like. Probably two pairs of sturdy flats. This song had played at his wedding, but Trip for the life of him could not remember it. They looked happy, Trip thought, watching them clutch hands and take steps in perfect stride, like they were ready to walk into this new life together. He remembered feeling that feeling with Daphne, only now he couldn't remember what the actual feeling was.

He was burning alive up here on this unbelievably sunny terrace. He looked in the distance and saw clouds doing a breaststroke across the sky and immediately wished they would breaststroke faster. He wasn't unlike the clouds: racing to ruin a perfectly gorgeous day. Except that wasn't fair: his life with Daphne was not a perfectly gorgeous day. Not anymore. It was an unseasonably warm day in the late fall, after daylight savings and when you stop trusting anything that's good until at least mid-May.

Daisy was standing up next to Tiny, to her right and beaming, the sun bouncing off her pale-pink silk dress. His heart and his eyes and his memory couldn't decide who they were looking at, and when

Trip finally closed his eyes to try to quiet the anxiety, he saw a version of Daisy she hadn't been in twelve years. She was a senior at Williams again, all polo shirts and ribbons in her hair, making even chugging beer look feminine. They'd always had *fun*, he thought, opening his eyes back to the moment and seeing that above all else, Daisy looked tired.

Andrew stood next to Caroline, his own eyes nearly brimming over. Connie, next to Andrew, looked like a sullen hippie.

Trip, as the officiant, led the ceremony, his presence perfect for this crowd: puffy-chested and full of shit.

What was he holding on for?

~

The quartet stopped playing as Tiny and Caroline reached the makeshift altar bursting with palm fronds and stood facing each other and lightly holding hands. His cue.

"Welcome, everyone, to this joyous occasion." Trip caught Connie rolling her eyes, and when he flared his eyebrows in response, she looked away and stuck her hands in her front pants pockets.

"Please be seated."

Trip felt powerful up here. It wasn't often that he could get up in front of a group of people and say anything he wanted.

"Except you, Peter. You should stay standing."

Everyone laughed because they were supposed to, and Trip felt this and felt stupid. He looked down at his script.

"When Tiny and Caroline asked me to officiate this ceremony, I was honored. Tiny is my younger sister, but in so many ways, I've always looked up to her, especially her fearlessness and willingness to go against the grain in the spirit of her happiness."

Trip looked up in time to meet Bitty's eyes. She was beaming.

The brides looked at each other and held hands and smiled, though even Trip couldn't pretend not to see that Caroline's smile was more of a grimace and that Tiny's lips were pressed together like they were holding a coin. Trip was talking again, now about the importance of commitment and compromise, and he felt like he was watching a version of himself talk about the importance of commitment and compromise.

~

Trip turned to Hank and invited him up.

"Tiny and Caroline have asked our novelist-in-residence to say a few words on the topic of marriage. Hank, I'll leave it to you." He stood off to the side as a wobbly, slightly sweaty, and noticeably pale Hank took his place. Hank walked so slowly, Trip was tempted to carry him the rest of the way, but he could hear Bitty's voice in his head urgently whispering that the only thing to do in the unexpected is wait for the moment to pass in hopes that no one notices. If you intervene, it's a guarantee that everyone will notice. Even Tiny and Caroline briefly looked at Hank in alarm. Maybe asking him to speak had been a mistake.

Hank very slowly—very, very slowly—walked toward the center of the terrace and stood close enough to the women that should he faint, he would fall directly onto them. Daisy looked lost between petrified and horrified, making Trip want to reach over and hold her even more.

The wedding guests stood before Hank, eyes and ears ready for whatever he would say. They looked anticipatory, Bitty especially, her eyes frozen yet shining. Daisy's eyes shone too, but more like she was trying to prepare herself for anything. Hank clearly hated public speaking, and he was either a masochist or simply unprepared. Trip caught Andrew give Hank a coy wink.

Hank took a deep breath, bowed his head, closed his eyes, and looked convincingly like this was a real moment for him. The guests started to shift on their feet.

He turned back around.

"Beloveds," he opened. Beloveds? Should Trip intervene? He couldn't read Tiny's face well enough to know.

"Beloveds," he said again. Again? He said "beloveds" twice with nothing else?

"I'm honored to be here." Okay, well, those at least were words. Tiny and Caroline each smiled. Of course they smiled; they were the ones getting married. Tiny's eyes urged him on. "We all know Tiny and Caroline have worked hard to get here. And I, for one, am very happy to see this moment come to fruition. They aren't an obvious couple." His eyes fell on Bitty's face growing tighter and tighter.

"Caroline once said that love is hard, and I think that's really true. Love is hard, and so is writing." Now even Tiny had to look away, her entire body begging him to stop speaking.

"Life, really, is hard, so very hard, and I wish them luck in surviving it. Best that they survive together."

Not even the birds or trees rustling in the wind broke the silence. The guests looked at him and then looked down and then looked at him again, and it was as if Hank was so impressed by their unison that he didn't immediately walk back to the group. Trip gave him a soft yet stern nudge on his back, and he felt palpable relief from the guests as Hank finally made his way back to the audience. This was why Bitty preferred place cards at even the most intimate of gatherings: one cannot overplan the chemistry of a moment.

"Thank you, Hank," Trip said without missing a beat, his face so fixed that it felt like wax. "That was memorable and also true."

Trip continued with the rest of the ceremony, announcing it was time for the vows.

By now, the clouds were nearly overhead.

CAROLINE

Trip didn't ask if anyone opposed the marriage. This flooded Caroline with relief, because she was petrified Connie would say something. What, she wasn't certain, but something certainly. But he hadn't asked and she hadn't dared look in Connie's direction. Trip kept the ceremony moving, treating Hank like a mere stumble in the woods of marriage, and before she knew it, she was kissing Tiny as wife and wife. It was a short kiss, a peck, really, because Tiny didn't want to seem vulgar in front of her family. Caroline understood and also didn't understand.

Then she and Tiny were walking back down the aisle, their arms tangled and everyone clapping as they passed by. She was married. A married woman to another woman, and that fact felt like a revolution somersaulting into the room. Caroline had never thought she'd get married, having let that dream die as soon as she'd told her parents she related to a Melissa Ferrick song on a carnal level. Her parents had been accommodating to Caroline's news, generally and especially for 2003.

She and Tiny stopped walking near the bar set up on the far edge of the veranda, and as Caroline noticed the sun hit Tiny's highlights and make her head shine gold, she decided she would do everything she possibly could to make this right. Last night had been a mistake, and Tiny standing in front of her was not a mistake.

Bitty and Dick and Andrew and Trip and Daisy and poor Hank and even her parents streamed out past the chairs and formed a line at the bar. Caroline wasn't surprised to see this group lining up, despite it being an intimate gathering. WASPs lined up for things, especially drinks. They liked order and knowing where to go. It was why they were such bad international travelers. Tiny had walked over to greet her parents and Daisy.

In the time Caroline had stopped to notice the clouds moving across the early evening sun, Connie appeared with two drinks in her hands.

"The signature," she said, handing Caroline one. It looked pink and suspicious. Caroline cocked an eyebrow.

"Have a rum swizzle. Swizzle my zizzle," Connie said unironically and took a long sip.

Caroline let out a laugh much louder than she'd expected.

"Who came up with these drink names? The other one is a tequila mockingbird."

Caroline raised her glass in Bitty's direction. "To my mother-in-law, ladies and gentlemen."

"Do you remember that time we went to Hardly Strictly Bluegrass and you were so determined to find me the beer I wanted that you actually snuck under the bar rope and fished out the can yourself?"

Caroline laughed at the memory. It had been in 2011, when being in your midtwenties made everything feel so possible. They'd gone out to San Francisco for the long weekend, so bold as to say that maybe they should move there.

"You were so into that band; we waited so long by that empty stage. Finding you the beer was the only thing to occupy me."

"We should be having fancy beer in a can right now." Connie was right—Caroline couldn't care less about the cocktail she was holding. But to drink a beer in a can right now would be vulgar, and Caroline could imagine her mother walking up and taking the can out of her hand and murmuring, "No need to broadcast, dear." She took a sip of her drink instead.

Caroline looked around at everyone speaking manically and wondered what there was to catch up about. It had been only a fifteen-minute ceremony, and, well, as with most weddings, hadn't they known how it would go? Bitty and Daisy especially were gesticulating wildly to Dick, who looked at best amused. Maybe it was a WASP thing, when they'd gone so far into small talk that it verged into passion. But she was one of them, at least by blood, and she found the entire thing ridiculous. It infuriated her, actually.

Trip stood in their makeshift semicircle, matching his father in yellow pants (the other Nantucket Reds), monogrammed white button-downs, navy ties with a single white anchor at the bottom, gold cufflinks, Gucci loafers. They even both wore tortoiseshell glasses. Bitty and Daisy also looked alike, Caroline realized, seeing how their similar blonde bobs were only the start of it. They stood wrapped into themselves the same way, like they were trying to take up no space and the entire world at the same time, their legs planted firmly into the ground but ankles bending and shifting underneath them.

"And I just told Tiny, the best part of marriage is getting to approach the world hand in hand with your best friend." Daisy was positively beaming at this, and Caroline felt a nudge.

"Will you stop staring," Connie commanded.

"I'm not staring—I'm listening. These are my people now," Caroline corrected.

Connie rolled her eyes and took a sip of her rum swizzle. "They don't have to be your people, you know."

"What's that supposed to mean?"

"You've told me you don't like Bitty. You don't understand Dick. Daisy overwhelms you. And you don't believe in marriage. So you're making a go of it with Tiny."

"Not believing in marriage because you don't think you'll ever be allowed to get married is not the same as not believing in marriage," Caroline said. She felt sharp about it.

Connie pursed her lips. "So be it. But her people don't need to be your people."

"Because you're my people?" The line came out by accident and Caroline knew she was playing with fire.

Connie didn't know what to say either. They stood there in a staring contest.

"I want you to be my people." Connie said the words so quietly, Caroline couldn't be sure she'd heard them correctly. But she couldn't ask her to repeat herself. Not here. Not at her own wedding reception. Connie stalked off without saying anything, leaving Caroline to look out over the water. Tiny was still with her parents, and Caroline suddenly and desperately wanted her over here, standing with her.

Her parents approached her, Peter holding out a champagne flute and Mabel moving in to kiss Caroline's cheek.

"Congratulations, bird!" her father said, holding his glass up to cheers with the other two. Caroline clinked her glass and sipped.

"Thanks, parents," she said.

Mabel looked around without moving her head.

"Tiny looks radiant," her mother said. "A beautiful bride." Caroline smiled without opening her lips. "This is a good union, one to be proud of. And your family appreciates it." She looked at Peter, who was nodding in agreement.

"Well, as soon as we get back, we'll know the best next step in terms of setting you up," Caroline said, feeling icky as she said it but clinging to her mother's affection. Mabel's approval of her had always been just out of reach but still close enough that she could strive for it.

"Doing right by family pays off." Mabel patted her daughter on the shoulder one more time before gliding over to where Bitty and Dick stood.

"Thanks, bug," her father said, trailing a few inches behind Mabel. Caroline breathed in and out a few times, positioning herself so it looked like she was taking a moment to admire the water. This was Caroline Schell on her wedding night: absolutely powerless.

She gave it a few minutes, then stepped toward a table where a Coral Beach chef was making mini poke bowls with tuna and avocado in crisp shells. Andrew was hovering over there, eating one after another, and Caroline was relieved to have someone to mock the day with. As she stepped closer, she decided she had never been so excited to see Andrew in her life.

"Andrew!" She couldn't even hide the excitement, which he very clearly noticed, raising his eyebrows, a mix of confusion and skepticism. They were best friends, but they weren't enthusiastic about it or each other.

"Hello. Mini poke bowl?" He motioned toward the table. The poke bites were perfectly placed with mango salsa and spicy aioli.

"What'd you think?"

"I thought it was pretty sweet," Andrew said quickly. "And you make a handsome bride."

"It was sweet," she agreed, looking down at herself in her dress and fidgeting. She should have worn the suit and the little bow tie Connie had suggested. Tiny would have been fine with it.

Andrew put another bite of tuna in his mouth.

"Andrew," Caroline said, and he instinctually took a step back.

"What's up?"

"You know you're playing with fire here. Forget that I asked you to skip the shenanigans this weekend, but Hank? Come on. You don't attach your car to a train that's already crashing."

"That isn't fair. Hank and I have a lot in common. We have a connection." Andrew said this proudly.

Caroline cocked her head. "Don't be ridiculous. You do not have a lot in common, and you need to get your shit together. It's not fair to Daisy that you let Hank get out of control like that. Be careful," she said, meaning it.

Andrew looked at her in such a way that it felt like it was the first time he was seeing her all day.

"*You* be careful," he said.

"What's that supposed to mean?"

"Promises in front of people make them loud promises."

So he knew. He had to: he'd have no reason to say that otherwise. Caroline felt her fingers go tingly and was afraid she'd drop her glass.

"I—"

"Don't. Not here."

Caroline nodded and inhaled.

"Go find Tiny," he said, his own eyes now on Hank.

She needed to pull herself together. It was only cocktail hour and the night was sure to stretch until morning.

She saw Hank cowering to the left of the door going into the kitchen and kept her gaze moving, then watched out of the corner of her eye as Andrew approached him. For the first time since the ceremony, Caroline noticed there was music, a local band playing an island blend with steel drums, and Connie was swaying along and breezily talking to Caroline's parents. Tiny and Daisy and Trip and Bitty and Dick were swaying too; they looked jubilant. Her eyes darted between the two groups, amazed that she could feel awkward and excluded from literally the closest people in her life. Where was she supposed to go next? Caroline looked down again at her dress and touched her stomach. She shouldn't have worn a heeled sandal. The white dress, linen and already wrinkly, hit a few inches above her ankle and made her legs look like two submarines that threw up into shoes. She'd gone for Sharon Stone and instead channeled a taller Danny DeVito in drag. All that was missing was a fedora.

Caroline looked between the groups again. Out of nowhere, the wind picked up with enough ferocity to blow a stack of custom cocktail napkins and the rock holding them down across the terrace, a flutter storm of white and pink. This got everyone's attention, and conversations paused as bodies bent down to retrieve the "T+C 9.14.19" napkins off the ground. Tiny appeared next to Caroline and grabbed her waist.

"Hello, my wife," she said, kissing her shoulder.

Trip walked up holding a New York State marriage license.

"Should we sign this and make it official?" He asked Andrew and Daisy to come over to act as witnesses.

"Let's do it in a little while," Caroline said, not sure why but positive she didn't want to make a scene while they all signed. Tiny cocked her head but didn't say anything.

Caroline pulled Tiny away and toward the bar. "Let's get some champagne."

RECEPTION UNDER
THE STARS

TRIP

Trip hadn't planned to drink tonight but he did anyway. The problem with sobriety was that people cared only when you slipped up; otherwise they gave you a pat on your shoulder and sent you on your way. Trip found the entire prospect boring and lonely. Daphne disagreed, of course; that's why she wasn't here. He'd given not drinking a real try and even made it a full year, nothing but seltzer and the occasional cigar. He had been bored to tears, going through the motions with those husbands of Daphne's friends. And after a while, he realized his sobriety didn't make Daphne like him more. It just kept her from hating him. Then one night, he'd realized maybe he hated her, and the Bulleit bottle was sitting there, glowing in the shadows of the bar. He poured a few fingers into his favorite lowball glass and thought maybe a few sips would help him hate her less. It hadn't worked, but it had relaxed him enough to pour a few more fingers.

The damage was done, and the more Daphne showed her contempt for him, the more he drank. And yet no one seemed to notice, not even Tiny, who had been onto him long before anyone else. He'd messed up; he knew that, taking two sips in quick succession. But he'd lost his words with Daphne. Nothing he said made any sense at all to her, and he was lonely, and he missed his children, and he hated that he'd failed them. He stood slightly away from the dance floor, lost in his thoughts while counting each sip.

It was cloudy. That seemed unfair, after all this, that their sunset would be squashed by mud-colored clouds. He tried to think if, at any point today, someone had mentioned the weather. Bitty loved the weather because everyone cared about it: no one could ignore rain, making it the perfect topic to begin every conversation ever. She even asked him about the weather, Trip thought, sipping again, suddenly and unexpectedly thinking about how she'd asked about the weather when he'd gone to rehab one town over from theirs. The only two questions she knew to ask were "how is the weather" and "how is work." She couldn't ask how he felt or why he'd done what he'd done, but she did ask if he'd noticed the rain and whether he thought it might clear up later so he could play tennis. Bitty couldn't talk to him about anything that mattered, and he couldn't talk to Daphne about anything that mattered, and he wondered at this moment if he would ever talk to anyone about anything that mattered. He sipped.

He drained his glass and turned to the bartender.

"More bourbon, sir?"

"No, vodka seltzer, though whenever I come over tonight, I will be asking for just seltzer. Understood?"

The bartender nodded and turned his back to pour. Trip slipped a twenty to him when he reached for the glass.

"You can expect that all night," Trip said, offering his own nod and turning back around to his corner.

He felt a tap on his shoulder.

"Expecting someone?"

It was Connie, one of Caroline's friends, appearing ever so slightly lopsided.

"Hi there," Trip opened. He'd just skip the name altogether.

"How's this corner? You know, I counted ten guests earlier, myself included of course, and was so confused because I thought there were eleven. I went through the entire group, counting out the guests sitting, and then of course Daisy and Andrew and the brides. And I couldn't get back to eleven. But then I looked and saw you lurking over here and realized I'd forgotten our humble officiant! So here we are." The woman beamed a little oddly.

"So here we are," Trip said, sucking his drink through a stirring straw.

"So here we are."

"So here we are."

"So here—" The woman cut herself off. "I can't say that again, can I?"

"Well, you could." Trip was loosening up. Maybe in a past life, this woman had been funny. "How do you know the bride?"

"Which one?"

"How do you know both brides?"

"Well, one I went to college with and one I met through the other one. How do you know the brides?"

Trip looked at her again. Her pupils were swimming a bit, and even as he started to feel the warmth coming back under his skin, he knew she was far drunker than he was. He'd learned from his mother that the best way to handle a drunk woman was to play along. It was also the best way to handle a drunk man, but that came with its own set of rules.

Talking to drunk people was like finding the point in the river where the current was strongest: find it, put yourself in position, and float on until it's over.

"Well, I'm Tiny's older brother, and I suppose I know Caroline through Tiny." He answered as if he had not just stood in front of the crowd and spoken to how he used to hold Tiny when she drooled enough to fill a large bowl.

"Of course that's how you know them! The officiant! I mean, I even said that just now." Connie stumbled a bit back and Trip caught her. She cocked her head and shrugged.

"Guilty as charged." Whenever he said this, he felt like he was mimicking a Pierce Brosnan movie.

"You forgot to ask the question," Connie said, her words falling into each other, a bit like word soup.

"Pardon?"

"The question. If anyone objected to the union. You forgot to ask it."

Trip couldn't tell if this woman was flirting with him or chastising him.

"You're right. I didn't ask it. I assumed if someone did object, they might not want to object to such a large crowd. Might be better to do that later, maybe when the guests have gone to bed but before the couple signs the marriage license."

This got her attention.

"Tiny and Caroline haven't signed yet?"

"They haven't. They wanted to sign it when they got back to New York. On their home turf. Plus, I don't totally know that we love gay marriage here?"

"Why did they get married here?"

"It was either because they'd been here before and liked it or that they got a really good deal for this weekend."

Connie considered this a beat too long for either of them to feel comfortable. She caught her own attention and nodded toward the other side of the terrace.

"There's a lobster guacamole station over there, you know," she finally said, gesturing widely.

"That's fantastic. It's a nice evening, isn't it," Trip said. He could at least be polite.

"I guess so."

Trip let the line linger. Maybe she'd know enough to walk away.

"So if you are the brother of the bride, why are you all the way over here?"

"I wanted a moment away. And given the people here, the same could be said of you, no?"

"I also wanted a moment away," Connie said deliberately.

He turned back to the bartender.

"Another seltzer, please," he said, the bartender nodding and turning around. He pushed another twenty across the bar.

"They shouldn't have done it," Connie said, staring into her glass and stirring the drink with a small straw.

"What do you mean?"

"It was a mistake. All of it. They shouldn't have done it."

Trip looked between Connie and the brides, his sister standing while Caroline spoke, her arms loose and her hands gesticulating. He didn't know what to say and he didn't know if he wanted to hear more.

"I guess time will tell, then, won't it?"

Connie swallowed and looked over toward the sea. "I just wish we could be honest, you know? All of us."

Her swimming eyes now filled with water. Trip silently begged her to hold it together. Bitty's was at least a manageable kind of drunk. She talked animatedly for just under an hour, disappeared into herself, and then Irish goodbyed before anyone was really the wiser. She would never cry in public. He looked around for Bitty and tried to catch her eye. She was deep in conversation with Mabel, but as he peered closer, he saw that it was really Mabel who was in deep conversation with his mother. For every word Mabel said, he could see Bitty lean back a fraction of an inch. Soon she would be in a backbend.

"I'm going to find my mother," he said abruptly, cutting Connie off from whatever rabbit hole she'd fallen down. Connie didn't object and simply turned her body to face the water.

He crossed the distance to Bitty and Mabel, putting a hand on his mother's shoulder.

"Hi, you two," he said, effectively cutting off Mabel.

Relief flooded Bitty's face. "Trip!" She held out her glass to cheers him.

"Mother. Mabel. It's a lovely night, isn't it, if not a little breezy?"

Both women nodded, Bitty perhaps too vigorously.

When in doubt: the weather.

BITTY

Bitty wished it weren't about to rain, and she wished Tiny had agreed to serve proper wedding cake. Instead, she cut into a rum cake with caramel sauce and bargained with God that if she could have a few minutes to rail on what was wrong with tonight, then she would put on a brave face for the rest of the party.

She wished she'd tried the fish instead of the steak. She wished she'd had only one glass of champagne instead of three. Her head was now fuzzy in that way where she didn't know if she was about to burp or cry. She wished Dick weren't so good at working a room. She wished Tiny would come sit by her for a minute. She wished Trip weren't drinking again, and she wished they could stop pretending that he'd ever really stopped in the first place. She wished Daphne had come; without her, it was impossibly hard to pretend everything was fine. She wished Caroline and Tiny had better-looking friends. She wished Tiny had thanked her when she'd thanked Dick, her toast casting a net over the entire group except Bitty. She wished Mabel hadn't bothered her about when they should throw the big party and whether the four of them could all throw it together. Mabel was too desperate sometimes, and this matrimony was not going to help. This weekend had exposed the fact that while Mabel easily flitted from group to group, she was also too desperate to belong in each one. Even families. Bitty missed Robbie.

Oh, how she missed Robbie; she should have never let him drift so far away from the rest of them.

Mostly, she wished it weren't about to rain. It didn't seem fair, after all she'd been through, to have it start raining now.

Dick interrupted her musing. "Do you think Tiny and Caroline would like to dance?"

The island music was at a soft hum, and the girls stood at either side of the room, deep in conversation with other people. Tiny and Caroline had absolutely refused to do a wedding dance. "It's too much," Tiny had said, her voice shrill. "Admit it: no one wants to actually see two girls dancing." Bitty hadn't disagreed soon enough to change Tiny's mind.

"You mean dance together? Do you think they want to do that?" Bitty asked.

"I'm not sure, but you and I could dance, and then if they want to, it'd be easy to start."

"I guess we could," Bitty said, taking Dick's hand. "If you think it wouldn't be too odd? To start dancing out of the blue?"

"Follow my lead." Dick nodded at the band and they started singing "Isn't She Lovely," the volume getting louder and louder. Bitty looked at Dick in time for him to say, "I told the band we were ready for something more festive."

They were off. Bitty was viscerally relieved she'd forced Tiny and Caroline to include the dance floor, despite their protestations. Weddings had dance floors. It's how it was done. At first it was all eyes on Dick and Bitty, a cross between affection and wonderment, and Bitty caught herself suddenly feeling very safe in her husband's arms. He was strong, paunch sneaking out of his dress shirt or not, and he was home.

"You've always been a great dancer," Dick murmured right into her ear, so close that he nearly nuzzled her lobe.

She breathed in her husband. Everything familiar and exciting at once. She loved this man.

"We should get away," Bitty said a little impulsively.

"When?"

"How about next week? We could get home and recover from this weekend for a few days, then head out to Nantucket for the tail end of the season." Bitty's mind was swirling now with images of golf and dinners on the terrace and dinners with friends they saw only during the summer months. It would put everything off for a few more days.

"We could get away," Dick said, clearly considering the idea. He spun her out and back in. Bitty felt warmth in the bottom of her stomach.

"Should we give our wedding gift to the girls tonight?" Bitty asked, suddenly feeling festive. This was her daughter's wedding night, after all.

Dick smacked his lips. "Oh, I think we can wait for a bit," he said.

"Why?"

"I still need to figure out the particulars. It's been busy, and I haven't had a chance, you know," he said, and she could tell he was working at sounding innocent.

Bitty opened her mouth to protest—the kids all got the same gifts; Dick was obsessed with being fair—but he cut in before she could say anything.

"We're dancing, Bit; let's talk about this later."

Bitty looked at Dick and could see that his eyes were bloodshot and sad, that his face was drawn, the bags under his eyes nearly down to his chin. How had she not seen this before?

"What is it, Dick?"

He tried to spin her again and she didn't let him, stopping abruptly midspin.

"Bitty, let's keep it light tonight."

"So it is something?"

The noise, the music, the energy, and the wind fell away as she waited for him to answer. He wouldn't look up, instead moving them both off the dance floor and toward the bar.

"Nothing to worry about," he said, spinning her again.

"But something? Is it us? Are we okay?" She didn't mean to sound so urgent.

"We're fine," he said quickly. "I just have this funny feeling. About Peter. Something is off with him. With both of them." Dick lifted his arms for Bitty to go under.

"What will you do?" she asked.

"Nothing tonight," Dick said, flashing her a smile and throwing her into another spin.

Bitty came out of the spin and stopped moving in eight counts, timed with the music. She stood up and straightened her shoulders.

"Go get your daughter, then," Bitty said softly to her husband, nodding toward Tiny. "She needs a dance."

Seconds later, Dick and Tiny were in lockstep on the makeshift floor. He spun her around and dipped her, gradually getting everyone's attention. They were joined now, first by Caroline's parents and then by Daisy and Hank, who danced like they were in front of an audience, their body language as choreographed as it was rigid. Connie and Caroline were still deep in other conversations, somehow not noticing the energy moving to the center of the room. Bitty watched her daughter realize it first and look across at Caroline. Bitty watched Tiny watch her wife and couldn't discern her expression, whether she was simply waiting to be seen or afraid of what Caroline would see when she looked up. It was Andrew who finally got Caroline's attention, snaking his way to the middle of the group and loudly calling, "Caroline!" until she looked over.

She moved away from Connie and toward the dancers, her arms over her head like she was leading a parade. The group made a circle around her, and the band played "My Girl." Caroline pulled Tiny into the circle with her, her hands around Tiny's waist and her lips kissing Tiny's cheek. They kissed on the lips and their friends cheered.

Bitty stood off to the side, conscious that she was smiling and swaying along but her thoughts melting into worry soup. She missed

Robbie so much, it felt like a wound. She wanted Dick to take her to Nantucket. She wanted to know that Trip was fine, even though he was getting soused in the corner. She couldn't be sure Tiny should have gotten married, but she couldn't be sure Tiny should not have gotten married.

For a moment, Bitty forgot all about the cake.

CAROLINE

It was late, after midnight, and the music had ended and the party was over, at least as far as the Coral Beach Club was concerned. Caroline left Tiny in bed and sneaked out of their room, putting one foot in front of the other as she decided over and over again that this was really what she was going to do. She would end whatever this was with Connie once and for all. They met in the same veranda as the night before.

"Hey," she said as Connie came into view. "Thanks for coming."

"Of course."

"Last night was not okay. You can't do that ever again. We need to stop whatever this is," Caroline said. She meant it. Tiny was her wife and she was asleep in their bed.

"I need you to say it. What this is," Connie said, reaching up and touching Caroline's shoulder.

Caroline clenched her jaw and tried to breathe, but her body felt locked in place. Even her body waited with bated breath to hear what she would say.

"How can I?" was all Caroline said. "What will that do?"

"When you name something, you take away its power."

Connie was right. Caroline had felt so much for her for so long, though she'd never equated her with fear. Name her fear.

She looked Connie right in the eye and almost lost her nerve. She had to close her eyes before she could get the words out.

"You were the first girl I ever loved, and often I'm scared I'll never love anyone like I loved you, but we can't go back and forth waiting for the other person to make the first move. There's too much hurt. Sometimes I feel like I only have scar tissue left. And I couldn't keep waiting for both of us to heal at the same time."

There it was: exactly how Caroline felt, naming it with words. She felt smarter but she didn't feel better.

"You were the first girl I ever loved, and often I'm scared I'll never love anyone like I did you," Connie said, parroting back Caroline's first line. Her words sounded brand-new, hitting Caroline somewhere in her brain she tried to keep asleep. Connie's hand was still on her shoulder. Caroline took a slight step forward, her body once again out of sync with her brain.

"I don't know what I'm doing."

"I don't either," Connie said back.

"But I know I can't do this."

"Why can't you?" Connie asked.

"I promised I wouldn't."

"Promised? Promised whom? Tiny?"

Caroline shook her head and put her hand over Connie's.

"I don't know what to do," she said, starting to cry. Her stomach felt like it was falling out of her body. "But I know I need to do this one more time and then never again." She kissed her best friend on the mouth and she closed her eyes and she felt something she hadn't felt in many years. Connie kissed back, and she put her fingers delicately on Caroline's jaw. This was a kiss that had been hundreds of times before.

Caroline pulled away. Connie waited.

"I fly to Paris tomorrow and I want to fly to Paris tomorrow," Caroline said. Connie nodded and bit her lip. "I need to choose Tiny."

Caroline watched Connie's eyes fill.

"I'm sorry I choose Tiny," she whispered. She turned around and started to walk back up the path, back to their room where Tiny was sleeping.

"Why?" Connie asked to her back.

Caroline turned around. "What?"

"Why do you need to choose Tiny?"

"Because I have to."

Caroline turned back around and kept walking.

Tiny was fast asleep when she got back, her body circled into itself. Caroline watched her sleep for so long, the stars started to fade. *I love you, I loved you, I will love you,* she thought over and over, willing it to be true.

THE UNEXPECTED

CAROLINE

The storm exploded like a secret. At first it was just rain finding its way down to the earth, and then it came down in sheets, the wind beating it against the roofs and windows. Caroline woke up to the rain, her arms around Tiny, clutching her, her body pasted against Tiny's back. Her thoughts were like a wasp's nest. She needed to get off this island and back home to her normal life and not think about Connie or her missteps ever again. She needed to never talk to Connie ever again.

The rain was hard enough to catch her attention, dragging her out of bed and to the window. Her head pounded and her tongue was dry and swollen, hogging her mouth more than usual. She couldn't see the beach or the ocean. The rain looked more like a wall blocking out the rest of the world, and even as she squinted to see outside more clearly, she could only barely see the shapes of the trees. They were nearly bent in half. The sky was so low, Caroline couldn't see where the clouds ended and the rain began.

She crept back into bed and nestled behind Tiny, inhaling her scent and trying to slow her heartbeat.

Caroline had seen Connie first, across the room at freshman orientation. Connie was standing next to a chocolate fountain, her head in a weird gray cap and her shoulders hunched. She was a brunette and she was poorly dressed, but there was something about her that caught Caroline off guard.

"Hi," she'd said, horrified because she knew she was introducing herself to a girl she liked. It was like there was no turning back from this moment: she was gay enough to say hello to a girl who caught her attention.

"Hello," Connie said, her eyes looking everywhere except at Caroline. She dug both hands in her front pockets like she was trying to scratch her knees.

"Where are you from?" Caroline didn't know any other lesbians in real life, and she didn't know if this girl was one either.

"Just outside of Boston. Like everyone else at this school," she said. Caroline laughed, not because it was particularly funny. "How about you?"

"Connecticut. Greenwich. Like everyone else not from just outside of Boston at this school."

Her eyes matched the chocolate fountain and Caroline couldn't look away. She also couldn't figure out what else to say, and a group of new friends was beckoning her from across the room.

"Well, maybe I'll see you around," she said, and Connie nodded, her own eyes darting around the room, looking for familiar faces.

~

It was like Caroline had implanted a tracking device on Connie, and for the next four years, she knew where she was. They were each other's first for everything, including the kind of breakup that happens in an instant and takes years to flesh out.

~

The first breakup came after Connie went too far with a friend from home, her phone call to Caroline short and after a month of increasing distance.

"Is it Polly?" Caroline had asked, sitting on the dock off her grandmother's house in Little Compton. Her feet were an inch above the water, and she kept trying to stretch her toe to touch it.

Connie was silent on the other end of the phone.

"Hello?" she said.

"It's not Polly and it's not *not* Polly," Connie finally said.

Polly was Connie's friend from home, either gay or intrigued enough to explore the possibility, and Caroline couldn't do anything about it. She was in Little Compton for the summer, teaching little kids how to sail Optis, and Connie was up in Maine, a counselor with Polly at some fancy summer camp.

"It seems a little unfair," Caroline said, "that after our spring, you could jump ship so easily."

"You're always there," Connie said.

"Isn't that how a relationship works?" Caroline asked.

"I'm sorry," Connie said, seeming to mean it. "I need some space."

～

Caroline had given her space, enough to find herself a perfectly nice lacrosse player to spend the nights with that fall. She'd purposely trotted Angie around campus, flaunting her, not-unconsciously hoping to run right into Connie. It worked. By Thanksgiving, they were back together, Connie completely uninterested in needing space anymore.

～

"I need to figure out who I am without you," Connie said their first year living in New York. "Our balance is all off."

Caroline sat across the table from her at The Smith and cried, her finger tracing the condensation on her pint glass.

"But I'm not really anyone without you," Caroline said. She couldn't believe they were here again: Connie suddenly needing space, without any warning, without any feedback that Caroline needed to do things differently.

"And yet you don't let me in, not really, not in the way that makes me think we're anything more than two girls who forgot they'd ever fallen in love." Connie could make anything Caroline's fault. It was like her superpower.

Connie left the restaurant without looking back and Caroline didn't get out of bed for a week.

~

Two years later, Caroline saw Connie across the room at a holiday party. They had enough mutual friends from college that this wasn't weird, but Caroline caught her heart in her throat. Connie was standing under a light and it was all Caroline could do to look away. Connie saw her and waved. Caroline waved back and mouthed, *Hi*.

"Hi, yourself," Connie said as she walked over. It was like the crowds parted just for this walk.

"How have you been?" Caroline asked.

"I've been really good. Really good." Connie said it twice like it was doubly true.

"I miss you," Caroline blurted out. She regretted it instantly.

Connie looked down before she answered, weighing her words. Before she could respond, a woman walked up and put her arm around Connie's shoulder.

"Hi, I'm Lauren," the woman said, sticking out her hand to Caroline. A girlfriend. Of course Connie had a girlfriend.

"Caroline," she said back.

Lauren raised her eyebrows and looked at Connie, who tried to smile through the moment.

"I was just about to tell Caroline about you," Connie said, her smile more like a piece of string stretched across her face.

"It's great to meet you," Caroline said; her mouth felt like it was full of marbles. "I need to go find my date, but, Connie, it'd be great to catch up properly sometime. If you want to."

Caroline snaked her way through the apartment to the door and left without so much as a nod to the party's hostess.

~

A few days later, Connie called.

"We could be friends, you know," she said. Her voice still reminded Caroline of an old Ani DiFranco album.

"We could," Caroline said, half believing it.

"Let's start with dinner. The three of us. And whoever you'd like to bring, if there's someone." There wasn't, until Caroline was walking near the courthouse during lunch and recognized Tiny on the street. That she'd been casually keeping her eye out for Tiny for the past few years and finally spotted her after Connie had suggested dinner felt like fate. Tiny rounded out the quartet.

"How do you two know each other?" Tiny had asked at their first double date.

Caroline paused, debating the best way to answer.

"Oh, we went to Middlebury at the same time," Connie had said with a breeze in her voice. "Sort of parallel friend groups, but you know how gays have to stick together at preppy liberal arts colleges in New England." Everyone had laughed at that.

They'd started a friendship of sorts, the four of them meeting for double dates every few months. And when Lauren faded from view,

Connie stuck around, brave enough to be the third wheel with Tiny and Caroline.

~

Caroline cuddled Tiny a little harder, half of her wanting Tiny to wake up and the other half of her wanting Tiny to sleep all day while she waited for her guilt to dissipate. Every minute she held Tiny canceled out a minute from the weekend. If she held Tiny until dinner, maybe everything from yesterday would disappear.

~

A quiet yet urgent knocking snapped Caroline out of her thoughts.

Andrew was on the other side of the door, sweaty and shaky.

"It's all ruined," he said, his words mumbly.

"What do you mean? How did you even get over here? The storm is insane," she said, opening the door wider so he could come inside. He stayed put.

"I need you. Come with me."

Caroline followed him out into the rain.

BITTY

The storm had started around 3:00 a.m. She knew because she'd checked the turned-around clock on her way to the bathroom, and by five, even Dick was stirring in bed. By six, they were up, leaning against pillows on the headboard and looking out the windows. The rain came down like bedsheets being folded, hitting the ground in layers. The rain and the ocean morphed into some sort of storm monster.

"Did the weather call for this?" Dick said first, his voice gravelly from sleep.

"I don't know," Bitty said as she pulled up her iPad. She hadn't looked since Tiny had yelled at her yesterday afternoon, and there it was, clear as day, alert after alert after alert of weather hitting the area just around Coral Beach. She was surprised the hotel hadn't said anything. The latest alert read simply, FLASH FLOOD WARNING IN THIS AREA UNTIL 2:00 P.M. EDT. AVOID FLOOD AREAS. —NWS. Bitty made a note to herself that if she ever sat next to someone from the National Weather Service on a plane or at a dinner party or luncheon, she would suggest they offer "but if" extensions to their alerts. Avoid flood areas, BUT IF you are in one, stay high. Avoid flood areas, BUT IF you are in one, know that the worst flood tends to happen after the storm is over. Avoid flood areas, BUT IF you are in one, steal a small boat.

Dick was now up and by the window watching the weather. Sunrise in a storm was more like a light switch: the world was dark and then it was not.

"Do you think we'll get out today?" he asked.

"So far, the flight's leaving," she said, thumbing through her Delta app but skeptical.

"Are any other flights taking off?"

"Not that I can see, but it's early."

"Or it's late—the storm started hours ago. Check New York and see if those flights are on time. A lot of those flights have planes originating in the islands."

Bitty moved on to Flight Tracker. Dick was right; flights looked grounded all over the place. Dick paced from window to window.

"I wonder if flights are grounded in Charlotte," he said.

"Why would Charlotte matter right now?"

"It would tell us how far-reaching this storm is. Are we in the middle of a tropical rainstorm, or is this a hurricane? One means a delay of an hour or two; one means we're here for a couple of days."

Dick's words hung heavy between them. Bitty did not want to be here a couple of days. It had already been three, two too many as far as she was concerned, and she wasn't sure how much longer she could keep it all together. Tiny was married, a done deal, and Bitty needed to leave this island so she could let it go. Her daughter had married a woman who did not love her, who Bitty was certain had gone through with it for some other motivation she would stop at nothing to find out. Bitty didn't have another couple of days in her kindness reserves. She thought of Mabel waving excitedly and she shuddered. It was a twenty-year friendship of convenience now made legal and she wanted to throw up.

A series of alerts from Delta filled her screen.

FLIGHT 1879 BDA/JFK CANCELED

Inclement Weather

Our attendants are currently rebooking you on the next available flight.

Next available flight departing BDA Monday, September 15th.

FLIGHT 583 BDA/JFK

"I can't do a couple of days, Dick," Bitty said, surprised and embarrassed and immediately regretting her vulnerability.

This sort of confession went against their pact: whatever it takes, keep things moving. The flip side to unspoken agreements was that certain things remained unspoken. Like Bitty's nerves, or Dick's weird ritual of circling the house after he ate dinner, or the time Bitty once woke up outside without any idea of how she had gotten there. Dick turned around to face her, his eyes a mix of confusion and concern, like a dog given a new command out of the blue.

"What do you mean?"

"I just mean it was supposed to be the weekend."

"And?"

"And now it might be longer."

"That's not so bad, right? That we're all here together?"

Bitty paused.

"I just want to get home," she said, like she was admitting something.

Dick started pacing quicker. His hands clasped behind his back. His pajamas made him look like a cross between a prisoner and a clergyman.

The wind made a sudden howl, shaking the walls as it blew against the building.

Dick's phone vibrated on the nightstand.

"Who is texting you now?"

Dick held the phone while it kept vibrating as new text messages came in. He didn't look up when he answered.

"It's Robbie."

Bitty looked at her own phone, void of any sort of communication from their son. She bit her lip too hard on the inside of her mouth.

"What's he saying?"

"Nothing important," Dick said, silencing the phone and putting it in the drawer. Bitty shifted her seat on the bed, realigning her back against the headboard.

"Dick?" she asked. He turned his head. "How often does Robbie text you?"

"As often as he texts you, I'm sure," Dick said, now rustling around for warmer clothes.

"Robbie doesn't text me," Bitty said. "He asked me to stop texting him, remember?"

Dick looked up from his clothes and considered Bitty. "I'm going to brave the rain and see about finding Peter. Maybe have a cup of coffee up at the clubhouse."

Bitty looked between her husband and outside. "Are you insane?"

Dick was dressed in head-to-toe rain gear, complete with a hat, thanks to Augusta National.

"I'll be insane if I stay inside all day."

Bitty looked at the clock. It was seven thirty.

"Well, you certainly didn't make it very long."

He gave a half wave before opening the door, putting his hand over his hat, and walking into the storm.

The door hadn't clasped shut before Bitty was in the drawer, picking up Dick's phone and thumbing in his pass code. She found his text messages, and then she found his text messages with Robbie, pages and pages of them, her thumb scrolling so far back that the phone needed a second to reload more. They texted all day every day.

She went back to her own phone. The last text from Robbie had been the day before, telling them both he wasn't coming, but the one before that had been months earlier, when he'd asked her to stop texting him, said he was in a place of deep introspection and devotion and would reach out when he was ready.

Robbie had been *hers*, she thought, sitting against the headboard of the bed with her knees hugged at her chest. Why would Dick have kept this relationship from her? All those times she'd ached with worry about whether he was all right, and Dick had sat silent, assuring her that he'd come home when he was ready. Her memory played like a montage, all the way back to when the kids were actually kids. Maybe Robbie had been looking at Dick all those years she'd thought he was looking at her.

She read the most recent messages more closely.

It's weird for me too, buddy. But Tiny is on her journey and we can't change that. Dick had written this the day before, based on the time stamp, on his way to golf.

Robbie had responded immediately: Sins of identity run deep and hard. She scrolled back to the text from a few minutes earlier. I prayed this morning for Tiny. I will pray every morning for her.

And Dick's response: Thanks, son.

They did have a party line.

She went to the bathroom and picked one pill from each bottle, then walked out into the living room to the bar cart. She placed the pills on her tongue and pulled hard against the vodka bottle, already holding her breath and swallowing deeply. She sat on the bench and watched the storm, pinching herself if a feeling came on too strong. This wasn't the party line she wanted.

Avoid storms that threaten to destroy everything, BUT IF you're caught in one, do whatever it takes to survive.

TINY

Tiny woke up alone and to rain. The rain was torrential; there was no other word for it, and it cast such a gloom inside that even the bedside lamp could not shine through. Tiny squinted around, her world layered shadows. She looked around the room for a note, swearing that if her new wife needed to be somewhere other than right here, certainly she'd say something. Tiny could feel her heartbeat accelerate as she ran out of obvious places to look, and when she finally found it—*Andrew needed me. Back soon*—written on the hotel stationery and waiting on the small table by the door, she felt her body wash itself with relief.

~

Caroline had been the one to ask her to get married, and Tiny did her best to cling to this fact whenever her anxiety started to spin her out. It'd been their second anniversary, celebrated at the Little Owl downtown: for Caroline, a splurge. Caroline was not poor—she was an attorney, and she'd grown up down the street from Tiny, for God's sake—but she was exceptionally cheap. It drove Tiny crazy, when she was honest with herself, but she'd never dated someone her parents were excited by, and that meant something. Like she could be herself and also belong.

"What have you been thinking?" Tiny had asked, suddenly thrilled that Caroline could be thinking of *her* and *them*. It felt like getting chosen for something.

"I think we should get married."

Suddenly Caroline was shifting in her seat, moving her hand around her pocket until she pulled out what Tiny recognized as her late grandmother's engagement ring. It was an oval-cut diamond with smaller yet sizable round diamonds wrapped around a yellow-gold band. Tiny had always loved this ring, and she'd always assumed the ring could not possibly go to a girl marrying another girl.

"You got my attention as soon as I met you for the second time, Tiny McAllister, and I want to see where this might go."

Tiny moved the ring over her finger before she said yes or even thought about what Caroline was asking or saying. She thought about it now, how Caroline made her feel safe and worthy, then stretched back across the hotel bed, with rain banging against the small terrace directly outside.

~

There was a knock on the door.

"Tins, are you in there?"

Daisy.

Tiny got out of bed and walked across the room, opening the door as she tied a robe closed.

"Daise? What's up?"

Daisy looked horrible. Her makeup was streaked, her hair was matted, and she was still in the same dress as the night before. She was a cross between a walk of shame and a slutty Halloween costume.

"It's Hank," she said, almost too quietly to hear, walking over the threshold and sitting on a wooden chair in the corner. Tiny closed the door.

"What is it? What happened?"

"I haven't seen him in hours, not since last night," Daisy said.

Tiny nodded. He'd been in rough shape last night and he'd probably wanted the party to go on when everyone else had died down. Everyone except Andrew. Cocaine did that.

"Things with Hank have been much worse than I've let on."

Tiny looked at her friend, her mouth opened slightly. Of course everyone knew this, but Tiny had never suggested it to Daisy.

"He hasn't written a single page of his novel," Daisy continued. "And he's been using again."

Tiny nodded again.

"He never stopped."

Tiny knew this too, of course.

"Most days, I come home and find him in his study snorting lines of cocaine and playing sudoku."

"Sudoku is such a stupid game," Tiny said. She put her hand over her mouth and flared her eyes. She hadn't meant to say that out loud.

Daisy laughed despite herself, and Tiny laughed at Daisy's laugh, and then they were both actually laughing.

"Sudoku is *such* a stupid fucking game," Daisy said between laughs, tears forming in the corners of her eyes. "And he's not even good at it! I looked at one of his sudoku books the other day and most of the puzzles were wrong!"

"But we should find him," Tiny said when their laughter faded.

"He's been using all weekend, and last night I finally lost it. I came back to the room and found him in a pile of the stuff, out of his mind, mumbling something about finally being seen for who he is. I can't take it anymore, Tins."

"Of course you can't; it's an unbearable amount of pressure."

"What do I do?"

Tiny knew immediately what Caroline had meant by warning her not to tell Daisy about walking in on Hank in Andrew's bathroom. No good would come of the message. She would forever be the person who confirmed what Daisy had tried so hard to keep secret.

"Well, for starters, where do you think he is?" Tiny knew at once that Caroline was with Andrew, who was with Hank. She hoped he was okay and she hoped she could somehow avoid Daisy ever knowing that she knew what she knew.

"Given the rain, I hope he's in someone else's room. I've checked all the common areas—the clubhouse, the veranda, the bar, reception. It's like a ghost town with this storm."

The rain came down with a sudden gust, a cacophony of storm against the building.

"Have you called the front desk yet?"

"I just want to keep looking for him myself."

"But why?" Tiny finally asked.

Daisy went quiet, her body folding into itself.

"What is it?"

Daisy was quiet a few moments longer before finally starting to speak.

"He, um, he did . . . big business on the hotel room floor yesterday morning."

Tiny knew better than to say anything. She bit the insides of her mouth to keep from laughing.

"When I was just waking up. I think he thought he had more time, or maybe more control, and had tried to come to his side of the bed to get a copy of *The Atlantic*, and then suddenly he was squatting and an immense amount of it came out, right onto the rug. I thought housekeeping was going to blow a gasket."

Tiny kneaded her hands and focused on her breathing. Her best friend's husband had pooped on the floor on her wedding day. She counted the flowers on the curtains.

"You can laugh if you want to."

A laugh escaped Tiny's mouth before she could properly introduce it.

"My husband pooped on the floor." Daisy's laughter was one-third laugh and two-thirds tears.

"Your husband pooped on the floor," Tiny parroted back.

~

"So we should knock on the doors, I suppose," Tiny said a few minutes later.

"And say what? 'My husband is missing from a very intimate destination wedding'?"

Tiny thought for a moment.

"We'll say that Hank went out for a cigarette after the party, just before the storm started, and it started with such ferocity that we imagine he ducked into a room for shelter, and given that the storm is still going, he hasn't had a chance to leave yet. We are the brave ones in this scenario, willing to find him and bring him to safety."

Daisy's face briefly brightened.

"You're a genius, Tins."

Tiny thought about waking up alone the morning after her wedding day. She thought about the entire weekend so far, a series of moments precariously held together by tradition and desperation for things to be something they weren't. She thought about her parents and Trip and Robbie and about how there had not been a single day in her life when she didn't feel alone. Daisy stared at her, waiting.

"I'm just good at optics."

Daisy furrowed her eyebrows and turned her head to look around the room. "Wait, where is Caroline?"

Tiny darted her eyes toward the bathroom as quickly and subtly as she could. She exhaled when she saw the bathroom door was closed.

"She's taking a bath." Tiny said this with the air that Caroline bathed all the time, that this was an indispensable part of who she was.

"Should we start knocking on doors?"

"Not yet," Tiny said.

"Is it still too early?"

"No," Tiny said, cocking her head as kindly as she could manage. "If you don't want to raise any suspicion, then I think you need to clean yourself up. Take a quick shower, put your hair up, brush your teeth, wash your face, put on some comfortable clothes intended for the daytime. Then come back here and we'll go together. We can also pretend we're rallying the troops for breakfast."

Daisy got up from the chair and embraced her friend.

"Thank you, Tins. Thank you so much."

Tiny closed the door gently behind her and leaned against it. She exhaled. Then inhaled and exhaled again, trying to calm her heart. She knew she had about a half hour to find Hank before Daisy would be back.

Tiny needed to be the one to find him, not Daisy. By finding Hank and getting him back to his room, she could help Daisy believe for a little longer that no one knew just how unwell her husband was.

She pulled her hair into a low pony, slipped into a loose cotton jumpsuit, and stepped into a pair of flip-flops as she walked out of the room.

COUNT THE
GUESTS

DICK

Dick went in search of other men in the main lounge of the clubhouse. He most wanted Trip but would take Peter. He'd even take Hank. He was less interested in Andrew. The walk up the path toward the clubhouse was treacherous. The wind was so strong, he walked nearly bent in half and with both hands plastered over his hat. He didn't fight it: the storm felt deserved. He was confused by the world changing around him, but he also knew, leaning into a particularly hard gust of wind, that he was indulging his son's particularly destructive thinking to stay in his life. Robbie was not correct here: Dick knew this—he could feel it in his soul—but he had never said to Robbie, *You are wrong*. He hadn't said it to his daughter either, but he also hadn't ever said to Tiny, *You are right*.

~

Peter was tucked in by a modest fire with a newspaper.

"Is that from today?" Dick asked, breaking the silence and making Peter look up abruptly.

Peter turned back to the paper's front page. "Friday."

Dick nodded and didn't move. Peter's glance turned into a questioning look.

"Do you want to sit down?" he finally asked.

This shook Dick out of whatever it was freezing him in place.

"Yes, yes. I think I will." He sat in an armchair turned toward Peter's.

"Well, this is some storm," Peter said, looking and pointing out the window for full effect.

"It really is."

"How's Bitty? Mabel is either still in bed or in the bath, but she told me that out of solidarity for the sun, she wouldn't come out until it stopped raining."

Dick laughed at this. Peter laughed behind his laugh.

"She's about the same."

"Any word from the brides?"

"I imagine they'll surface soon." Dick made a show of checking his watch, as if his lack of mentioning them were more about allowing them their space. "I know Bitty said something about a brunch later this morning."

Peter shifted in his seat and put down the paper.

"I actually wanted to ask you something, Dick."

Dick nodded for Peter to go on.

"About this weekend. The matter of the bill."

Dick nodded again.

"I know we talked about splitting it, being two brides and all." At this, Peter attempted a half grin. "But the thing is, it's been a tough year for us. A tough few years, really."

"I'm sorry to hear that," Dick said. "Everything okay?"

"To be honest, we're moving in a few months."

Dick felt for Peter. They'd been in their house on North Maple for twenty years.

"Hopefully somewhere nearby?"

Peter moved his head from side to side. "There's a new complex in Riverside that'll work for the time being. While we get everything sorted."

"You'll be back on your feet in no time," Dick said, adopting a coach-like tone. The situation was clearly dire. Dick didn't know any adults who lived in a condo. At least not as their primary residence.

"Mabel and I were wondering if we could set up some sort of arrangement. I'm good for my half—you know I am. It would just be so appreciated if I could, you know, wait a little while."

Dick considered his friend. They'd made an agreement to split the wedding, and here Peter was, going back on that. He'd been right to think something was off.

"I wish you'd said something sooner—" Hadn't they saved for something like this? Dick took his end of any bargain very seriously. How could Peter be so trite after thirty years of friendship?

"I'm good for the money, Dick; you know I am. It's just been a hard year."

Dick nodded. He could feel his mouth turn itself downward, and he tried to fix this. The last thing he needed was Peter to see him frown. But the attempt went haywire, and then Dick was smiling—with teeth—and he didn't need to see a mirror to know that he looked absolutely creepy. Peter looked away.

"It's nothing. We'll take care of it," Dick said.

Relief flooded Peter's face. "Thank you so much. So much." He was profuse. "And thanks for not mentioning this to anyone."

"I wouldn't dream of it."

"I've got another favor, if you can bear it," Peter said.

"Sure?" Dick thought his paying double for this wedding was favor enough for now.

"The Country Club of Connecticut membership is a little jeopardized. The minimums went up, as you know, and, well, it's a bit of a struggle to meet them."

Dick felt like a puppet as he nodded and said he'd make a call. Peter seemed quite boosted by their entire exchange, and Dick felt like he'd just been taken for a ride. Dick was a principled man, and this felt entirely unprincipled. Unscrupulous. Downright deceitful.

"I'm glad this little union worked, marrying of the families and all that," Peter said. Dick looked at him curiously, but Peter didn't seem to notice. "Just glad our daughters could fall in love in the nick of time!"

At this, Peter stood up and started to walk away. He turned at the door.

"Peter," Dick said, catching him before he left. Peter turned around. "When did you say the trouble started?"

Peter cocked his head to the side and ground his teeth.

"I hate to admit it but almost four years ago or so. The fund took a turn and we've been chasing it ever since."

"Fair enough," Dick said, repositioning himself in the chair.

"So we'll see you at brunch?"

"See you there," Dick said, giving a little wave. He turned back toward the fireplace and picked up the two-day-old paper, then put it back down again. Caroline's arrival to Tiny's life felt too convenient, almost staged: the run-in on the street, the string of fast and increasingly lavish dates. Dick had kept track through Bitty, who was overcome with relief that Tiny had found someone so relatable. Paying for a wedding was one thing, Dick thought, now folding the paper into a perfect square, but pretending to pay for a wedding was quite another. Maybe this was the ammunition he needed to set Tiny's life back on track.

CAROLINE

Caroline stood in Andrew's room looking between Andrew, who was standing by the window and could collapse at any moment, and Hank, who was curled up in bed, not ready to face the world.

"I see why you needed me," Caroline said.

"I don't know how to get him back to his room without Daisy seeing. She can't know we were together," Andrew said. Caroline didn't think she'd ever seen him consider consequences before. It was refreshing.

"Do you really think you're protecting Hank here? By doing coke with him all weekend and then trying to hide it from his wife?" Caroline asked. The storm was like the perfect noise machine, the rain tapping against the window like a thousand metronomes going at quarter-second intervals.

"No," Andrew finally replied, his eyes cast low on the ground. "But maybe I like him?"

Caroline winced. "You don't like him. You got a buddy for the weekend. But he isn't some guy you picked up at a bar. He's connected here. His wife is Tiny's best friend."

He was crying now, the shame spiral in full force. Caroline knew this was bad even for Andrew, to so boldly disregard everyone around him.

"What happened exactly?"

This question ignited more tears.

"We met back on the beach. After he had a fight with Daisy." Andrew stopped talking, lost in thought.

"Keep it moving," Caroline said.

"Sorry. We had a bottle of tequila and an eighth, and then I guess we both passed out. Then the rain started and it felt like it was going to wash us away. Hank was curled into the sand, little-kid-like, and I heard footsteps and I had a feeling those footsteps would lead to something very bad, so I woke him up and told him to run and we both ran back here."

Hank started to stir in bed. His eyes opened and caught Caroline's.

"We aren't ready for you yet," she said to Hank. "Go back to sleep."

He pulled the duvet over his head and turned away from the window.

"Okay, so what you're saying is you found a drug buddy in my wife's best friend's straight husband, who happens to be fake sleeping in your bed right now while the storm of the century traps us all on this island. Is that what you're saying?"

Andrew nodded.

"Stop smirking. This isn't funny."

Andrew nodded again. "You're right. Of course. This isn't funny."

There was a knock on the door and an urgent, "It's Tiny. Let me in."

Andrew raised his eyebrows at Caroline.

"Open the door. Clearly Daisy got to her."

"But why would she know to come here?"

Caroline scrunched her eyebrows until her face was all but contorted. "Are you out of your mind? Do you not remember yesterday at all? When I came in to grab my makeup bag and *you were in here with Hank*?"

"Coming!" Andrew called to the door.

Tiny looked like a wet kitten and Caroline felt immediately protective.

"Are you okay?" She embraced her and kissed her forehead. "Are you cold?"

"I'm fine," Tiny said, pushing herself away from Caroline's tight hug. "But I'm curious as to what's happening in here." Now it was Tiny's turn to look between Andrew and Hank. She added a suspicious glance at Caroline for good measure. Caroline felt her neck go limp and she looked at the floor.

Tiny walked over to the bed and sat next to Hank. She patted his shoulder and let her hand trail down his back.

"Hey," she said in an almost-whisper. Hank turned so he faced her.

"Hey," he said back. Caroline and Andrew stayed out of this moment.

"How's it going in there?" Tiny gently tapped Hank's head.

"It's not pretty."

"I bet it's not."

Tiny repositioned herself on the bed so she was facing only Hank.

"So here's where we are. You are married to my best friend, who is extremely worried about you and who I was able to stall by telling her to change out of her wedding attire and into a daytime outfit."

Hank's mouth turned ever so slightly upward.

"But that was at least a half hour ago and she's going to come right back to my room, ready to start looking for you. I'm going to give her the gift of being there when she gets back and I'm going to give you the gift of letting you tell her yourself."

Hank opened his mouth—

"This isn't a negotiation." At this, she turned to include Andrew. "I'm sure he's great, you've had fun, and it would be so much easier if Daisy let you be. That's for you two to sort out. But I got married last night and my best friend is about to get her heart absolutely broken because the secret she's worked so hard to keep isn't really a secret at all, and I don't want her to ever know that I knew any part of this."

Hank closed his mouth and nodded.

"Understood?"

"Understood." Hank was still nodding.

Caroline had never loved Tiny more, had never seen her puff out her chest and be so strong. She was like a tiny block of steel.

Tiny stood up and faced Andrew and Caroline.

"Are we all on the same page?"

"I love you, Tins," Caroline said. "That was amazing." She said this as if they were the only two people in the room.

Tiny raised her eyebrows and side smiled. "I've been known to have my moments."

"Well, have more," Andrew said, breaking them out of their trance. "That was hot."

Tiny kissed Caroline on the mouth before she left the room.

TINY

Tiny stepped down the steps into the rain, a vertical lake washing over her, knocking her on her heels every few steps. The grounds were a ghost town, save for the hotel workers running around asking anyone outside to go back to their room. Palms had fallen and scattered along the pathways, never in one place for long before blowing somewhere else. Coconuts, beaten and cracked, rolled like kicked soccer balls. Each wave crested higher, closer to the cliffs, flooding the steps leading up to the Frozen Hut. Tiny walked from memory the path connecting the various cottages, squinting to see the ocean beyond. The wind was too strong, and she couldn't hold her head up without saltwater stinging her eyes closed. Her clothes were soaked, but that was the least interesting thing about this moment, she thought, actually holding on to a railing as she stopped to catch her breath.

Tiny had almost gotten back to their cottage when she saw Connie hovering in the doorway.

"Connie?"

Tiny realized she was standing three inches too close to her and stepped back.

"Hey, Tiny."

"What are you doing?"

"I was out for a walk before the goodbye brunch, or whatever this meal is, given that we're all stranded here." Connie said this too tentatively to pass off, and it made Tiny more confused than suspicious.

"Out for a walk?"

"Yes."

"May I ask why?" Tiny gestured obviously at the weather.

Connie wasn't used to Tiny having so much presence, and Tiny wasn't used to having so much presence either, but right now she was exclusively focused on protecting Daisy, and that meant everyone being in their rooms, away from here.

"I needed some air."

"You needed some air."

"I needed some air."

Tiny repeated her again. "And you just happened to fight the storm all the way to our room?"

Connie didn't say anything back. Tiny moved to wave the key card over the doorknob.

"Where's Caroline?" Connie asked before Tiny could close the door behind her.

Tiny hesitated.

"She's taking a bath."

"Caroline doesn't take baths."

"How would you know that?" Caroline's aversion to the bathtub was something Tiny had thought only she knew.

"Caroline hasn't taken a bath since the second grade and a cockroach crawled out of the drain." Connie said this like a threat. For a moment, Tiny wondered what else Connie knew, and the thought sent a bullet into her gut. She didn't know why, but her Spidey sense was going ballistic. "Are you going to let me inside or would you prefer I drown out here?"

Tiny held the door open wider. Connie stepped inside, and within seconds, there was a pool of water around both of them.

"What's this about, Connie?"

"I need to talk to Caroline."

"She isn't here."

"Okay, so where is she?"

"She's not here, Connie. I don't know what to tell you."

"Just tell her I'm sorry."

Tiny saw Daisy fighting her way down the path and physically pushed Connie outside. "You need to go. We'll do this later, but you need to go." The door was closed before Connie could get a word out.

～

Tiny counted to ten before she opened the door and waited for Daisy to finish her way down the path. This time Daisy had braved the storm with an umbrella, and Tiny couldn't believe how she'd transformed into a lady who lunched again. She was even wearing bright yellow rain boots and a matching slicker.

"How on earth . . ." Tiny trailed off.

"Always be prepared!" Daisy said this too brightly. Tiny looked down at her own soaking body. Never in her life had she ever thought to pack rain gear.

"Should we go look for him?" Tiny asked.

"Your mom still wants us to do the goodbye brunch. The hotel called while I was getting changed."

Tiny looked at her own room phone and saw the message light blinking.

"Do you want to find Hank first?"

"I don't want to be late for your parents. Put on something dry and we can go," she said. Tiny found the white linen jumpsuit she'd planned for the final meal of their weekend. She opened the door.

"Here," Daisy said, stepping outside and opening the umbrella, "we can both stay dry."

Tiny knew not to ask anything more. She couldn't stop thinking about Connie.

FAREWELL BRUNCH

BITTY

Bitty sat at a large round table in the restaurant, the staff scurrying to keep the doors and windows closed and locked to block out the storm. They'd started with thick plastic flaps, but those were no match for the wind. There were six of them, moving so nimbly that it all looked coordinated. Obviously no one was feeding the fish, and Bitty wondered if fish ate during storms. Was it like the bears in Yellowstone, who now only had a taste for human food? There were signs all over the resort requesting guests not feed the fish, and Bitty understood perfectly: unexpected changes can destroy an ecosystem entirely.

The others were supposed to be here. She'd had the front desk call each room announcing a celebratory brunch. "We'll call it the Eggs in Terminal Four Brunch, because Terminal Four is where I know everyone wants to get to! Well, or LaGuardia." Bitty started to overthink it. The attendant on the phone hadn't found this funny. "Just please invite everyone for eleven thirty and tell them it's on Dick and me."

Now it was nearly twelve thirty, and Bitty was the only one here. The servers were either too polite to nudge or assumed this group just ran an hour late. They weren't even moseying around the table refilling her water. Daisy and Tiny finally walked in just as Bitty was starting to think the manager had never called the rooms at all.

"Over here!" She waved as if they weren't in an empty and otherwise silent restaurant.

"Bit!" Daisy said too brightly.

"Hiya, Mom," Tiny said.

"You look incredible," Daisy said. Bitty looked down at her turquoise slacks and matching tunic.

"Just beachy," she said. "Trying to dress for this weather."

Both girls were in good Sunday outfits, loosely fitted but short, Daisy in a dress and rain boots and Tiny in a jumpsuit and carrying sandals. When they got to the table, Tiny slipped the sandals on her feet.

"Smart to prevent backsplash," Bitty said, getting up from her seat to kiss both girls on the cheek.

The three sat down. Tiny dived into a roll sitting in the basket. Daisy asked if it was too early for champagne.

"Never too early," Bitty said, matching the affirmation with a firm nod. A waiter appeared out of thin air, uncorking a bottle of Veuve.

"Where are your spouses?" Bitty asked after they'd all had a sip.

Daisy and Tiny said, "Coming," at the same time. Bitty thought it sounded rehearsed but knew better than to say as much.

~

Peter and Mabel and Connie filed in a few minutes later, their walk over clearly more treacherous, because they were absolutely soaked. Mabel needed five minutes of whimpering before she could even fully enter the room.

"How do you look so fresh for today?" she said to Bitty, air-kissing her on each cheek. Her hair looked like the humidity was holding it hostage. Bitty felt a little gleeful at Mabel looking almost ugly for a change, even if it was because of the storm.

"Where is everyone?" Peter asked in the same breath as he asked the waiter for a cold beer in a glass.

Dick and Trip showed up as the answer to Peter's question, and Caroline and Andrew appeared as soon as Dick made his way to the table. That just left Hank, who ambled in a few minutes later and wedged himself next to Daisy. Bitty could smell the booze from the other side of the table.

~

"So, Bit," Mabel began after everyone was eating. "I can't remember—did you say you and Dick could come to the Garden Club benefit next month?"

"Remind me the date?"

"Saturday the nineteenth."

Dick gave her a glance she couldn't translate. A cross between alarm and warning.

"Of course," she said, ignoring him.

"We were hoping you might get a table and invite some others," Mabel said.

Bitty knew Mabel probably hadn't bought a table at all. This had always been her strategy: convince several friends to buy their tables instead and join one at the last minute. The charity equivalent of wedding crashing.

"Mabel," Bitty said in her kindest voice, "you know you can't host a benefit without buying a table, right?" She knew Mabel and Peter were having a hard time. Their house was probably in foreclosure by now. Mabel had told her one night after way too much chardonnay and half a Valium.

Mabel went a little white and swallowed. Bitty could suddenly hear the table go silent around them. This was mean, even for her, but she was tired of being the fool in everything.

"Mom," Tiny said, trying to soothe the moment. Bitty paid her no attention.

"So two tables, then? Side by side?"

"Side by side!" Mabel said, her jaw betraying her intonation.

TRIP

Trip took a spoonful of lobster bisque. "Should we call this hurricane soup?" he asked no one in particular but hoping Daisy would laugh. She did not. "We could call it lobster tsunami," he tried again.

Daisy looked at him and cocked her head. But she didn't say anything. It was a stupid joke. He knew this.

Hank was at the other end of the table, alternating between taking humungous bites out of a burger and large sips of a beer. He had two glasses in front of him already.

"Did you know lobsters mate for life?" He said this looking directly at her.

"Trip," she said.

He raised his eyebrows, full alert. Hopeful.

"Shut up."

Everyone around her laughed.

Trip was sitting between Tiny and Connie. He'd run out of things to talk to Connie about so turned his torso to Tiny.

"Why is Hank already hammered?" he whispered.

"Not now," Tiny said through the side of her mouth. She was pretending to listen to Bitty and Mabel talk about the Garden Club.

"Seriously, though. It's early to be so drunk."

"Stop it—I'm serious," she said, this time more urgently.

He took a sip of beer. Unexpected hurricanes called off any rules he had for day-drinking.

"Daisy," he said, waiting until she looked up. "Is everything okay with Hank?"

"Trip, seriously," Tiny said.

Daisy pursed her lips up toward her nose. "What do you mean?" she asked, her voice even.

Hank didn't seem to notice he was the topic of conversation. Trip saw a fresh beer had been delivered in the past few minutes.

"Just that the day is young. Should you help him out a bit, maybe make sure he drinks some water?" Trip was poking the bear like it was an out-of-body experience. He was utterly aware that he was the kid on the playground picking on the girl he liked without an ounce of self-control to right this ship.

Daisy looked at him long and hard, the rest of the table falling away. He was scared now, thrilled by her attention. Maybe this was why little boys pushed little girls. Because it worked. His fear turned to excitement and then anticipation.

"At least my spouse is here."

Her words hit him like pellets in his chest. Suddenly everyone was watching. Even Hank had looked up.

"Daphne had to stay with the kids this weekend."

Daisy smirked at this.

"Tiny's niece and nephew couldn't come to her wedding?"

"Something came up. And it was just better if . . . they stayed." Trip was trying to be careful with his words.

"Everyone knows she's gone, Trip."

"Daisy," Tiny said, putting up her hand. "Don't."

"Is that true, Trip?" Bitty asked. Trip thought for sure everyone could hear his heart pounding. He could feel sweat prickling at his hairline. His fingers tingled. His stomach went to putty just enough to momentarily distract him.

"Son?" his father asked, the only one with concern in his voice.

Tiny reached over to put her hand on her brother's shoulder and he shook it off. When he raised his eyes, he saw every single person at the table looking at him. Forks were down. Glasses were ignored. This was as much a stage as he'd ever been on.

"Daisy and I are taking a break," he finally said, only realizing he'd said the wrong name too late. There was an audible gasp from the table. "Daphne. Daphne. Obviously I meant Daphne. *Daphne* and I are taking a break."

More silence. Daisy looked like she was about to cry.

"Why did he say Daisy?" Trip heard Hank drunkenly ask. He wore a white polo shirt that was too big for him.

"It wasn't my fault," was all Trip said before he got up and walked back into the storm.

ON HOLD WITH
THE AIRLINES

DICK

Dick wanted the mixed nuts sitting on their bar cart, but Bitty sat directly in his path on a wing chair reading a *National Geographic* and he knew if she intercepted him, he would have to talk about either the wedding gift, Robbie, or Trip's potential divorce, or he would have to share what he'd learned from Peter—she would know he was hiding something. He didn't want to talk about any of those things, and despite the fact that salted bar nuts were his favorite, he abstained. He would not approach the bar cart.

Then again, if he just sat here like a dummy, she would eventually look up and see an opportunity to ask whatever she wanted. He couldn't risk that either.

"Any word from the airline?" he asked, breaking the silence.

"Not one. Even their app is freezing," she said without looking up.

"What are you reading?" he asked.

"Something about fish."

She looked birdlike on the chair, her legs like spindles sticking down from her torso. Had she always been so frail?

"I bet we leave tomorrow," he said.

Bitty didn't say anything back. So she was angry, he thought, clueless as to why.

"Peter and Mabel are broke," he blurted out.

"I know. Mabel told me." She didn't seem nearly as nonplussed as he'd expected.

"She did? When?"

"Months ago."

"Don't you think we should be concerned?"

Bitty looked at him, an expression somewhere between confusion and disgust.

"You never honestly expected Caroline to provide, did you? They've never been worth much. They waited all those years for Mabel's mother to die only to learn that the old money had long since dried up. And you know Peter's attitude toward work has always been to do a little bit but later." Bitty said this like it was entirely old news. She was right, he thought, cataloging the string of dead-end-but-I-swear-this-will-be-the-one jobs Peter had started over the years.

"Well, no," he said, sitting back in the chair and a little confused about why he was somehow in the wrong here. "But I just think people should be honest." That was it. People should be honest.

Bitty raised her eyebrows but said nothing. She went back to her magazine and he went back to thinking about how people should be honest.

~

A knock broke his train of thought and he looked up to see Tiny at the doorway.

"Mind if I come in?" she said. When she walked through their door, he thought back to Peter and his odd turn of phrase about unifying their families.

"Of course!" He got up and walked over to hug her. She was still so small in his arms, and when he inhaled, he pretended she was still the schoolgirl excited when he picked her up from soccer practice.

Bitty remained seated but she had put down the magazine to acknowledge their visitor.

"Mother," Tiny said.

"Daughter," Bitty said back.

Tiny sat down on the couch and Dick sat on the wing chair opposite Bitty.

"Where's Caroline?" Dick asked. Did Tiny flinch when he asked that?

"She's organizing in our room before games in the clubhouse."

At this, Bitty perked up. "Is that happening? Do Mabel and Peter know? Does Trip?"

Tiny nodded while she answered. "Everyone knows. Everyone knows to meet in the clubhouse at four."

Bitty went back to her *National Geographic*.

"So, Dad," Tiny said, shifting her weight so she was leaning ever so slightly toward him.

Dick raised his eyebrows as an answer.

"Now that I'm married, we should probably talk about what happens next. Trip said there's some stuff that happens. And Caroline and I are trying to figure out where we want to live and all that. So I should know what we're talking about here." Her words came out in fits and starts; she was nervous and had clearly thought a lot about this moment.

Dick's heart fell into his stomach. Of course she'd thought about this moment: Dick prided himself on what he was able to gift the children. But Peter was in his ear again, and he didn't feel right.

"Well," he started, "we haven't talked about it yet."

Tiny dragged her lips into a straight line. "Yes, that's why I'm here, you know, to talk about it."

"So let's talk."

Even Bitty had looked up from her magazine.

Tiny crossed one leg over the other. "I guess I'd just love to know what we're talking about here. Maybe you could just tell me what Trip got when he and Daphne got married? So I can prepare or plan?"

"He didn't tell you?" Dick asked.

"We don't really talk about money," Tiny said.

"Good girl," Bitty chimed in. She cocked her head at Dick.

Trip had gotten a million. That was six years earlier, and each child was supposed to get the same amount. That's how Dick had set it up when the children were so young that matrimony seemed impossible.

Tiny looked at him expectantly.

"I think, instead of talking about amounts, we could talk a bit more about your and Caroline's financial health."

"Our financial health?"

Dick nodded. "How do you and Caroline spend your money? Do you think you'll have a joint account or maintain two separate ones?"

"I'm not sure. I imagine joint, right? Isn't that what most married couples do? Isn't that what you and Mom do?"

Tiny looked between her parents.

Dick kept speaking.

"Your mother and I are different. We both knew exactly what we were bringing into the marriage and what we wanted our financials to look like."

"Where is this coming from?" Tiny asked. Her voice was thinning out, almost shrill, and Dick could see her wringing her hands in her lap.

"Your mother and I just want to be sure before anything happens."

"Sure about what? We're married. Pretty sure this is it, Dad. Sorry if you were hoping for a different outcome."

"Dick," Bitty said quietly from her chair. Her expression told him she didn't know what he was doing. He could have told her that: it was like he'd lost control over everything coming out of his mouth.

He leaned back in the wing chair and crossed his ankle at his knee. He exhaled. He inhaled.

"Dad?" Tiny's eyes were wet, and Dick felt his heart plummet from his chest.

"Is this the right thing to do? With Caroline? Are you sure?"

"What does that have to do with our wedding gift? With our financial health?" she asked. Everything was coming out wrong. Bitty looked like a china doll about to shatter. "Is this a gay thing?"

"What? Of course not—"

"It is. Isn't it? You went through this weekend because you knew you were supposed to, because your good friend Peter was, but really, when it comes to treating your children equally, you can't do it. Why do I have a hard time imagining you asking Trip and Daphne, who has never worked a day in her life, by the way, about their financial health?"

"That's not it at all," Dick said, horrified. He looked at Bitty for support. She sat tight-lipped.

Tiny stood up.

"I should have known. Of course a girl from Greenwich, Connecticut, can't be gay and expect to get away with it."

She left the villa before he could respond.

TRIP

The phone in Trip's room rang too much like an alarm. High-pitched and piercing. Trip tried to hide under the pillow. What he needed was sleep. The ringing continued.

"Hello?" he finally said, for a second thinking maybe it was Daisy and how that would help.

"Trip, it's Dick. I mean, it's Dad." His father was nearly sputtering. This got his attention. He sat up and shook his head a few times. Of course Daisy wouldn't call him. Daisy hated him.

"What's up?"

"Can I come over?"

"Can you come over? Like to my room?"

"Yes."

Trip looked around at the clothes strewn on chairs and sofas and piled in corners. The bathroom was in far worse shape. He was the child turned man who still left wet towels on the floor.

"I guess so, yeah."

"Great. I'll be right over."

~

Someone knocked on his door not two minutes later.

"That was quick," he said, opening it, only to find Tiny on the other side. "Tiny. Hey."

She didn't look good, and as Trip looked closer, he saw she was actually shaking.

"What's up?" He opened the door wider, though he then started to worry his father needed him *privately* and, in that worry, closed the door almost completely, then realized this was his little sister and he couldn't close the door on his little sister and so he opened it again, only to get stuck in the same cycle. It was as if he were trying to fan out the room.

"Should I not come in?" Tiny asked after Trip almost closed the door for the third time.

"No, no, come in. Dad's just on his way over here."

At the mention of their dad, Tiny froze.

"What does he need?" she asked.

"Didn't mention it," he answered, now certain he was about to be in the middle of something. "What's up?"

"Do you think Mom and Dad are homophobic?"

Trip realized too late that his sister was crying. He braced himself. "Come again?"

"You heard me. Do you think Mom and Dad are homophobes?"

The weight of a lie could break a man, but being caught in one could ruin him. Trip knew this, and he lied anyway.

"Absolutely not. No." He shook his head vehemently for effect. "Nope. No. And I'm not either."

Tiny crossed her arms and sniffled. He'd gone too far. Especially on the last bit. He shouldn't have exclaimed it like that. He exhaled and softened his approach.

"What happened?"

Tiny said she didn't want to talk about it, just that Bitty had been silent and Dick had been rambling and it had all happened over the question of a wedding gift. Trip winced and looked out the window and wished for the hundredth time that day that he wasn't stranded here. He clasped his hands behind his head and stretched out.

"Look, they probably just don't want you to have a harder life. I don't either, for the record. They don't want you to suffer."

Tiny closed her eyes and shook her head so imperceptibly that Trip couldn't be sure she'd really moved at all.

"You aren't ever going to understand, are you? In the world out there, I'm actually okay the way I am."

Trip put his hands up in surrender, apologizing and shrugging.

"How much did Dad give you and Daphne? When you got married?"

Trip shrugged again and tried to play it off. "Well, they helped right after the wedding but then also when the kids started preschool. So it wasn't just once, but right after the wedding, they helped with the down payment." He sounded like a liar and he knew it. Tiny knew it too, but she kept her mouth shut, already defeated. "I'm sure they give us all the same amount," he said for good measure.

"But how much did Dad actually give you?" Tiny asked again.

"Honestly? I think our down payment was like, three hundred and fifty thousand bucks." He prayed this sounded like enough. He had no idea what his father was brewing, but he knew for sure not to mention that it had been the down payment and then some.

She said, "Okay," and "Goodbye," and "See you at the clubhouse in a little while," all in one breath while she walked out the door, leaving Trip to wonder what their dad could have possibly said.

~

"Trip, you in there?" he heard a few minutes later, his father standing in his threshold wearing a plaid button-down tucked into khakis, a Patagonia vest, and a pair of gray Allbirds. The WASPy man's athleisure.

Trip ushered his father inside.

"Dalwhinnie?" Trip asked, already pouring two tumblers.

Dick nodded and held out his hand for the drink.

"Are you supposed to be drinking?" he asked.

Trip shrugged. "Sobriety has always been more of a suggestion."

"Is that why Daphne and the kids aren't here?"

"I'm not a falling-down drunk, if that's what you're asking," Trip said, the defensiveness sneaking out with the words.

"I'm not, actually," Dick said.

"It turns out that Daphne does not particularly care for me regardless of how many I've thrown back," Trip said.

They each took a sip and sucked in air through their teeth.

"I care for Daphne because she gave us our grandkids, but you know we'll support you through this," his father said. Trip was unexpectedly touched.

They took a few sips without saying anything and looked out the window. It was still pouring, but the destruction phase felt over. Trip made the first move to sit down. Dick followed suit. After their drinks were nearly gone, Dick finally spoke.

"I might be in a bit of hot water with Tiny," he said. Trip instinctually got up to refill their glasses.

"How's that?"

"Well," Dick started, repositioning himself on the wing chair and widening his manspread. Posturing for something, and Trip could only imagine what. "To be honest with you, I'm not entirely sure about Caroline."

Of all the things he'd expected his father to say, this was not high on the list. Trip knew better than to question anything going on in his sister's life, and when they'd announced they were getting married, Trip had assumed he was somehow missing something.

He stood up. "Let's go for a walk."

They both left their glasses on a dresser by the door. Trip led the way as they walked outside, the air humid and warm and wet. The rain had lost its power, the water slipping off the clouds as opposed to shooting from them. They walked as a pair, their feet in unison. From behind, they looked like two cavemen dressed for golf, their backs slightly tilted forward, their arms hanging at their sides. It was not a walk that could easily turn into a run.

"You don't like Caroline?"

Dick shook his head. "I didn't say that."

"Okay, you don't think Tiny and Caroline should have gotten married?"

"I didn't say that either."

"Would you like to tell me what you did say?"

His father bristled. "Jesus, Trip, I just said I'm not entirely sure."

It was a brave feat for Dick to admit he wasn't sure about something. They walked a few strides in silence. Trip leaned his head side to side as he figured out what to say next. No words were coming.

"Does it matter?" he finally asked.

"Does what matter?"

"How you feel about the whole thing?"

His father considered the question.

"Maybe it doesn't."

Trip waited.

"I hate that her life is so much harder. It's not fair."

Trip put his hand on his father's shoulder and squeezed. He didn't say anything, and they kept walking. He knew this feeling: he fell into it whenever he went to a party or a wedding or church and saw a single gay couple in the crowd, their tokenism as much celebrated by the self-proclaimed progressive or ignored by the mass that easily avoided change. His father had never admitted this before, and Trip imagined one of the twins growing up gay. What would he do? What would Daphne do?

"You know, Dad," he said after a while, "I'm not sure we've got this one right. Tiny's navigating it just fine. No thanks to us."

They walked by a Coral Beach staffer and nodded hello.

"I might need a little help here, with Tiny," Dick said.

"How so?"

"Can you talk to her? Tell her it's not a gay thing? Smooth things over."

Trip whistled and shook his head. "I can't. That is a minefield waiting to happen and I'm not walking into it."

"It's not a minefield."

"Are you trying to avoid giving her the wedding gift?"

"I just don't completely trust Caroline. I don't think it's right."

"What is *it* exactly?" Trip asked.

"All of it," Dick said, gesturing around them.

Trip frowned and put his hands on his hips, planting his feet like a golfer's stance. They could make jokes, but he loved his sister.

"I'm not getting in the middle of this," he said. He was firm about this.

Dick stopped walking and faced him. Their shoulders were both squared.

"Don't be a prick," Dick said, now on the offensive.

Trip put his hands up. "Don't put this on me."

"This isn't how I raised you."

"A woman named Trena raised me. And you taught me to make sure the lead horse is always fed first."

"That isn't fair, Trip," Dick said.

Trip looked at his father and, for the first time in his life, saw a man who had never walked into a room and not felt like he belonged. The wind pricked at his skin under his raincoat, and Trip felt suddenly exposed. His mind was racing, and in the stream of thoughts there was Daphne, asking him over and over again to see her. To hear her. And there was Tiny. Always there, always willing to smile. Witty but never sharp. They were wrong here; he was sure of it.

"We're wrong, Dad. About Tiny. About everything. There's got to be more to life than what we think there is."

He left Dick standing by the croquet field and walked up toward the clubhouse.

CAROLINE

The rain had lessened just enough so the outdoors were no longer an all-out threat. Tiny had suggested the group reconvene in the game lounge at four for gin and tonics and board games and told Caroline she was going to discuss their wedding gift with her parents. Caroline went back to their room to start packing.

An hour later, Tiny was still gone and Caroline saw Connie walking outside, just below their cottage, relieved to see her alone.

"Hey, Con," she said from the terrace. "Hold on—I'll come for a walk with you."

Connie turned around and waited for her. "Hey."

"Hey." Neither woman knew if she should embrace the other. They settled on an awkward shoulder pat.

They stepped gingerly along the path, alternating between real steps and mini jumps over puddles or stepping just on their toes to avoid getting the rest of their feet wet. The rain was more of a mist now, and Caroline noticed Connie's hair was already beginning to frizz. That meant her hair was already beginning to frizz. It was now or never.

"What did you say to Tiny?" Caroline blurted this out more than she wanted to.

"What do you mean?" Connie asked.

"At brunch. Tiny said you'd told her you were sorry and that you'd been looking for me. What was that about?" Caroline felt herself getting mad and she tried to slow down her breaths. This wasn't the time to get mad.

"I didn't mean anything by it," Connie said, her steps slowing so much, it was like she was walking in place.

"But you meant something. You had to—you said it. Why did you tell her you were sorry?"

"Because I was. I am. I shouldn't have come. And I'm sorry I did. But she doesn't deserve this, you know."

"Doesn't deserve what?" Caroline couldn't help that it came out as a yell. Connie stopped walking altogether.

"She invited me! Not you—she did, thinking she was doing this generous thing for you. And it's not fair."

"What isn't fair? She did invite you. Which means this isn't my fault. I didn't cause this," Caroline said, not hiding her defensiveness.

"She doesn't deserve someone who is on the fence." Connie said this so evenly, Caroline almost believed it.

"I'm not on the fence," she said. Connie kept her gaze. "I'm not," she said again.

"Are you sure about that?"

Caroline suddenly felt like she might fall through the earth at any second.

"Am I sure about what? The fence?"

"You just told me you aren't on the fence."

Caroline and Connie did this: parrot and mirror the other until one crumbled, making the other the winner by default.

"I'm married now," Caroline finally said.

"And what would you do if I kissed you?" Connie said, taking a step so she was mere inches from Caroline's face. Caroline took a step back.

"Don't," she said, shaking her head and closing her eyes and wishing for this moment to be over.

"Don't what?"

"Don't." Caroline couldn't look up. She couldn't move away. Her feet felt cemented onto the ground.

"You have to say it."

"I have to say what?"

"You have to say what you want."

Caroline felt the tears only after they hit her cheeks. She licked up the salt and tried to swallow.

"I can't."

"Is it because you want what you can't have or you don't want what you've got?"

The tears fell harder now, and Caroline could feel herself shrinking. She knew this was a trick question.

"That isn't fair," she said.

"What isn't fair?"

Caroline looked up before she spoke.

"You could have had me at any moment for so long. For so many years, I loved you and waited for you to come back and you didn't and I found Tiny and she at least wants me all the time, not just some of the time or when I'm perfect or when she's in the mood. Why did you have to come do this now? Why this weekend?" Caroline didn't care how loud her voice had gotten. She wished for a moment that she were the type of person who could turn her rage into something physical.

"I didn't know, and now I do. It's you; it's always been you."

Connie grabbed Caroline's face and kissed her in such a quick motion, it took too many seconds for Caroline to realize what was going on. Her reflex was to kiss back, but when her hand finally grazed Connie's neck, she snapped back into the moment and moved away.

"I can't do this," she said, shaking her head for effect. "Not now."

She looked up just in time to see Tiny standing there, her face a mix of shock and horror and rage and an utterly pure sadness. Connie stood between Caroline and Tiny, her hands now up in a surrender position, as if the whole moment had happened by accident. Tiny furrowed her eyebrows and leaned back on her heels and then turned around, and Caroline got enough feeling in her legs back to follow.

Tiny stopped in place, then turned toward her. "Don't follow me."

"How much did you see?" Caroline asked.

Tiny turned back around and kept walking.

GAMES IN THE CLUBHOUSE

TINY

They would play games in the clubhouse, Tiny decided. It was a natural next thing to do after one catches one's brand-new wife kissing her best friend the day after one's wedding and one also finds out one's parents aren't nearly as accepting of one's sexuality as they claimed. Not to mention one's brother not showing up at all. Suddenly, Daisy's behavior at brunch, showing up and eating and drinking a glass of champagne and talking like nothing was wrong, made an entire world of sense. Tiny got to the clubhouse and started positioning the couches and sofas so everyone could sit in a makeshift circle. She found punching the pillows so they looked just so on the couches felt quite good. She wasn't angry, she thought, sliding a couch perilously close to a table hosting a china lamp. She was disappointed. This was not how she'd wanted the weekend to go. She asked the bartender to make a pitcher of rum punch and a pitcher of gin and tonic for the group.

Daisy arrived first and they greeted each other like everything was fine and their spouses weren't incredible liars. Daisy even beamed, which impressed Tiny and made her want to beam too. She smiled wider and gestured to outside.

"The storm is clearing up!"

"Just a little while longer and we should be good to go!" Daisy answered. They were good.

"What should we play?" Tiny asked, taking a sip of her drink even though no one else had arrived yet.

"Maybe something like Monopoly?" Daisy said, watching Tiny drink but not saying anything and not drinking herself. Tiny took another two sips for good measure. She needed a straw.

"I'm thinking more Truth or Dare."

"I *like* this Tiny," Andrew said, walking into the room and not stopping until he'd grabbed a glass from the bar. "Keep it up!" He winked at her.

"Really?" Daisy asked. "How would we even play that?"

By now, other bodies were trailing in, and as Tiny nodded hellos to her parents and in-laws, she noticed her father staring at the ground. Served him right. Bitty looked like she'd seen a ghost but was still dressed impeccably. Hurricane chic, if Tiny had to label it. Trip sauntered in next and made sure to sit next to Daisy, who sighed and rolled her eyes and looked like she might actually get up and move, but she stayed put. Hank sat on her other side looking sweaty, his arms and legs twitching a bit like they were attached by wire.

Tiny wondered if Caroline or Connie would dare show up. They needed to, or else people would know something was wrong, and Tiny knew Caroline wouldn't let that happen.

"We'll wait a few more minutes and then I'll tell you the game," she said after Bitty asked twice what they were playing and whether they all needed to play.

"I'm more a spectator than participant," Bitty said to whoever would listen.

"I'm sure you'll do whatever you want to do!" Mabel said, not unbitterly. She looked rumpled. Tiny had never seen her mother-in-law in a wrinkly shirt before.

Caroline and Connie came inside two minutes apart and Caroline knew to sit next to Tiny. She was about to lean in to kiss her cheek when

Tiny murmured, almost inaudibly, "Don't you dare," and Caroline pecked her on the shoulder instead. Tiny tried not to flinch.

"We're playing Truth or Dare," Tiny said, feeling a little maniacal.

"What on earth?" Bitty said, leaning back and chuckling and looking at Mabel and Dick for reinforcement.

"Truth or Dare," she repeated, "wherein one player asks another player whether they'd like to do a truth, so answer a question truthfully, or do a dare, so do whatever the player might ask."

"What if I don't want to answer the question?" Bitty asked, taking Tiny quite seriously.

Trip and Mabel both groaned.

"Jesus, Mom, just go along with it," Trip said. "The sooner we play, the sooner it's over."

"Then you should probably do the dare," Tiny answered, ignoring Trip.

"But what if I don't want to do the dare?"

"Well, Mother, that's part of the game. You have to pick a lane. Are you for the game or against the game?"

Bitty leaned back and shrugged. "I guess if that's what the girls want to play," she said over to Mabel, who was always ready for a party.

"I don't think I want to play this game," Tiny's father said, positioning his weight to stand back up.

"You wouldn't, would you, Father? You've proven that you're pretty antigame at this point," Tiny said, half-conscious of what she was saying.

Dick leaned back, a mix of disgruntled and trepidatious.

Tiny felt alive.

"Trip, how about we go first."

Trip let out a nervous laugh. "Okay, Tins."

"Truth or dare?"

"Dare."

"Go kiss Daisy on the lips."

Daisy gasped next to Tiny.

"Okay, then truth," Trip said.

"Why didn't Robbie come to the wedding?"

"Tiny—" he started, then closed his mouth. Tiny knew if she lit a match, the room would explode from the tension. Trip looked at Tiny long and hard, leaned back, closed his eyes, leaned forward, and kissed Daisy, a chaste though undeniably familiar kiss. Hank turned his head just as Trip's mouth hit Daisy's and he let out something between a grunt, a whistle, and a laugh but thought better of all three and leaned back into the sofa.

"My turn, then," Trip said after the kiss was over. He took his time looking at each person sitting around the clubhouse. Tiny followed his gaze and realized everyone looked a little scared. This absolutely thrilled her.

"Andrew. Truth or dare?"

Andrew sat up to attention, not expecting to be called on.

"Truth?"

"Why are you here?" Trip asked this lightly, the words inflected up. It was a fair question.

"You know, Trip," Andrew said, looking around like he couldn't decide if this was the best or worst day of his life, "at this particular moment, I have absolutely no idea what I'm doing here."

The tension in the room broke for a moment as real laughter ensued. It made Tiny simmer to the point of boiling over. Andrew held up his hand after a couple of minutes and kept the game going.

"Connie. Truth or dare?"

"Dare," she answered quickly, her arms crossed over her chest.

"Fair enough," he said, nodding, contemplating. "How about you take a shot of rum." Collective nodding started, making Tiny think she was looking at one of those singing-frog videos. She couldn't blame them: little bad could come from a shot of rum. Connie stood up and walked over to the bar, where she asked the bartender for a shot of dark rum. Shaken first with ice. He obliged, and she took the shot quickly and easily, then walked back over to the wing chair she'd been sitting in.

"Caroline," she said. Hearing her say Caroline's name made Tiny flinch. That was not the name she was supposed to say.

"Me?"

"Yep. Truth or dare?"

Tiny was holding her breath. She couldn't watch them interact.

"Dare, I guess?" Caroline answered. Tiny could feel how rigid her body was sitting next to her, and Tiny herself felt at once hollow and overflowing with rage.

"Then I dare you to—"

"No," Tiny said, shaking her head and standing up. "No, no, no, no. Absolutely not. Nope." She was walking in little circles in the middle of the room, not caring that there was literally a circle of people sitting around her, watching her pace. She stopped every few steps to take another sip of her rum punch, refilling it twice. "This isn't going to work. Not today. Nope."

She could hear murmurings around her, but they were all nonsense until Caroline said, "Tiny!" and snapped her out of her pacing and caused her to stop and look directly at her new wife.

"How could you?" Tiny asked. She could feel the tears welling up and she prayed to all that was good and holy that her eyes would stay dry. She knew the second she started crying that everyone would write this off as little Tiny McAllister feeling too much too fast and not understanding the ways of the world. She could already hear Trip explaining to the group that she just "needed a moment to sort herself out."

Caroline held up her hand like she was calming a horse. "Not here," she tried to whisper, going so far as to stand up.

"Sit down!" Tiny said, unexpectedly loudly. Caroline sat immediately. "You are not to stand near me at this moment." The words were stilted and Tiny realized she was holding her breath.

"And you," she said, now turned toward Connie. "How dare you come down here, with your smug attitude and homely clothing and sarcastic little quips about me and my family and this weekend."

Connie was ashen.

"Nothing happened," she said.

"Do you mean nothing happened after I walked in on you kissing my wife? Or you mean nothing happened right before I walked in on you kissing my wife? I'm just trying to get the facts right, because I literally saw you kissing my wife." Tiny cocked her head while she spoke, the world suddenly making sense as she looked at it from this new angle.

"Tiny, stop," Caroline said. She was standing now, physically trying to rein in Tiny. "It's not what you think."

"What do I think, if you know me so well?" Tiny had never let her anger bubble over like this before.

"I choose you," Caroline said. "I choose you. I told her I choose you," she whispered. She tried to take a step toward Tiny, which resulted in Tiny dramatically stepping backward and nearly toppling over a rigid and silent Daisy and Hank.

"All of you are liars. You're a liar and a cheat," she said, pointing at Caroline. "You're a liar and a homophobe," she said, pointing at her father. "You're a liar and an addict," she said, pointing at Hank. "You're a liar and full of shit," she said, pointing at Trip. "And you," she said, pointing at Daisy, "you lie so much, there's no point in even wondering what's really going on. Your entire life is a performance."

She felt like a windup doll, completely out of control of her next movement.

"Don't do this," her father said, holding up his hands.

"Do *not* tell me what to do!" Tiny said with so much power, her father seemed physically touched by the words.

"I understand you're angry—" he started to say.

"Don't use that voice on me, Father," she said. "That's for Bitty when she's had just a little too much of the grigio." She made sure to lock eyes with her mother as she spoke, miming a wineglass. Bitty looked down.

"I don't understand why you're doing this!" Dick said, now getting angry too.

"And I don't understand why you're still hung up on the fact that I married a woman." Both Dick and Bitty looked especially struck by this, which only invigorated Tiny. "Just because I'm gay doesn't make me less. I'm gay! I think women are sexy! I want to sleep side by side, *with* a woman, for the rest of my life. Get used to it!"

A chorus of "well, I never" erupted, led by Mabel and culminating in Trip hugging his head and moaning, "Why is this my life?"

Tiny turned to her brother. "Oh, for the love of God, you're a loser, Trip. Why *isn't* this your life? What have you honestly done that would result in something better? You can't even get into Wing Foot. And you're a legacy!" Trip stared at her, his eyes widening by the second, his mouth slowly opening like he was about to say something. But like a short gust of wind, it was over and his mouth closed, his eyes went back to their normal size, and he looked down.

"What was the point of this weekend? Huh?" She was screaming now. "To make a fool of me? What, did you think if we could just marry off poor, pathetic little Tiny, I wouldn't be anyone's problem anymore? But at the last minute, you decided you couldn't bear to have a daughter married to a woman? And you"—she looked Caroline square in the eye—"what was the point? I have always been true to you. Always. I'm honest. I'm loving. I love *you*, and I was never good enough and you knew you wanted someone else. All of you—" She took a few steps back and closed her eyes, willing herself to find the words. No one else dared speak. "All of you are so busy living in your perfect castles, you have no idea that everyone else can see you for the frauds you are."

It was time to leave. Tiny looked among Caroline and her parents and Daisy.

"Some friends. Some family. Some wife."

She walked out into the storm.

INCREASING
DESPERATION

CAROLINE

"What on earth was that about?" Caroline's mother asked her, not caring at all that the entire group was listening.

"Stop it, Mom," she said, but she didn't get up and run after Tiny and she didn't tell her mother that anything would happen if she didn't in fact stop. Caroline wasn't sure she was up for awarding a punishment. She squeezed her eyes together. Why wasn't she running after Tiny? When she opened them, Connie was looking at her.

"Must everything be so hard with you?" Her mother whispered this in her ear, pretending to embrace her. Caroline felt like her bones were snapping one by one.

"I'll fix it," she whispered back. Mabel pushed away in one fluid motion.

"Well, that was awkward," Trip said, breaking the silence. The group laughed uncomfortably in a round, each person letting out their own little chuckle.

Caroline was out of her seat and outside before she really knew what she was doing, but when she came to, she was walking quickly toward their cottage.

~

"Tiny!" she called out. Tiny was twenty steps ahead of her, walking with purpose and looking slight against the palm trees lining the path. "Tiny!" she called out again, picking up her pace. "Tiny!" she called a third time, close enough now to put her hand out to her shoulder.

Tiny stopped in her tracks and turned around too slowly, like she was afraid of what she might see. Caroline winced despite herself.

"Hi," Caroline said. Her hands were raised in surrender.

"Hello," Tiny said back.

The rain had turned to a mist and it felt prickly on Caroline's skin. She shivered into herself.

"Hi," Caroline said again. "Sorry," she said quickly. "Sorry."

"Hi and sorry? Is that all you've got?" Tiny was glaring; she almost looked amused, which made Caroline forget her words entirely. She took a deep breath and tried to stay even.

"I'm sorry, Tiny," she started again. "For everything. For my attitude leading up to this weekend, for this weekend, for how I took out my awkwardness on you and made it your fault, for how when I'm uncomfortable I spin these webs that leave the people I love the most caught in the middle."

"And?" Tiny cocked her head.

"And I'm sorry about Connie." Caroline was crying now, the tears free-falling down her cheeks, and she could taste that her nose was running. She used the back of her hand to wipe her face.

Tiny nodded as she took in Caroline's little speech. "Thank you," she finally said. "I'm not sure where we go from here. I feel so stupid." Tiny was crying too.

"Why do you feel stupid? I'm the one who is stupid."

"I invited her! She wouldn't have even been here if I hadn't gotten all excited about surprising you."

Caroline took a deep breath and counted to three, then gently cupped Tiny's face and kissed her. Tiny at first resisted and then gave in, her mouth opening slightly, her tongue grazing Caroline's teeth.

Caroline gained courage with this and moved in closer, putting her arms around Tiny. This kiss was so familiar and yet felt foreign: her lips completely new from the ones she'd kissed before. Even her tongue was different, searching now, none of the timidity of a young mouth, deft in navigating teeth and tongue and lips. Maybe they'd needed this fight to get to this moment.

"What is this?" Tiny finally said, breaking away.

Caroline tried to kiss her answer and Tiny moved back.

"Tell me. What is this?" Tiny needed to hear Caroline say she chose her. Not Connie.

"What do you mean?" Caroline asked deliberately, her hands coming up to Tiny's face to bring their mouths back together. Tiny let her, dipping her mouth down again to keep kissing.

"What's the point of kissing me right now? To apologize? To wordlessly say you were wrong? To ask me for another chance?" Tiny asked, pulling away. Her eyebrows furrowed. Her eyes flecked gray in the sun.

Caroline didn't answer her. They kept kissing.

Caroline's mind flew from one thought with Connie to the next, and she kissed Tiny desperately, willing her mind to get back to her wife. But her memory was suddenly a montage of their buildup to this weekend, complete with a soundtrack. That Indigo Girls song she didn't even like that much but every time she heard it, she was back in the student center of Middlebury staring at her phone, waiting for Connie to text back. It was "Fugitive," and she'd never looked at the beach the same way.

Connie calling her first after she was promoted. Connie stopping by her apartment unannounced when she'd broken up with Michelle. Connie laughing at how they always ordered the same thing. Caroline laughing at Connie dancing. This was love, wasn't it, when the people at the end finally showed up to the same place at the same time and made some affirmations and then began kissing just as the sun started to go down? Was Connie her choice? She couldn't be. She'd promised

Connie wouldn't be. And Caroline was here, kissing Tiny. She wanted to be here, kissing Tiny. Tiny was her choice. She had promised that Tiny would be her choice.

"You didn't answer." Tiny pulled away again.

"Didn't answer what?"

"Don't deflect."

Caroline looked at her and cocked her head. "I'm not deflecting."

"So answer the question."

"Ask it again."

"What is this?"

"Why does it always have to be so complicated?"

Before Caroline could take back her words—so stupid! Tiny was her choice; it was all she needed to say!—Tiny looked like the air had been vacuumed out of her lungs.

"Complicated?" It came out as a whisper.

"I meant you. I choose you."

Tiny stepped back, shaking her head side to side.

"You kissed me. You married me. You proposed to me. You courted me. You met me on the street in New York and asked if we could get together sometime. And here we are. The day after our wedding, and you've just said that kissing me feels complicated."

"I didn't mean it," Caroline said. It was too late. Tiny was walking away and Caroline knew she couldn't follow her. Not yet.

Her heart was breaking, and she didn't know how to make this right.

AN EXTRA SUNRISE

TINY

Sun streamed through the blinds, which told her it had stopped raining and that she'd actually fallen asleep. Tiny turned slightly toward the window and watched the sun stream through the blinds onto the half of her bed that was still made, which told her Caroline was still gone. They hadn't talked since last night, when Tiny had been too angry to see straight and told her she wasn't welcome in their bed. Of course, Tiny had thought she'd come back anyway, that she'd crawl into bed and hold her from behind and whisper that it had all been a dream, that Connie meant nothing and Tiny meant everything and all they needed to do was sign the marriage license and go to Paris and put everything behind them. But the sheets were tight against the made bed. Tiny imagined the maid smoothing the bed's surface with her hands, a move she did a hundred times a day, assuming her work would be forgotten as soon as the couple returned to their cottage.

This moment felt like dead air on the radio. She wanted to be left alone and yet kept waiting for a knock on the door, some sort of confirmation that she wouldn't die alone in this bed. Wasn't this what mothers were supposed to do? Lie in wait for their daughters to stumble and come swooping in for the great rescue? Where was Bitty? Where was her dad? Where was her brother, the goddamn officiant, and where was her other brother, all but disappeared from her life? Where was anyone who ever saw her for anything beyond a nice, small girl living a harder life than other people?

"Open up!" came along with banging on the door. "It's me! Daisy! Open this door. I know you're in there!"

Tiny wasn't prepared for Daisy. Out of everyone, she felt worst for blowing up at Daisy. She put a pillow over her head and hoped Daisy would go away.

"Seriously! Open up! The pillow-over-the-head trick will not work. I'm not going anywhere."

Tiny let out something between a cough and a sigh and a groan and rolled herself out of bed, nearly busting the landing. Daisy knew her friend too well.

"Coming, coming," she said, willing her legs to make it from the bed to the door.

Daisy was on the other side of the door holding two iced coffees. "Come on. You need to get out of here."

Tiny scrunched her eyebrows.

"Don't give me that look. Let's walk. Don't forget you left an entire room of people yesterday afternoon and then disappeared for the rest of the night. Everyone is impressively confused about what the issues are, but I'm here to actually say that I love you and you are my person."

~

A few minutes later, after Tiny had trouble deciding which spandex to put on and Daisy said, "Oh, for the love of God, it doesn't matter! Just put on shorts—we're in the tropics!" they were outside. They walked in silence to the croquet field, where they sat on a bench that faced the water.

Tiny finally started.

"I walked in on Caroline and Connie kissing. And my dad made some pretty homophobic comments and then Trip didn't say he was wrong. Then Caroline ran after me yesterday and said Connie didn't mean anything, but she also didn't say I meant anything."

"Worse than my wedding," Daisy said. "And Hank peed the bed."

Tiny stayed quiet, her thoughts racing. She hadn't known Hank had peed the bed at their wedding, but she didn't have it in her to ask more.

"Well, what do you think?" Daisy asked. They had left the bench and were walking on the part of the beach where the waves only lapped over their feet every so often. Even the ocean was telling her to make a choice: either walk into the waves or walk where the sand was soft and dry.

"I don't know," Tiny said.

"Who's there when you feel happy? In your mind?"

The problem was, Tiny was slowly realizing, that there hadn't been a Caroline before Caroline, so she didn't have a reference point. Her old boyfriends couldn't compare: she'd never needed any of them to breathe.

"I think it's Caroline. Caroline is there, and I'm happy. In my mind."

Daisy waited a few beats to speak again.

"Then you need to forgive her."

Tiny stopped walking. It all felt too hard. Too much up to her.

"What about Connie, then? What about her? And them together? What about that?"

Daisy took Tiny's hands in hers and squeezed like only a best friend could, at once intimate and sisterly and affirmative.

"Sometimes we put too much value in the past, and when we're afraid of what's coming up, we suddenly think that if we move backward, we'll be safe. And it never works."

Tiny looked at her friend, standing tall in the daytime, the sun highlighting her hair and casting her face in bronze. She looked strong, stronger than maybe Tiny had ever seen her, and she looked like someone desperate to see her friend happy again.

"So I forgive her?"

Daisy nodded.

"You try. And if you can't, then you leave, but you decide either way. She doesn't get to. She can only have you if you want her to have you."

Tiny started nodding with her, hoping Daisy's confidence would be contagious.

"I'll go tell her that I'll try."

"Good."

Tiny took a deep breath. "Also," she started. "I'm really sorry for everything I said yesterday. I was, I am, so angry, and it all came out at once and I couldn't control it. You aren't a liar."

"I am, though," Daisy said, shifting her body so she faced the ocean. "I am a big fat liar." She was crying now, and Tiny wasn't sure if she'd ever seen Daisy cry, beyond drunk tears in college. Daisy was always so stoic, and now she was crumbling even more than Tiny was crumbling, and Tiny reached out to hold her friend's hand and squeeze in a way that said, *We'll get through this. I promise you we'll get through this.*

"You just wanted it to work," Tiny said.

"I just wanted it to work," Daisy parroted back. "But it's not working. It hasn't been working for a very long time and we both deserve so much more than this. He uses and I nag and he uses and I nag and I can't remember the last time we didn't start and end the day fighting."

This was Daisy uncensored, and Tiny felt her heart swell as Daisy let her completely in, her guard down and her words not in their typical measured delivery.

"Okay, so we both deserve more—is that it, then? The point of this entire weekend?" Tiny said, crying now too.

Daisy laughed, a chuckle at first and then a real laugh. "Yes. Exactly. The point was to realize we both deserve to be happy and that no amount of Bitty's pinot grigio will make that happen if we don't do a single thing for ourselves."

"Wouldn't it be nice to be Bitty, though? Always protected with a steady stream of wine and Dick following her around?"

Daisy grimaced and inhaled sharply. "Isn't she just as imprisoned by those things too? We're all a little imprisoned by the same things that keep us safe."

The girls sat down at the water's edge, their butts and legs and feet lapped up by every wave's final stretch. Tiny looked around them, the water and the sun catching the palm trees and the sound of birds and waves and wind. She squeezed the sand with her toes. She'd chosen water.

DICK

By now the storm was really over: the blue sky and chirping birds and waves lapping the beach were almost ironic next to the fallen branches and shingles scattered all over the premises. This was regret, Dick thought, nearly to the club's entrance gate, when the world tried to move on but you couldn't look past the destruction. He needed to find his daughter, but he was scared. So he walked. He'd been walking for close to an hour, trailing the perimeter of Coral Beach until it was fixed in his memory, learning after two times around that a combination of paved road and paved walkways and a stone path and then a few steps over fresh grass made a complete loop. The distance between the cottages at the far east end and the rocks leading out to the water where the cove met the sea was his favorite. He knew he was wrong about Tiny. But he didn't have a road map for how to be right. The world changed without him and he was scared by the idea that his daughter might be happy even if he wasn't happy for her. The two were supposed to go hand in hand. Weren't they?

He saw Peter standing outside the pool area between the tennis and squash courts. The courts were just starting to dry in the sun. Peter called out his name and did a dramatic one-armed wave, as if Dick were out at sea, scanning the coast for life.

Dick one-arm-waved back.

"Morning," Dick said, reaching him.

Peter said, "Morning," back and patted Dick on the shoulder.

"How's the day?"

Peter tilted his head side to side. "Pretty good. Think we'll be heading out to the airport soon. I wanted to make sure we said goodbye!" The last part came with an odd inflection.

"And if you hadn't seen me walking, what, would you just have gone?"

"Well, no. I mean, we wanted to see you, o-of course." Peter was sputtering.

Dick stepped back from Peter and put his hands on his hips in a power pose.

"It's a little suspicious to slink off, don't you think?" He was suddenly extremely unimpressed by his old friend Peter.

"How do you mean?"

"It's one thing to not hold up your end of the bargain. You're broke now, fine. I'm not." Dick let himself smirk a little with this. He knew he was being mean. "But your daughter is the one kissing someone else at her own wedding, leaving my daughter heartbroken and distraught. I'd think you would want to make sure everything between us was okay before slinking back to Greenwich."

Peter took a step toward Dick, putting his own hands on his own hips in his own power pose.

"I didn't say we're broke. I said it had been a few hard years and we need to make some adjustments."

Dick sucked his lips into his mouth. "You also let us plan a bogus wedding to make sure your daughter would marry well. That's what happened, isn't it? You and Mabel realized your portfolio wasn't all it was meant to be and you needed an exit strategy for dear old Caroline?"

"Well, at least my daughter isn't accusing me of being a homophobe. She knows I actually want her to enjoy her life." Peter sneered.

Dick picked up his fist and wound it behind his shoulder and punched right into Peter's face, his knuckles cracking into the other man's cheek. It hurt mightily, something he would have expected if he'd ever punched someone before.

Peter fell back, his hands cradling his cheek and jaw, yelling obscenities.

"What the fuck?" he shouted, now on the ground and trying to move into a sitting position. There was no blood that Dick could see.

"Don't tell me how I feel about my daughter. And don't pretend this was anything more than a bunch of money-grubbers realizing they could marry into a family actually worth something."

"You'll pay for this," Peter said, still on the ground.

"I'll pay for the wedding. You'll pay for the fact that I oversee membership at the Country Club of Connecticut."

Peter put his head between his knees. Dick started walking back to their villa before turning around.

"Oh, and Peter?"

He looked up.

"Your daughter is an asshole."

TRIP

Trip was returning a CBC-owned cruiser bike to the designated cycle parking when he looked up and saw Daisy rolling her bag past him. She wore a floppy hat tilted down, like she was in hiding.

"Wait up!" he called, kicking out the kickstand and jogging a few steps to reach and then pass her. The sudden burst caused him to pant slightly. She stopped in her tracks but didn't say anything.

"It's always been you. I think," Trip said, looking up from his feet. He felt his eyes moisten and this embarrassed him. Daisy didn't notice or pretended not to notice, but her eyes softened and she let her hat flop away from her face.

"What do you mean?" He thought she looked hopeful.

"We were so young," he said.

"We were so young," she echoed. Trip parted his lips, but Daisy kept talking.

"We were so young, and you were so mean! Your temper. Your stubbornness." She gained momentum as the memories flooded back. "Do you remember leaving me in Newport after Hannah's wedding? Because I wanted to go to the farewell brunch, and you were afraid traffic would be bad back to the city? So you drove back alone. You said, 'You summer on Fishers; you'll figure it out,' and then you said I should probably hitch a ride with someone who doesn't care about timing."

He grimaced. That hadn't been great. It had been near the end, when Daisy had grown wise to Trip's anger and realized it had turned into the third person in their relationship.

"Traffic is *really* bad—"

Daisy held up her hand.

"Do you want to win me back or not?"

Trip nodded.

"Then don't remind me of your shitty argument ten years ago."

He nodded again.

"You are so angry, Trip."

He nodded. He felt like a puppet.

"But I didn't cause that anger. Just like I didn't cause Hank to spend our savings on cocaine. If this weekend has taught me one thing, it's that I have to stop waiting for someone else to walk up and tell me what to do to be happy."

Trip felt like he was staring Daisy down. When had she gotten so strong? He was transfixed—at once longing and adoring, watching Daisy transform from the college girl he was always in love with to the adult he knew he needed to know.

He couldn't lose her again.

"Daisy," he said, the name like music. "Daisy," he said again. "I am an angry, curmudgeonly old man who has never been totally right in this world. Daphne changed the locks for a reason, and I can't sit with Bitty for more than a few minutes before wanting to run away screaming." This felt like a confession. He could feel the sun burning the back of his neck. She waited for him to continue.

"Eat dinner with me," he blurted. She furrowed her eyebrows. "In New York. When we're back."

"Eat dinner with you?"

"To start. If I can get through dinner without being an angry prick, then maybe we could have another dinner after that."

Daisy smiled with half her mouth. "It's going to be complicated. Whatever happens. I'm not even sure what I can do. I have to get Hank some help, see if I can do right by him after all this."

"Just have dinner with me," he asked again.

"Dinner, then."

Trip was smiling so much, his cheeks hurt. "Can I kiss you?"

"No."

He reached out to put her hands in his.

"You need to go help your sister," Daisy said. "And I need to figure out what to do about Hank. I can't do anything until I know he's going to be okay."

She turned around and finished rolling her suitcase to reception.

AN INAPPROPRIATE
DISPLAY OF
EMOTIONS IN
PUBLIC

CAROLINE

Caroline was standing on the terrace off the clubhouse, her body pointed to the sea and her mind racing. How was she going to fix this? She should never have said that to Tiny, to imply that it was only Tiny who wanted this. The sun was nearly overhead and the beach so reflective it looked like a mirror. Caroline noticed two bodies swimming out by the rocks and squinted to try to make out who they were, only getting as far as knowing it was two men.

"Caroline," her mother said, startling her enough that she jumped.

"Mom. Hi." She turned around and they hugged but only lightly, their chests not touching.

"What's going on?"

"What do you mean?"

"I presumed after yesterday's ordeal that you would have done what needed to be done, but Dick just punching your father on behalf of his daughter implies in fact you have not at all done what needed to be done. Were you hoping we wouldn't notice? That you'd, what? Fly on to Paris with that woman and Photoshop Tiny in later?" Her mother squinted at her, like she was seeing her for the first time, and Caroline shriveled from her gaze. "Surely you can't be that stupid."

"I was going to come talk to you. But I was waiting for the right time."

"The right time? What on earth would you wait for? Until Tiny is happily married to someone else and all you have to show for yourself is the memory of ruining a perfect arrangement?"

Caroline clenched her jaw and smoothed her hair with her hands, wishing she had a hair tie. "I'm doing my best."

Her mother pursed her lips and crossed her arms, blocking Caroline from leaving the terrace. "Would you say your best is working?"

A lifetime of failings streamed through Caroline's consciousness, her mother's voice the loudest on the tape: Caroline not getting accepted to Harvard. Caroline not getting into honors English. Caroline getting cut from varsity lacrosse. Caroline crashing the car weeks after she got her license. Caroline being ditched time and again by the girls in her class at Greenwich Academy. Caroline not knowing what to wear to church. Caroline trying so hard to look appropriate for dinner at the club that she tried to wear her mother's clothing. Caroline overhearing her mother say she wished her daughter knew how to wear a dress. It was a cacophony of humiliation and Caroline almost shouted out for the voice to stop. She wasn't supposed to ruin this. Finally, she would do something that would make her parents proud.

"I told you I will figure it out." She hated that she was crying.

"You should have never allowed that woman to come down here. You should have never allowed her to stay."

"This isn't Connie's fault, Mother."

"Don't say her name."

"Mother, you've known Connie for years. You know what she means to me. What she meant to me."

"She's young love. Don't you understand that she could never be your choice? That matches need to make sense? Otherwise you'll spend your life justifying it to everyone else."

"Connie is more than young love. She could have been my choice," she whispered.

"If she were," her mother said before cocking her head to the side in a way that made Caroline shrivel into a raisin, "then you would have eloped. Run away. Declared that nothing mattered except for you two. But you never did that. You stayed here, in this life."

"This weekend isn't her fault." Caroline said this into the ground so quietly, it was as if she were simply mouthing the words.

"Is it yours, then?"

Caroline felt like her legs would give out at any moment. Did it even matter what she felt?

"It's just complicated. You have to understand." She tried not to plead.

"We can't afford complicated. You know that. You take after your father. An utter inability to ever think with his head. And you know what I tell him?"

Caroline waited. Her mother had never protected Caroline from her father's indiscretions, and neither parent had ever fooled her into believing their marriage was one built on love.

"Discretion is rewarded with freedom."

Caroline nodded.

"Remember why we're here," her mother said.

"How could I forget?"

"This is a good union, Caroline."

Caroline closed her eyes and hung her head back. "I know, Mother. I told you I am trying to fix this."

When she opened her eyes, her mother was already retreating, tapping her kitten-heel sandals on the limestone, her white linen pants swaying ever so slightly with each step, her arms loosely at her sides. Her mother had always walked with such purpose, Caroline thought, her stomach a mix of acid and nerves as she realized just how badly she needed Tiny to come around. Her parents had been angling for this since before Tiny was even in the picture. That Peter's fund had dried up and Caroline had learned just how much Tiny would be worth one day happened a year to the day of each other felt like a cruel confirmation that her parents were onto something.

Caroline turned back to the sea. The bodies were Hank and Andrew; she could see them now, their arms and legs in easy unison as they crossed from one side of the swimming area to the other. They made it to the western buoy and turned, and for a split second, they used each other to stay afloat, and Caroline watched this simple movement and realized she was drowning, right here on this island, her heart submerged, with no hope of getting out.

She had one shot—she knew this, turning around from the sea and walking back to the room.

~

A few minutes later, Caroline saw Daisy walk with her suitcase through the main clubhouse to reception.

"Daisy!" Caroline called out, stretching her legs into longer strides to speed walk from the Longtail Terrace inside. Daisy turned around. "I know, you don't want to look at me right now," Caroline confirmed. This made Daisy relax her posture.

"Hi, Caroline," she said evenly.

"Hi."

Daisy raised her eyebrows for Caroline to continue.

"Can you tell Tiny I'll meet her at the airport?"

"Caroline, I don't mean to interfere, but I don't think leaving Tiny here is going to win her back." She added a "you know?" to sound nicer.

"I know," Caroline said quickly. "I know. I'm not leaving her here. I'm just meeting her at the airport. I have to do something first."

Daisy opened her mouth and Caroline exclaimed, "Jesus Christ, just tell her! Seriously! I've got a thing!" Caroline would have never described her voice as shrill before, but there it was. So shrill, she could break glass.

Before she knew it, she was running, her plan falling into place as she realized exactly what she would do. She would fix this.

TINY

She kept throwing rocks as she walked up the path and nearly threw one at Trip, who had appeared out of nowhere wearing a damp sea turtle–motif Vilebrequin bathing suit and faded Saint Barths T-shirt. Not a soul on the beach, but he was ready to be seen.

"Watch where you're going," she said, a near shout.

"Watch where you're throwing rocks, asshole," Trip said back.

"At least I'm not secretly drinking and pretending that my wife and children haven't left me." Tiny's rage was escaping her.

Trip stopped in his tracks. "What?"

"You heard me. At least I'm not pretending that I'm not getting divorced."

"Tiny—" he started.

"Whatever, Trip. Leave me alone."

"I would, believe me, but we're kind of stuck here."

"Why are you making a joke out of this?"

"I'm not—" he started to say.

"You are just like Mom and Dad!" Tiny properly exploded, tears starting to sting the backs of her eyes. "You can't ever just talk about something like it really is. It's always a joke with you."

"Tiny. Dude. What the fuck?"

The tears came now and Tiny couldn't stop them.

Trip put his hands on his hips. "Yeah, my wife left me. Daphne actually changed the locks, if you want to know the truth. She can't even look at me without storming away in the other direction."

"So she's really gone?" Tiny asked.

"She's really gone. I fucked it up."

"Wow," Tiny said without meaning to. Trip arched his eyebrows. "I don't think I've ever heard you say you did something wrong before."

Trip shrugged and kicked the sand. "I fuck up all the time." His words came out like pellets shot into the ground.

"I think everyone fucks up all the time."

Trip looked at her. "You think so?"

Tiny nodded.

"I don't want to tell you this next thing," he said, his hands now dug far into his bathing suit pockets.

"What is it?"

"Caroline left."

"How do you know that?"

"I saw her leaving the hotel with Andrew. They had their bags."

This news jolted Tiny out of this sweet sibling moment and back into her body.

"They had their bags?"

So it was real. It had been a mistake, every single moment of it, and Tiny couldn't believe she'd been so stupid. Andrew had probably been in on the plan from the second they'd all arrived in Bermuda. She was always going to be left. She only wished she could leave herself behind too and float into someone else's life.

And to think, she'd invited Connie in the first place. The joke of the century was on her.

Trip moved to hug her, but Tiny knew if he did, she'd collapse. She held up her arm and he stopped in place.

"They had their bags. I'm really sorry."

The fight left Tiny suddenly, her spirit going with it. She felt utterly defeated. "Was Connie with them?"

Trip shrugged but in a way that said *maybe*. He didn't know.

"What do I do?" She didn't know what else to say.

Trip embraced her in a hug far tighter than they'd shared in years. She was used to Trip hugging her without touching his body to hers. It felt good.

"Let's please get off this island."

~

Connie walked into the lobby as Tiny was walking out. She tried to turn around when she saw Tiny, but it was too late.

"Tiny."

"Connie."

At first, she was flooded with relief that Connie wasn't with Caroline. But that meant Caroline had left her anyway.

Connie was looking everywhere except at Tiny.

"I didn't think I'd see you."

"In the reception area of the club where I was married two days ago?" Tiny asked, her voice dripping with sarcasm.

"I just thought maybe you'd left."

"Still here." It was unclear if Connie noticed her family standing nearby, but Tiny was starting to feel brave. She took a deep breath. She let the breath out. She was not going to cower.

"Well, where is Caroline?"

"Taking a bath, Connie." The tone rolled Tiny's eyes for her.

"Where is she really?"

"I can't believe you. I invited you here, and what did you think? That you would come all the way down here for what? To steal her back? To make me the fool? Well, let me tell you something, *Connie*: if you come down to break up a wedding but don't actually break up a wedding, more like stir the pot around until you figure out there's nothing actually in it, if you do that, does that make you a fool or just pathetic?" Tiny was shaking, the energy coursing through her entire body. She was about to throw up and she was about to become a gladiator. Connie looked struck. Trip and her parents stood off to the side, pretending not to watch.

"I'm sorry," Connie said, staring at the ground.

Tiny heard it in her voice: she thought she'd merely been caught.

"She left, by the way. A few hours ago. With Andrew."

Tiny watched the news hit Connie between the eyes. Her face fell for a flash before she regained her composure, but it had been enough for Tiny to see: Connie hadn't thought Caroline would leave without her.

"Guess it wasn't worth it, was it? Getting in the middle?"

Connie looked down, her hands wringing each other out like towels.

"I'm so sorry, Tiny." It came out a whisper. It was more than Tiny wanted to hear, and she turned around before Connie could say another word.

"I thought everything would be different," Connie said, louder this time, as Tiny made her way out of the lobby and down the steps toward the beach, her brother and parents passively looking on.

∼

Tiny let out a guttural growl and fell to her knees. She felt like the entire ocean couldn't fill the hollowness inside her, and for a moment, she considered letting the water swallow her whole. She'd been brave, but Connie had also confirmed everything she didn't want to confirm: that Caroline had never loved her or never loved her enough. This weekend should never have happened, and she was to blame. If she hadn't invited Connie, she and Caroline would have gotten married. Nothing would have happened. Was this God laughing, or was this God playing a joke?

She was as alone today as she'd ever been. Her family wished she were straighter. Her wife wished she were gayer. She was caught somewhere in between, futilely trying to convince herself that was okay. The tears came now, robust and soaking, covering her face in a sheen of salt and snot. This had been her wedding. This had been her *life*, and no one actually wanted *her* in it.

Movement came from behind her. She turned around to see Bitty standing there.

"Go away." She didn't have the defenses up for her mother's criticism.

"I come in peace."

"Like hell you do," Tiny said, anger starting to push out despair.

Bitty cleared her throat.

"Go *away*."

Bitty turned around and started to walk off the beach before stopping in her tracks. She made eye contact with Tiny and held it. "You crawled away from me."

"What?"

"When you were younger. And you were learning to crawl. You crawled away from me, and I could never catch up." Bitty bit her lip.

"Who was I crawling toward?"

"Sometimes your father. Most of the time, you just crawled away, looking for your own adventure." She paused. Tiny had no idea how to fill the silence. "It's why I push you so hard," Bitty finally said. "Because I know your spirit."

"Then why have you worked so hard to push it down?" Tiny asked.

Bitty closed her eyes and spoke. "I'm sorry you feel small."

The women hugged, tentative and not totally touching at first.

"You are brave being who you are." It was barely above a whisper, and Tiny almost didn't hear it, but the words hit her heart in a way that made her feel heard, and she fell into her mother in a way she hadn't since she was a very small girl.

ESCAPE

CAROLINE

Caroline got to the airport two and a half hours before their flight to Paris (by way of JFK), praying mightily that she would beat Tiny and have time to get situated. She had caught a glimpse of Hank when she'd arrived, but he'd hurried to the gate and she hadn't called him back. It was hard to know who was in more trouble, him or her. She suspected it was him, and that did not actually make her feel better. She debated forgoing her American Airlines ticket and finding another airline, or flying into a different airport, or even throwing everything to the wind and flying into an entirely different city. The only thing that would make her feel better, she knew, looking around for the front of the departure entrance, was to fix everything with Tiny. And that was why she was here, alone, prepared to make a gesture.

She tinkered with the makeshift poster, haphazardly constructed in the back of the taxicab with computer paper, too much tape, and a permanent marker.

An hour later, she heard a voice behind her. "What are you doing?" *The* voice.

She turned around. Connie was standing right there. Right *there*. Not where she was supposed to be.

"I'm waiting."

"For what?" It was a fair question. Caroline looked up and caught Connie's eye and knew she'd meant to ask, *For whom.*

This was Connie. *Her* Connie. She was yesterday and today and tomorrow. She was a convertible with the top down in the rain.

"I'm waiting," she said again.

"For Tiny?" Connie asked like her oxygen depended on the answer.

"For Tiny," Caroline said. The poster felt like bricks in her hands.

~

When Caroline's parents had first sat her down, she'd thought one of them was sick. Connie had just left again, and Caroline was heartbroken, knowing it had been her fault this time.

"Bird, do you have a sec?" her father had said, entering the living room with Mabel one step behind him. Caroline had been spending a lot of time at her childhood home.

"Of course." She sat up on the couch.

"Dear," her mother started. Her parents were seated on either side of her in tufted armchairs.

Caroline waited.

"Dear," her mother said again. "As you know, your father and I completely support you and your alternative lifestyle." Her parents smiled and Caroline smiled back.

"And I'm so appreciative of that," she said.

"That's why we wanted to talk to you. About how you going down this . . . path does not mean everything else gets thrown out the window." Mabel shifted in her seat and crossed one leg over the other.

"Your mother and I have been talking about the best way to handle this in a town like where we live." Her father motioned around the room, as if introducing the concept of Greenwich, Connecticut, for the first time. Caroline nodded along, genuinely interested.

"What your father is trying to say, dear, is that it's just as easy to fall in love with a rich woman as a poor woman." Her mother said this and folded her hands on top of her knees.

"So you're saying I should marry someone rich?" Caroline asked, her head cocked so far to the left, it almost fell off her neck.

"Not at all," her mother said, shaking her head for full effect. "What we are saying is that it is just as easy to fall in love with a rich woman as it is to fall in love with a poor woman. It's a matter of where you look for a mate."

Caroline took it in. Connie, she knew, was the poor woman here. Raised two tax brackets shy of the top, privileged enough for an education, but nothing to show for it beyond a good vocabulary.

"We need this," her mother said, urgency flooding her voice. "Your father's fund is not what it used to be." She closed her eyes before she said the next part. "We are on the brink of life dramatically changing."

Caroline knew what she had to do, and she knew this was the only way she'd ever really win over her parents.

Bitty had called Mabel a few weeks later. The union had been decided before Caroline even saw Tiny on the street.

~

Caroline felt Connie moving closer to her. Sometimes it felt like the attraction was out of her hands, like it had just happened to her and kept happening. Caroline moved closer too, and then they were standing, almost touching. Almost.

"What will you do?" Connie asked, not brave.

"I don't know. Fly home. Give Tiny some time. Try to figure it out."

Connie closed her eyes. She wasn't part of that answer. Caroline didn't know what else to say: *I broke everything, and it's still broken, and I'm broken, but I'm not sure I can even be fixed.*

"What about me?" Connie said after too many silent moments, looking everywhere except at Caroline, who in turn looked everywhere except at Connie. It took forever for her to answer. The din of the airport went up and down, bodies moving around them in the way anonymous bodies do: only noticeable when they enter your breathing air.

"You aren't Tiny," she finally said, her voice no more than a whisper. Her eyes were closed. She shook her head slightly. "I'm so sorry." She kept saying it, *I'm so sorry*, over and over again, her mouth moving but no sound coming out.

There it was. Connie had never been first, and that was the problem. She couldn't be—not when Caroline's parents cared so much about who she married. Caroline was so close to their approval that it felt real, and she knew she wouldn't stop trying until she had it. She didn't have the strength to run away and elope.

"I'm not Tiny." It came out like a sigh, the words disappearing as soon as they'd been spoken. What she didn't say: *I don't need to be Tiny.* Caroline's eyes met with hers and she knew Connie was saying goodbye. It was over in a blink. Goodbye.

Connie walked away, not looking behind her, not even giving her a little wave. Of course, Caroline knew, hating every fiber of her being, walking away was the only thing she could do.

BITTY

The McAllisters would ride to the airport together. Bitty called both Trip and Tiny and told them to meet up by reception at one. She'd learned Caroline had already left for the airport, her no-good parents minutes behind her, and this made her furious, regardless of the fact that Dick absolutely losing his shit with Peter may well run them out of town. All she'd asked for was a pleasant weekend. Why everyone had needed to bring all their baggage down here and light it on fire was beyond her. Dick especially, all that pent-up anger simmering for years and years, mocking her for experiencing any emotion ever.

Bitty started throwing items in her suitcase, letting out little yips with each throw. When she threw her hairbrush from the bathroom, sailing it past the suitcase on the bed and right into the wainscoted wall, she howled.

"Will you pipe down?" Dick said, sweat pooled under his neck. "The last thing we need is for someone to knock on that door and ask if everything is all right."

"There's Dick, always with appearances! Lest anyone know his daughter's a *lesbian*! Everything is A-OK! Haven't heard from our missionary son in five years? Well! He's just saving the world! Haven't seen our grandkids in six months because their mother thinks we're degenerates? Well! They're so busy with school!" She was flailing items into the suitcase now: clothes and her hair dryer and makeup and shoes.

"Thanks, Dick! For this wonderful life!" She screamed this and chucked the heel she'd worn to the wedding at his head. He ducked and it sailed through the open terrace door and over the railing.

"My shoe!" she said, running after it. "How could you?"

"How could I duck?" Dick said, his exasperation like a cloak.

"How could you let my shoe go over the railing? What kind of animal are you?"

"What kind of animal am I? What kind of animal pelts a shoe at her husband?"

"The kind of animal who is sick of pretending everything is always okay! The kind of animal who has realized that her husband bottles everything up and the kind of animal who thinks maybe it's time to see what else is out there."

Dick's eyes were wide. "What is going on?" he asked, the fight in his voice gone.

Bitty started crying, a deep sniffle and cough, and then the tears were flowing. "I can't bear it if we lose Tiny too."

Dick walked over and put his arms around her. "We won't let that happen."

~

When Dick was packing in the other room, she went into the bathroom for her bottle of pills and poured too many into her hand. She paused before throwing them back. The only way to break the cycle was to break it, and she willed her hand to lower down onto the counter, to slowly dump the pills onto a washcloth by the sink. Her heartbeat was like a metronome through her chest, and still, she let the pills stay there. *Just for this dose,* she said to herself. *Just skip this dose and don't worry about anything else.*

Her hands shook ever so slightly and she could feel her heart rate accelerating even more. She looked between the pills and the mirror. The only way to break the cycle was to break it. Could she skip these pills? Could she even dream of facing the outside world without them?

She swallowed one with water, putting the rest in the bottle, the bottle in her embroidered cosmetics bag. She would talk to Dr. Larkin this week. The thought alone was enough to make her want to swallow six more pills, but she willed herself to breathe and count to three. The only way to break the cycle was to break it.

~

Trip and Tiny were waiting for them just next to the lobby, their bags in tow. Bitty was fighting and then submitting to and then bargaining with a headache, her left temple throbbing at even beats.

"About time," Trip said, his stance one that suggested they'd been there awhile.

Dick proceeded to the reception desk to close out the bill.

"Thank you, Peter, for nothing," he muttered, shaking his head and humming a little while he looked through each item. Bitty and Trip and Tiny stood nearby, making idle chatter.

~

"No Caroline?" Dick half asked and half confirmed to Tiny a few minutes later when the town car pulled up.

"She said she wanted to meet me at the airport. Whatever that means," Tiny said.

Bitty barely registered getting into a waiting car, barely registered the car starting to drive away, but at the last minute, she turned to see the resort in its midday glory, shining right there in the sun. The palm trees stretched upward, their leaves folding down, like a mother patting her children on the back. The pink clubhouse was still upright after the storm, and Bitty watched workers sweeping away fallen coconuts and branches. Despite it all, the Coral Beach Club really was beautiful.

Bitty looked at her son and her daughter and her husband. Trip sat with his head leaning against the window, his skin ashen against the sun. Tiny was next to him, her body at once slumped and rigid, her arms birdlike and protective over her chest. She looked broken but also like her pieces still fit together. Dick was red and sweaty, his polo shirt loose at the neck.

And there it was, right in front of her: her son, her daughter, and her husband all needed her and there wasn't an ounce of power to take. They were powerless, shoulders hunched and eyes squinting from the sun pouring in through the windows. After all this time, she knew she had only one thing to offer and it cost nothing: love.

She counted to three.

"I want to help," she said, breaking the silence. Everyone turned to her a little skeptically.

"What?" Tiny asked.

"I want to help. I love—I love you. I love you all." She was nervous. As nervous as she'd ever been, telling her family that she loved them.

No one said anything, but Tiny turned her head and met her eye. Then Trip. Then Dick.

"I don't know what comes next." She'd never uttered such an honest statement. It felt good. It also felt petrifying. But it worked: Bitty watched the tension and anger start to lift out of her family members.

"I don't know what's going to happen with Caroline and me," Tiny said.

The first die had been cast.

"Daphne left me. She locked me out of our house. I'm angry but I think I'm also relieved, to be honest," Trip said, giving Tiny's shoulder a squeeze.

"Tiny, I'm sorry for what I said," Dick added. "I never should have stepped in the way of you and Caroline."

"You didn't step in the way of us," Tiny said.

Dick looked relieved. "Oh—"

"You were worse than that," she continued. "You are one of those people who think if they don't say anything, it won't exist. I've been out for twelve years, Dad. Twelve years. My comfort with who I am is in sixth grade. And you've never ever talked about it. You threw me a destination wedding, but you never asked how I was feeling. Think about that."

Everyone held their breath, waiting for Tiny to stop talking. Bitty and Trip both looked at Dick.

Bitty felt like she was looking through glass, her family magnified and morphed in the lens. They were shifting before her eyes, their secrets overtaking them, sending a mist through the car. Would the driver notice? Would they run out of air? Dick and Trip and Tiny looked at her, waiting. She had no idea what to say. She'd never looked truth in the mouth before.

Dick coughed and turned his head toward the window. Tiny sighed next to her and kept talking. "You have to talk about things sometimes, Dad. You can't just go for long walks and wait for whatever you're avoiding to go away."

Bitty's eyes were wet as she reached over and almost touched her daughter's hand.

"Let your father be, sweetie. He knows he messed up."

Tiny ripped her hand away. "You can't just smooth this one over."

Dick turned away from the window and looked into the back seat. "You're right. I'm better at walks."

"Can you look me in the eye and say you are okay with me being gay?" Tiny asked.

Bitty inhaled sharply. Her daughter had never been so forward before, always treating her sexuality like something to be kept in a box under the bed.

Dick looked right at his daughter.

"I can't," he said, his voice quiet and resigned. Tiny's chin started trembling. Trip looked like a balloon after it'd popped. The whole car felt suspended.

"But I promise to try," he said a few moments later. "I promise," he said again, reaching out and taking his daughter's hand. Bitty watched Tiny squeeze her father's hand back.

Bitty reached for her phone in her purse and took it off airplane mode and went to her text messages. She clicked on Robbie's name and began typing.

I should have sent this years ago: come home. We need you. I love you and we love you.

She didn't know if it would work, but at least she'd finally tried. Her pieces were being put back together, one at a time.

TINY

Tiny saw Caroline in the terminal standing at the large departures and arrivals board. Tiny was with her family and Caroline was alone. When she got closer, she could see Caroline was holding a sign with writing in all caps:

*INDECISIVE ROMANTIC LOOKING FOR BIGHEARTED
GREENWICH GIRL*

"You're here," she said, the din of the airport falling away. She read the sign again. And again.

"I'm here."

Habit told her to move closer and kiss Caroline's cheek, but Tiny stood still.

"I like your sign."

"I'm sorry for everything," Caroline said, closing the distance between their bodies. "I'm so sorry."

Tiny let Caroline kiss her cheek and put her head on Tiny's shoulder. She breathed in her scent and for an instant closed her eyes. This was too easy to fall into again.

She stepped back, and when Caroline moved toward her, she held up her hand. "Wait."

Caroline stopped in place.

"I need you to be honest."

"Okay."

"What happened this weekend? Why *this* weekend and not any other time in the last three years? I'm trying to think—did I push you? You proposed to me. Is it my family? Yours is the same with a different last name. Did you wish it was Connie, but then you kept waking up next to me? We laughed. We like the same food. What was it?"

Caroline shook her head at Tiny's suggestions.

"Explain it to me, then. I'm trying to go back, over and over again. All weekend, I've traced every single moment of the last three years, and I keep coming back to this: that you never wanted to be with someone so small."

"I'm sorry," Caroline kept saying, over and over. The apologies hit Tiny like tiny bullets, and she was scared if two hit the same place, she would cave. She loved this horrible woman, even now, standing at an airport two days after a wedding that hadn't ever turned into a marriage. If Caroline asked her to run away at this moment, Tiny couldn't be sure she would say no. She could feel her family in the background, encircling her like human wagons. She wanted to be strong for them. She wanted to be big.

"What was it?" Tiny asked one more time. Despite everything, she still wanted to be saved.

Caroline opened her eyes and closed them again. "You aren't Connie."

There it was, the truth she'd been avoiding for three years. Somewhere inside her, she'd always known she wasn't the first choice.

"And why *not* Connie?" she asked, finally brave enough to want to know the answer.

"My parents . . . ," Caroline began, trailing off.

"Your *parents*?" Tiny suddenly saw Caroline in a new light: one where she was positively small, shrinking under the glare of her parents and their own set of expectations. Of course, Tiny thought, she was a nice girl from Greenwich. To Peter and Mabel, she was marriage material.

"I think I deserve more," Tiny said, realizing it as she said it out loud. "And I'm *not* Connie," she said, her voice stronger. She was not someone else at all. She looked at Caroline again, noticed how her forehead cast out like a desert, her nose pointy, her long, lithe body actually softer and less athletic than Tiny had ever registered. "Actually," she said, smirking and shaking her head, "I'm not Connie and I don't wish I was."

Tiny had one thing she wanted to do before this weekend officially ended. The thought had come to her yesterday, with the rain pouring down and the realization that Caroline would never be hers. She pulled out the piece of paper, their marriage license, and held it up for Caroline to see. Did she want her to reach out and try to grab it, signing it and making their union real before Tiny had the chance to run? She didn't let herself think about the answer and tore the piece of paper in half, a line down the middle, the ripping sound slicing right through the air. She swore she heard a whoop escape Bitty's mouth.

"I should go," Tiny finally said, ignoring her family huddled around them. She looked over at the board of departing flights and scanned the locations. She could not go to Paris alone or back to New York, not with this voice, with this fight in her. She needed a fresh start, where she could arrive and no one needed to know she'd ever been tiny. Sun bounced between the shiny white airport floors and the walls, calling her attention outside, to the destroyed area around the airport. The waves lapped gently onto a ruined beach, as if they had no idea that the waves before them had taken the sand under siege, beating it mercilessly as the rain poured down. In the waves' defense, the sand hadn't put up much of a fight. Tiny didn't want to be the sand anymore.

Then she saw it: Atlanta. Atlanta was a hub to the rest of the world, and when she arrived, she would go on to Austin. She was always supposed to go there with Caroline, but it was better this way. She had no idea why. She didn't know anyone there or care about music or barbecue or any of the things that people tended to talk about when they talked about Austin. But she'd been once—before Caroline, before she got so small—and she'd liked how the energy felt on the streets, like the bars and restaurants and clubs and life couldn't possibly be contained indoors. She needed that energy to start over. Without Caroline. Without Bitty. Without her father being able to look at her only halfway. Without Daisy pretending everything was always fine.

"I should go," she said again, louder, now addressing the entire group. Caroline was white, utterly defeated.

"Caroline, I've always loved you, and until this exact moment, I thought it was my job to make you love me. It's not. It's not my job to make anyone love me. Not Bitty, not Robbie, not Andrew. Certainly not you. Not anyone."

She'd found her words. That's what it had always been: Tiny trying with every ounce of her being to get people to love her. And it wasn't working.

Mabel stepped out of the group and toward Tiny like she was going to intervene. Bitty blocked her. Peter stood to the side with an obviously no-longer-cold ice pack on his cheek.

"I always envied you, you know," Bitty said. Mabel questioned her without any words. "I envied how you can bend yourself into different groups while still somehow staying yourself. I envied your seemingly perfect marriage to Peter. Even how it looked like you didn't miss a beat when Caroline came out. But you're just like anyone else: desperately hanging on to a life that could blow away at any moment. You're a fraud, Mabel, and your plan to infiltrate our family didn't work." Bitty looked at her daughter. "You are the bravest one here."

"Tiny—" Caroline started, her voice pleading.

Tiny put up her hand to stop her. She looked back to her mother and they locked eyes. Bitty was standing up straight and beaming, the pride emanating from her entire being. She was watching her daughter get big again.

"My name is Georgia."

With that, she walked away from her group and toward the counter, ready to buy a one-way ticket out of this place.

The counter attendant greeted her, asking her for a last name and passport.

"How many are in your group?" the attendant asked.

Tiny didn't hesitate.

"Just me today."

ACKNOWLEDGMENTS

It's a true act of bravery for an agent to represent a friend, Alexandra Machinist, and you handled this challenge with the best parts of both. Thank you for reading, believing, sending me that scary email, and most of all, for all these years of friendship. Alicia Clancy, you're a star and a wonderful editor. Thank you for getting this book so perfectly. Sophie Baker and Josie Freedman, thank you for bringing this book abroad to the screen.

To my Verve family: you welcomed this book nerd with open arms, and it didn't take long for you to root yourselves in my heart. Thank you isn't enough. You helped cement my agent career in purpose. And to my clients: thank you for trusting me to copilot your journeys.

Wendy Wolf, mentor, friend, fairy godmother, Boss. Where do I begin? Thank you feels too insignificant for all you've offered since hiring a well-intentioned yet utterly underqualified kid right out of college. But I'll say this: I trust everything you say and any good I'm doing now can be directly sourced to you.

To my early readers, in particular Connie Tallman: thank you for your insight and wisdom into what this story could be.

I had three teachers particularly encouraging about my writing: Connie Blunden, John Palmer, and Kathy Skubikowski. Your support stayed with me. Thank you.

Mom + Dad, thank you for letting me be me. You drove three hours to hear me read a short story in high school. That deserves proper Acknowledgments Section recognition and says it all in how supportive you've always been about my writing. I'll call you at dinnertime. Mike, I love you, brother. Thank you for teaching me about asking people questions about themselves. Gie Gie, you are just weird enough to join this family. And we are so grateful for you to join it.

Sarah Tallman, eight years with you only makes me want eighty more. Thank you for being you, for loving me, for being the funniest, kindest, oddest girl I know. While I've been verbose all my life, you bring out my best words.

A few years ago, two experiences made the necessary room in my brain to consider actually writing a novel: when Ryan Doherty and I worked on a treatment for a television series and when my essay was published in the *NYT* Modern Love column. Ryan, this book couldn't have happened without you. Thank you.

ABOUT THE AUTHOR

Photo © 2020 Phil Toran

Liz Parker is a literary agent at Verve Talent & Literary. She has written for the *New York Times*'s Modern Love column, and she lives in Los Angeles with her wife, Sarah, and their two dogs.